ETRUSCA'S VOW
AFV DEFENDER #3

By Michelle L. Levigne

Ye Olde Dragon Books
P.O. Box 30802
Middleburg Hts., OH 44130

www.YeOldeDragonBooks.com

2OldeDragons@gmail.com

ISBN 13: 978-1-952345-78-4

Published in the United States of America
Publication Date: September 15, 2022

Chapter One

Nisandros
Ba'e'do'stra Clan House

M'kar heard the shrieking and wailing and banging approaching the gates on the northern side of the clan house only because of the short lull in the current storm. The lull wasn't long enough for those two intruders from Rissor Clan to jump in their land-cart and go home. Ke'Jor and Ke'Niq had showed up four days ago, nearly thrown across the threshold by the oncoming storm. M'kar wished her grandfather could have refused the boys and their servants shelter, but Ba'e'do'stra and Rissor were on friendly terms right now, and Ke'Jor was the heir of the heir to Rissor Clan.

That friendship wouldn't last much longer if Ke'Jor's grandfather kept demanding a marriage alliance between their clans. M'kar wanted to heave every time she thought about marrying Ke'Jor. She was only eight years old and he was fourteen. Besides, he was a nosepicker.

And now, the wailing of doog horns came through the momentary lull in the storm, to make her miserable day even worse. Even sitting in the high tower in the southern wing of the house, where she went to hide from Ke'Jor, she heard the horns wail. Only self-appointed prophets used doog horns nowadays. Only the crazy-nasty kind traveled the Ring Mountains to Ba'e'do'stra's gates while storms prevented land-cart travel.

M'kar wondered which Ancestors this prophet served, and what threats he would make to have the half-blood girl (her) be handed over to him, supposedly for the good of the planet. In between wails of wind gusts, she guessed the distance of the approaching nuisance and calculated when she would hear the clatter of prophecy sticks against the gates. Less than half an hour.

The prophet probably knew her parents were away. She tried to calculate which of her many uncles and great-uncles and cousins were preparing to catch her and hand her over.

What was the best tactic this time? Stay here in the crumbling old tower room, because moving targets were easier to spot? Or find some place new to hide? At least a dozen servants knew she holed up here to avoid the Rissor cousins.

Maybe she should take shelter with Great-grandfather Aquid. She liked him best of all her relatives. During his lucid moments, Aquid told her incredible stories and taught her about the secret passageways of the house. Of course, if he was insane today, thanks to the winter storms, he might decide the prophet was in the right and turn her over to him.

M'kar didn't care if the messengers from the Ancestors insisted she was an abomination or a fulfillment of prophecy. The basic story was always the same: if the half-blood girl wasn't handed over, Nisandros was doomed. Her father, Ashrock found it only slightly amusing that the prophets could never agree on which bloody ritual to use for the sacrifice. Or what ceremony to make her a high priestess to rule the planet. M'kar didn't care. Nothing could persuade her to go live in one of those dark, filthy, disgusting-smelling crumbling rockpiles designated as holy sites. Especially not if the spirits of several thousand Ancestors inhabited the damp, dark, windy rooms and hallways. She couldn't quite persuade herself the inimical spirits weren't going to eat her if she stepped out of line. She believed Enlo was stronger than any dark spirits, but sometimes that wasn't enough. Despite the scars she earned fighting off assassins, she was still a child, and her imagination was stronger than facts. With her parents gone on clan business, she had to protect herself.

Great-grandfather Aquid might be the wiser choice today. He hadn't talked about trying to court Etrusca, the legendary warrior woman, in nearly three luns. She would settle in his quarters until the prophet gave up, or her parents came home.

The two-story-tall doors of the main entrance swung ponderously open when she was halfway through the central courtyard of the house, lined with stairs and balconies, fifteen stories high on all sides. Even from a dozen hallways away, she heard them. Someone welcomed the prophet. She braced herself as the winds that tore into the house reached her, but she didn't catch the expected, disgusting smell that accompanied every prophet she had ever seen. As Ashrock said, there was something very wrong with people who equated holiness with filth and insanity.

"This one isn't so bad," her cousin B'keerimo said, from the landing of the crooked stairs two levels above her. He leaned over the banister, clutching one of the huge volumes of transcribed ancient philosophy books he loved. It was large enough she expected it to pull his skinny frame over the railing and down several flights of steps.

She ignored him and leaped the last two steps to reach the landing one level below him. B'keerimo was always reading and pretending he could hear the Ancestors whispering in the wind and storms. While he was the least violent of her cousins, he lived for arguments and twisting people's brains into knots. M'kar wasn't going to give him the pleasure of getting her into an argument and delaying her. Not when other cousins were likely even now looking for her.

It was too bad her three half-brothers had left the planet. She didn't think they liked her, but they honored their father enough to do the right thing and defend her. They would be looking for her right now to stand between her and whatever had just come through the main doors. The youngest, Shauq, had even taught her a few defensive leap-kick moves that worked quite nicely, before they left to seek their fortune.

"No, I'm serious," B'keerimo said, coming down the stairs to try to intercept her. "This one wants to protect you from all the others."

"Until he can find a use for you," Ke'Niq said, stepping out of the shadows of the hall ahead of her.

M'kar kept moving and clutched the knife at her waist. Ke'Niq hadn't sided with her cousins against her so far, but now was a good time to reveal the real reason he and Ke'Jor pretended to get themselves stranded here during the storm. Killing the half-blood girl would earn them honor debt with at least a dozen clans, and two-thirds of Nisandros's prophets. Then there was Ke'Jor's nasty habit of insisting she had to marry him when they were grown up.

Better to keep several rooms between her and the Rissor cousins. If that failed, a knife blade would do. Her knife wasn't a large one, but she was good with it. Until she was taller and her reach was longer, her father focused all her knifework lessons on teaching her acrobatics and moving swiftly enough to make her attackers dizzy. The last would-be assassin had laughed at her leaps and twists -- until she climbed up him. He hesitated just long enough for her to clobber him between the eyes with the haft of the knife and send him tumbling down the stairs.

"Go back to your nursery," B'keerimo sneered.

"You'd better get to the women's quarter fast," Ke'Niq said.

"We don't have a women's quarter." M'kar kept moving, not paying attention to which hallway she took. All that mattered was putting space between her and the boys.

"Why not?" He raced to catch up with her.

"She's the first girl born to our clan in centuries," B'keerimo called after them. Of course, the big know-it-all had to answer, even though it was none of Ke'Niq's business.

M'kar wished Ba'e'do'stra did have a women's quarter, but the only women in the family had married into the clan. There had to be a daughter of the clan's bloodline to rule the women's quarter. Ashrock could have asked for the sprawling complex of rooms to be opened up when M'kar was born, but he and Jeyn had always planned to leave Nisandros, so why waste all that effort? Besides, there was no guarantee any of the uncles, great-uncles, and cousins would leave her alone if she retreated to the women's quarter.

"Why are you bothering her?" Ke'Jor called from a level above them and around the corner.

"He's not." M'kar sighed and picked up her pace, but she refused to run. This was her home, and Ke'Jor wasn't going to make her run. Hiding wasn't the same as running. What would it take to make him stop insisting she would marry him? Would she have to take the blue tattoos of Etrusca's vow, so no one could force her to marry? Ke'Jor wouldn't take the warning, or fear reprisals from the monsters of legend that enforced such serious vows. He would just switch from being irritating to using nasty tricks. The only tactic that seemed to work was to avoid him.

Which wasn't working right now. Ke'Jor was heading for the stairs that would bring him down in front of her, if she continued down that hallway. M'kar turned right. She muffled a growl when she didn't know for a few seconds where she was going.

That wasn't smart. How could she beat the assassins and kidnappers if she didn't know where she was in her own house?

Why did Ke'Jor have to be the heir? Not that she liked Ke'Niq, but she thought he was a better choice. He was nicer than any of her cousins, and yes, he didn't pick his nose. He believed her when she said her tattoos and scars were real, and not painted on to make her look tougher than she was. Not for the first time, she silently complained to Enlo over how much the cousins looked alike, almost twins: sharp chins, sharp cheekbones, thick manes of blue-black curls, gray eyes, wide shoulders. She always had to look twice before she let one of them get close, because Ke'Jor was always trying to hold her hand. With the hand he used to pick his nose. She had to admit they were both handsome, other than the white ink of their honor tattoos, which always looked like mange against the deep red-brown of their skin. That made her itchy.

A shout echoed down the hallways. The prophet was probably inside the house now and making his demands. She needed to vanish, and fast. M'kar threw pride to the winter winds and ran. She took the right turn at the next intersection.

Now she knew where she was. This hallway led to the air-car dock. She ran faster. Maybe twenty seconds later, she hurried through the door and was greeted with gusts of sandy air.

Uncle Ashreel's new air-car, painted in the clan's colors, eye-watering orange and poisonous blue, sat on the central landing pad, with the gates wide open to the sky. The hatch was open. Maybe she should try to hide in there. Could she try to fly out of here if someone came looking for her?

M'kar hurried to the open hatch of the air-car and stepped in.

Or maybe she shouldn't hide here. The gates wouldn't be open to the sand and wind of the winter storms unless someone still feared the Ankuar merchant who had sold the air-car to her uncle had hidden bombs in it. She had heard the servants laughing about Uncle Ashreel searching for someone he trusted to thoroughly inspect it. Not just for bombs, but poisoned boobytraps or spying devices. The first cursory inspection had uncovered several listening and energy-scanning devices.

When Ankuar chose spying over sneaky attacks and assassination, then trouble was coming. Many of the uncles and great-uncles blamed Ashrock for the continuing trouble from the Ankuar. Ever since he had married Jeyn, an Alliance anthropologist, the Ankuar had focused all their bribery attempts and attacks on Ba'e'do'stra, trying to convince the other clans to depose them as leaders and prevent Nisandros joining the Alliance. That was a mistake. The more other worlds tried to influence Nisandros to move in one direction, the harder they turned in another.

M'kar wanted Nisandros to join the Alliance. She wanted to go to the Academy and study on Le'anka, and maybe become an officer in the Fleet. Nisandros's membership would make that easier. Dr. Jeyn was close friends with Thean, a healer at the Academy. She and her husband, Master Reydon, had invited Ashrock, Jeyn, and M'kar to settle with them. They planned to leave Nisandros when Jeyn finished her preliminary studies of the culture, but M'kar wanted to leave now.

Especially with *boostifak* prophets banging on the clan house doors every few luns, trying to have her killed, or the relatives of disgusting boys like Ke'Jor demanding a marriage alliance. M'kar was only eight years old. Her own father was even more adamant than her that she would never marry a Nisandrian man.

Not that Ke'Jor counted as a man. Nosepickers who screamed two octaves higher than she did when a baby ykas dropped from the ceiling on their heads certainly could never earn the title of "man."

"I wish I could go up to the Alliance orbital platform right now," she murmured, stroking the control panel.

Too late, she heard footsteps scraping on the sandy floor behind her. Both boys had followed her into the air-car dock. She ducked back further into the vehicle, hoping they hadn't seen her.

No, stupid move. Now she was trapped.

Ke'Jor leaned into the open hatch and grinned at her. "Of course, this is the best place to hide. No one will expect you to hide here. Know why?"

M'kar said nothing. She had learned the hard way over the last few days that no matter what she said, Ke'Jor would keep talking.

"It's because girls don't like to fly air-cars."

"Our cousins and sisters don't want to fly with him, because he lectures them like he knows everything," Ke'Niq said. He flung himself into the air-car, avoiding Ke'Jor's punch, which hit the side of the open hatch instead of him. M'kar muffled a giggle.

"I can fly just fine," Ke'Jor growled. "You want to go up to the orbital platform? Let's go." He tried to vault through the hatch to the cockpit, caught his foot on the lip of the hatch and sprawled through the door, hitting his face on the support bar for the pilot's seat.

"Can this fly that high?" Ke'Niq said. He and M'kar settled on the bench seat across the back of the compartment and watched Ke'Jor wipe the blood off his face and reach, half-blind, for the control panel.

There was no security on the air-car, no alarms or locks on the dock. Only someone with a death-wish would take an air-car up before the winter storms had passed, so no alarms went off when Ke'Jor set about hitting the control panel.

"You don't want to do that," M'kar blurted, when the vehicle rumbled into life far too easily.

Uncle Ashreel would rage if Ke'Jor flew his new air-car before he did.

"If you sit with me, I'll take you anywhere you want to go." Ke'Jor patted the bench seat next to him.

"I don't want to go anywhere with you. Ever," M'kar snapped.

A loud rumble of thunder answered her words, followed by a wailing shriek of wind that swirled around their heads and filled the air with clouds of gritty dust.

"You're supposed to be nice to me." How did he talk clearly with his lower lip sticking out like that?

"Laws of hospitality don't count when you weren't invited."

"I mean when we get married."

"I am never marrying you!"

"Grandfather says you have to."

"Your grandfather can't make me do anything!" She stomped up to the pilot's seat, intending to punch him.

He reached for her. She flung herself backward, kicking up with both feet in a one-two swing that would have made her father proud. The toes of both her shoes slammed into Ke'Jor's chest and chin before her back hit the deck of the air-car. She hadn't mastered the somersault part of the maneuver yet.

Snarling, Ke'Jor swept his hands across the control panel. The air-car jolted straight up. Only proximity sensors kept it from hitting the roof of the dock. The hatch slammed closed. The car jolted forward, out into the open air and churning sandy winds. M'kar rolled and slid backward, her abdomen slamming into the support for the bench seat, knocking all the air from her lungs.

The air-car tipped hard to the right, then righted itself. It rattled. M'kar was sure it shouldn't make a sound like that. Maybe her uncles were right, and it was boobytrapped, rigged to fall apart when it went far enough into the Barrens to make rescue difficult.

A low rumbling came from outside. It sounded like thunder, or very strong, brutal winds. Or both. And got stronger, louder, shaking the vehicle more with every second.

M'kar needed to laugh, but she couldn't seem to get any air. A growing storm swirled around the air-car. She was sure they couldn't go very far. If Ke'Jor wanted to take her to his clan territory, he had to cross the Ring Mountains, which divided Rissor from Ba'e'do'stra. Storms were always worse in the mountains.

"You have to go back," she finally managed to croak, when she got her breath back.

"I'm not turning back until you apologize," Ke'Jor snarled.

"Apologize for what?" Ke'Niq shouted. "She didn't do anything wrong."

"She's supposed to be nice to me. Grandfather said."

"Your grandfather is a narding indiferp with delusions of being Human!" M'kar reached for the bench seat to pull herself upright.

"You take that back!"

"You take me back home, you thief!"

"You have to obey me. You have to be nice to me."

"I'll never be nice to you. You're an even worse idiot than your grandfather. And my grandfather says that!" She thumped her fist on the cushion for emphasis. It didn't do much good, but the gesture made her feel better.

The air-car jolted, dropping suddenly. M'kar thought about trying to crawl across the deck and reaching Ke'Jor before they crashed. If they were going to die, she wanted to hit him as hard as she could, first, as many times as she could.

The air-car jolted worse. She grunted. Ke'Jor cursed. The bouncing as they plummeted downward broke his curses into fragments and threatened to slam her into the roof. Shrieking alarms filled the air, deafening. Through the wail of the engine and the blatts and squeals of the alarms, the wind's howl grew stronger, and soon drowned them out.

"Alert," a mechanical voice said, while the alarms silenced for a few seconds. "Approaching Etrusca's Wall. Change course. Continuing on this course violates a blood edict of the Council of Clans."

"What does that mean?" Ke'Jor shouted, as the voice repeated the message.

How could he not know? Etrusca's Wall was the surbda crater on the dividing line between Ba'e'do'stra and Rissor clan lands. Didn't they teach them anything in the Rissor Clan?

This was the largest surbda crater, with a wall of rubble ten meters high surrounding it. Legends said the warrior Etrusca had pulled it up from the netherworld during one of her many resurrections from the dead. Navigation equipment and sensors refused to work within ten meters of most surbda craters, but that trouble zone reached fifty meters out from Etrusca's Wall. All transportation equipment refused to work. Animals refused to go into it. There were nine total surbda craters, scattered across the planet. All were forbidden, by ritual and common sense. All equipment, whether transportation, probes or drones vanished once they crossed into a crater.

If they crashed into Etrusca's Wall, they might vanish forever.

They were going to die.

"You have to turn back before we get killed, that's what it means!" M'kar shouted, as the alarms resumed their ear-splitting shrieks.

The craft tipped. Ke'Jor slid out of his seat, hitting the floor with a thud. Ke'Niq and M'kar slid sideways, he on his knees on the deck of the craft, and her falling sideways along the bench seat. Ke'Niq caught hold of her wrist with one hand and with the other hand caught a cleat in the deck used for tying off cargo nets.

"Get your hands off her!" Ke'Jor lunged at his cousin. "She's mine. Grandfather says so."

M'kar twisted around to kick Ke'Jor in the face. He shrieked like a goosigah, threatening to go so high no Human ears could hear.

The craft kept tipping, and the engines shrieked loud enough to cover up Ke'Jor's cursing and spitting and the slapping of his hands on the deck plating as he tried to climb the steep angle. M'kar got her own grip on a cleat in the deck. She stayed a good meter out of Ke'Jor's waving, slapping hands.

The craft tipped over on its roof, hard enough to knock them loose. They hit the ceiling. M'kar yelped. Ke'Niq swore. Ke'Jor shrieked for Ke'Niq to make the air-car behave.

Then the craft hit hard, bouncing all of them up to the floor, now the ceiling. M'kar's head hit. She saw stars and bit the inside of her cheek. Her neck snapped. She fought to hold onto consciousness as the craft tipped and slid, then hit and flipped up in the air, then turned over.

For a few heartbeats there was nothing but tumbling and trying to grab onto something. Ke'Jor shrieked for Ke'Niq not to tell their grandfather he crashed another craft.

Then blackness.

Good. She was tired of hearing Ke'Jor shriek.

~~~~~

M'kar woke to heavy, black, purple-fringed clouds boiling across the sky. Ke'Niq moved into her field of vision, waving a diagnostic wand over her. His face was muddy and streaked with bloody scratches. His nose was crooked and swollen, with blood smeared on his upper lip.

"Nothing broken," he muttered. Then his gaze shifted and met hers, and he grinned. "You're awake."

"I don't want to be." Her jaw throbbed from the minimal movement.

Ke'Niq patted her shoulder. That triggered new throbbing.

"Where are we?"
~~~~~

"All our equipment is dead. 'Jor smashed us up even worse than the last time he crashed. I took a look around ..." He shrugged. "I don't recognize anything."

"We sure aren't in Enlo's Rest." She sat up, choking on a groan. All her bones were trying to shatter. "It wouldn't feel like this."

"You believe in Enlo. Why?"

"He makes a lot more sense than trusting the Ancestors not to be nasty *a'go'sots* and refuse to let us into the Halls."

"True." He grinned, until a strong gust of wind swirled around them, dropping the temperature. "We need to find shelter."

M'kar looked around for the air-car. She found a crumpled lump surrounded by a spray of shattered pieces. She felt as sick as the time her cousin Bexqer had poisoned her.

The light was strange, that gray of twilight when the air turned to murky liquid, and she couldn't see more than a few meters away. Beyond the crumpled air-car there was little but boulders and pebbles. They were on a slope, but she couldn't tell where it met the sky or where it reached the bottom.

She had multiple scar-worthy cuts in her feet and legs and down one arm. Would they be considered battle wounds? Could this be considered another kidnapping attempt she had foiled? Great-grandfather and maybe even Grandfather would praise her and laugh at the boys for their stupidity. She expected Ke'Jor to blame her, maybe even say she had tried to fly the air-car and he had jumped in to stop her. Most of her cousins played such tricks.

Jagged furrows streaked the rocky slope, littered with shreds of ceramic hull and mangled equipment. She looked up, trying again to find the sky. That simple movement made her head hurt. Her neck crackled loudly enough she almost didn't hear the sobbing groan behind her. Ke'Jor was waking up. She had hoped he hadn't survived the crash. It was his fault, after all.

Thunder crackled, sounding like a thousand massive serving platters tipped off a shelf, bouncing and banging on tables and benches before hitting the flagstone floor. Rain slapped at her, blown nearly horizontal. Then a moment later she felt the wind.

That didn't make sense.

She had an awful idea where they had crashed, but her brain didn't want to give her the words.

"Come on." Ke'Niq stood over her with his hand held out.

She let him pull her to her feet, even though her body hurt enough all over to make her want to shriek. M'kar held her breath, bit her lip, and promised herself she would kick Ke'Jor soon. She might have to wait until they were rescued and he was on his feet again, but she would kick him.

All over. Until he hurt like she did right now.

They went downhill, toward a pile of rocks. Her vision cleared as they got closer. She saw dark gaps under some long slabs of stone that might be shelter.

The slope dropped and twisted under them, then flattened. The light turned an odd shade of green streaked with amber and rippled as if they were underwater. She couldn't see more than a few meters in any direction. M'kar clutched at Ke'Niq and closed her eyes when the ground kept turning, twisting them to the right.

Closing her eyes didn't help. She thought her empty stomach would come up her throat. She opened her eyes. That didn't help either.

"Get to the rocks." Ke'Niq's voice strained like he fought not to be sick, too.

They stumbled forward. Four downhill steps, and suddenly they were going uphill. Behind them, Ke'Jor wailed and whimpered.

With every step forward, they slid uphill a meter or more. The slope got steeper and in a few steps they hurtled uphill, headfirst.

They slid on their stomachs. Faster and faster. M'kar couldn't feel the sand rubbing against her. This was like sliding through soft, warm oil.

Ke'Jor let out a yelp as he slid past them, tumbling head over heels uphill. His shriek turned into glubbing and bubbling. He tumbled, splashing and kicking, into sand that became deep purple water.

Two seconds later, she and Ke'Niq hit the water.

It wasn't water. It was fermenting gondiberry syrup, thick and sticky and the aroma overpowering. Nisandrians used it for heavy-duty cleaning of machines. Her uncles sold it off-world labeled as wine. It was supposed to be very popular. The rotten-sweet smell made M'kar want to heave. The sticky turned slick. A strong wave of the awful purple stuff swept her and Ke'Niq apart. Another wave lifted her high and turned her around, then over. Just a dozen steps away, she saw those rocks again, and the promise of shelter.

"Wait for me!" Ke'Jor wailed, as M'kar started swimming. He splashed her, flailing and kicking and trying to get a grip on her.

"Leave me alone!" She kicked hard, trying to put him behind her.

The sea of syrup vanished. She rolled across rubble-littered ground. She was coated in dust. Her cuts stung and bled as the sandy dust filled them. The only wet and sticky came from her own blood. M'kar flopped onto her back. The sky churned with storm. She shuddered, positive it would burst open on top of her at any moment. She turned, and saw purple swirls of sand, with the rocks sitting on top of the waves, but not moving. The optical contradictions made her eyes hurt.

Chapter Two

The shelter sat right in front of her, but taller now, pillars of rock with a crossbar, forming a rough doorway. M'kar rubbed her eyes and paused.

She was entirely alone. What had happened to the boys?

The light softened, the air cleared, moving away from her in a visible wave, so now she could see to the horizon, a clear line where dark rocks and rubble met the sky. M'kar shuddered as she understood.

Etrusca's Wall. She was sitting in the deep bowl of the surbda crater called Etrusca's Wall.

Lore said anyone who went into the surbda craters went insane. Family lore said Great-grandfather Aquid had visited Etrusca's Wall many times. Every time he went missing, he could always be found heading toward the surbda crater. He claimed he was visiting his sweetheart, who lived in the crater. Clear proof he was insane. No one could live in a surbda crater, with no plants, no animals, no water. Yet his was a peaceful, mischievous kind of insane, and his health was that of a man thirty years younger, so maybe going insane wasn't all bad.

Was she going to go insane?

"Please, Enlo ... help me?" she whispered.

Then she heard her father's voice, as clearly as if Ashrock stood behind her, teasing her into fierceness. Her name was from ancient lore, a mighty warrior, shortened to mean *Little Blade*. Ashrock insisted little blades were far more deadly than great, long blades, because they could hide and get close, and wait for the right time to do the most damage.

"Come, my little blade, my *mi'sho'ki*, make me proud. Give me reason to laugh at those *agu'shi* in my old age. Get up!"

Her legs ached, like she had fractures in every bone, but she pulled herself to her feet. With each step, she braced for something new to hit her, for the world to turn inside out.

Nothing happened. Four steps brought her within arm's reach of the pillars. They were made of many pieces of rock, odd angles, long and thin pieces holding up massive squat pieces. The pillars shouldn't have stayed upright. They wobbled, and the individual pieces rocked in different directions, different rhythms, tipping and even spinning ... but the pillars stayed together. M'kar took a step back, watching those gyrating, always-on-the-verge-of-disintegrating pillars.

Swirls of color filled her eyes, a gossamer sheet blowing in a gentle breeze, between the two pillars. Colors spun outward from the sheet, some evaporating in the air, others staying in long streamers that twirled and wrapped around the pillars. Some oozed outward and down, reaching for her. Beckoning. She took two steps.

"Not yet," a woman said from behind her. "Well, you are something new, aren't you?" A gentle hand gripped M'kar's shoulder and turned her.

The rubble and wasteland vanished. A multi-colored haze filled her eyes. She stumbled, then she stood in a pool clearing. Short, fat fish in green and blue jewel tones chased each other. The plants surrounding the clearing were thick and green, heavy with moisture that drove away the sticky and dusty feeling. Her cuts no longer hurt.

"Sit, child." The hand guided her down, onto a folding stool.

The woman had long, blue-black hair with silver streaks at her temples. Multiple blue tattoo lines streaked away from her eyes, emphasizing the thin white scars surrounding them. More white scars and blue tattoo lines outlined her mouth, like laugh lines rather than silent testimony to a terrible battle for her life. Her eyes were bright silvery green in a face of sharp cheekbones and skin the color of dark honey.

"Who are you? And who do you serve with your soul?" She let go of M'kar's shoulder and reached to the ground at her feet, to pick up a glossy black stone bowl that fit perfectly into her cupped hands.

"I am M'kar, of the Ba'e'do'stra, daughter of Ashrock, second-born tri-born son, and Dr. Jeyn Fleetwind of the Alliance."

Her gaze dropped to the bowl as the woman dipped it into the pool. The water sparkled, drops falling with rainbow glints. The symbols of the woman's tattoos, on her scarred, bare arms, and the clan ornaments and battle tokens sewn around her collar and on her belt were rooted in the oldest, fiercest traditions of Nisandros. M'kar said a silent prayer for help and strength, and took her life in her small hands.

"I serve Enlo, the All-Maker. I want to go to the Academy and study on Le'anka and join the Fleet and help in the hunt for more lost Human worlds and find the Gatekeepers."

"Do you?" The woman's face was calmly unreadable. Grandfather said people who hid their thoughts so completely had much to hide.

M'kar braced for a knife to appear from the folds of the woman's skirt. Despite all the teaching of many Masters sent from Le'anka, too many on her world still worshipped and petitioned the Ancestors, instead of serving Enlo. Ashrock had put her to bed many nights with stories of brave warriors and teachers who had been killed for their efforts to turn Nisandros back to Enlo.

"Welcome, child. I salute you as a brave warrior who holds the power to change many worlds." The woman smiled, her face brightening. She handed the bowl to M'kar. "This will help while we wait for your sisters to come and take you to safety."

"I don't have any sisters." M'kar nearly inhaled the first mouthful of the water, shocked by its sweetness, its thickness in her mouth like pol-bug syrup, and the sparkling sensation on her tongue. She wanted to hold that mouthful for as long as she could hold her breath.

"You have hundreds. Thousands, if we look back through history. Drink. Be welcome in Enlo's name, brave one. Why did your parents name you Little Blade? And what is the Alliance?"

In between sips, to make the experience last, M'kar told her what Dr. Jeyn always referred to as the simplified history of the Alliance: the quest to unite the Human race while seeking out the Gatekeepers and the truth of just why all Human life had been evacuated from Core, the birth world, so many centuries ago. Then she explained how her mother had come to Nisandros to study the culture, had married Ashrock in what everyone thought was purely a political marriage, and the consternation and shock when they had produced a child. Nisandrians were supposed to be altered enough that they couldn't interbreed with other Humans. And yet M'kar had been born without any outside interference or help.

"Yes, that foolish experimentation with our genetics was taking place when I was your age," the woman murmured. "Aquid has told me about the silly belief that they succeeded in making themselves superior, a new breed of Human."

"Aquid?" M'kar considered the possibility someone else had that name. "Do you know my great-grandfather?"

"I have known many with that name. But your sisters approach. Do you speak truly, child? Do you serve Enlo, no matter how you are threatened and reviled, to make you serve the Ancestors?"

"I want to. Most of my cousins make fun of me, though, when I'm having morning prayers. And that *boostifak*, Ke'Jor, says I won't be allowed to pray to Enlo when I'm married to him. But I'm not going to marry him. He's a nosepicker!"

The woman laughed and reached to wrap her arms around M'kar. The embrace stung for a moment, like touching a live power feed.

"If you take my marks, you will warn the universe that you will give your life for Enlo, and you will not be forced." She touched her eye tattoos.

"Like Etrusca." M'kar grinned. She liked the blue lines, and all the stories she had heard of Etrusca. She had vowed she would never marry any man who served the Ancestors and denied Enlo. Many of her scars came from attempts to silence her, to blind her, and punish her when other women took up her vows.

"Yes," the woman whispered. "Like Etrusca. Come. Your sisters are here." She stood and gestured to the right.

M'kar turned. The pool and lush greenery vanished in a dizzying whirl as she went to her knees. Dust and debris surrounded her again, and her arms stung from her many cuts. Voices called out to her as the dust spun upward, filling the air, turning the light murky again. M'kar bowed her head, guarded her face with a bent arm while reaching out with the other, and aimed herself toward the voices.

The dust storm settled slowly. She found the crashed air-car in front of her, halfway up the slope of the crater. A line of people trailed down the slope, all dressed in heavy storm gear. The dust had settled enough for M'kar to see them passing Ke'Jor and Ke'Niq along, from one person to another, heading up to the top of the wall of rubble.

"Well, it's the Little Blade," a woman said, bending down to look her in the eyes. "I'm sorry for what you'll have to face, but another storm approaches and we don't have time."

M'kar didn't have to ask what that meant. A few moments of thought as her rescuers led her up the slope explained everything. The woman's protective gear bore Rissor Clan markings. Her rescuers were taking her to their clan house, which was closer than her own. She would be stuck in that clan core house until the weather relented, just as Ke'Jor and Ke'Niq had been stuck with Ba'e'do'stra.

The rescue craft was a three-part land-cart that rolled along the rough landscape on massive treads. Each compartment could be sealed. All three children were put in the middle compartment with the healers. As soon as Ke'Jor could sit up and talk, he declared he had rescued M'kar.

"That one couldn't rescue his own dinner from a half-dead ykas," the woman driving the land-cart called from the cockpit. The entire team was women. She let out a whoop of amusement. "Don't you worry, child, you're safe with us. Just make sure you're never out of sight or hearing of any of us, and you'll survive all their idiot schemes."

M'kar didn't ask. She knew what they were talking about, and it made her head hurt.

"I did so," Ke'Jor blurted. "And it's all Ke'Niq's fault we crashed."

"He never touched the controls," M'kar snapped. "You were flying and you weren't paying attention and you ignored the warnings when we were close to Etrusca's Wall."

"You take that back!" He sat up, resisting the hands trying to push him flat on the padded bench while the healer sealed up the long gashes on his leg.

M'kar stuck her tongue out at him. Several women chuckled. Ke'Jor cursed her and the oldest healer reached up and slapped his mouth. He stared at her, but instead of fury, fear twisted his face.

"She's the oldest of the aunts," the second healer whispered, pausing in washing the grit out of the cuts on M'kar's arm. She winked. "You never want to make her angry, and he just did."

"She has to take it back," Ke'Jor muttered, when the woman went back to working on his leg. "Grandfather says she's going to marry me, so she has to obey me."

"Not never!" M'kar ignored the sting of her cleaned wounds as she struggled to sit up. Words slipped into her mind like someone had written them down for her. "I call on Etrusca and take her vows."

Silence for several moments. Every woman in the compartment turned to look at her. Most smiled. Many met each other's gazes and nodded. M'kar had the awful feeling quite a few adult conversations took place in just a few seconds. The kind that said a hundred words with a raised eyebrow, a nod, a pursing of the lips.

Ke'Jor blubbered, insisting she take that back, too. He ordered Ke'Niq to tell them he was a hero, he had rescued M'kar. Ke'Niq scowled and turned his head to the wall. Half the women hurried M'kar out of the compartment. They sealed themselves into the third compartment, allowing her to ask questions without Ke'Jor interrupting.

Then she learned she and the boys had been missing three days. Search parties from both clans had been all around the area, but none had gone into the crater until Tayleen, the oldest aunt, received a signal from "our friend, the recluse," telling them to come get the children. That was the only reference to the woman M'kar had seen, the only proof that she hadn't hallucinated the entire odd encounter. After all, one of her wounds was a painfully tender, bloody patch on the back of her head.

Just before they reached the clan house, Tayleen took M'kar's hands in both of hers and looked into her eyes. Everything around them seemed to go still, as if the world held its breath.

"Little Blade, for the sake of our friend, for the love of Enlo, do not speak of what you saw and heard and tasted during the time you were lost. It is enough to say you were injured and you do not remember, and nothing is clear. Will you do that for us?" She waited until M'kar nodded. "You called upon Etrusca. Are you willing to take her mark? Willing to serve Enlo?"

M'kar didn't have to think long on that. Etrusca's blue tattoo lines around her eyes would warn the universe that she had vowed herself to Enlo's service and to purity. She called upon the monsters of Nisandros's darkest legends to defend her choice in marriage and in soul-service.

When the rescue craft reached the Rissor clan house, she was whisked away to the women's quarter, and the boys went into their parents' quarters. Two days passed before any of the men who led the clan gathered up their courage to invite her to enjoy clan hospitality.

When M'kar emerged, the deed had been done, dealing the plans of Rissor Clan a serious blow. She wore the tattoo lines of her vows to Enlo and to Etrusca. Even the most brutal Ancestor worshippers lacked the courage to gamble that the monsters of the deep darkness who had protected Etrusca wouldn't leap to the defense of her new adopted daughter. The monsters were said to den in the surbda craters. Too many would-be heroes had gone into those craters and never returned. Better to fear than to risk their lives to prove those fears wrong.

To make sure no one tried to drug M'kar into compliance, Desra, eleven years old and wearing Etrusca's marks, was her constant companion whenever she left the women's quarter. By the time the storms calmed enough that her parents could come on the ten-hour overland drive to retrieve her, M'kar and Desra had vowed sisterhood to each other, with matching starflower tattoos on their right shoulders.

Other than regular attempts by Ke'Jor and his father and grandfather to have private conversations with her, M'kar enjoyed her stay in the Rissor clan house. The women ensured she was never alone, even when she slept, so no man could claim she had agreed to betrothal. The women's quarter was her refuge, and an entirely new world for her. With the permission and cooperation of the Rissor women, she took extensive notes to aid Dr. Jeyn's studies. The women's quarter, the domain of the women born into the clan, wasn't to cut them off from the affairs of the men, but rather to keep men from interfering in their lives and give them some privacy. Dr. Jeyn was a welcome visitor in any clan house that was on friendly terms with Ashrock's clan, but she had never stayed overnight in the women's quarter.

M'kar had female friends of her own age for the first time in her life. At home, she had no female playmates at all, because the Ba'e'do'stra hadn't produced daughters in centuries. Ashrock blamed that on some extra genetic tinkering his ancestors had performed in the Nisandrian search for superiority.

The tradition of alliance marriages to force peace among the clans meant several of her cousins would marry Rissor girls. M'kar's new friends deserved every bit of help she could give them, so she warned them about which of her cousins were tolerable, which ones needed a good thrashing every day before breakfast, and which ones could be trained to be civil. Her new friends did the same for her, recommending several brothers and cousins who were much more agreeable possible husbands than Ke'Jor. They all agreed he was an overbearing, arrogant snot. M'kar thanked them for their advice but didn't tell them Ashrock didn't want her to marry a Nisandrian man.

"I know from personal experience what arrogant, selfish, narrow-minded brutes Nisandrian men can be. I don't want my *mi'sho'ki* bound to one of them for the rest of her life," Ashrock had declared. "Actually, the rest of *his* life, which won't be very long. I want to spare you the trouble of having to kill one idiot after another. Blood can be very hard to wash out of your good clothes." Then he laughed and discussed another handy weapon to use on unwanted husbands.

Communication bands were open despite the storms, and the women made sure M'kar spoke with her parents every day. Her father made her laugh, telling her about the visit from the smelly, self-appointed prophet. He had instructions from several Ancestors that M'kar had to marry the heir of every clan whose land touched Ba'e'do'stra land.

Grandfather Ba'shiq, the high chieftain of Ba'e'do'stra, asked just how M'kar could be married to eight different men at the same time. Uncle Be'dosho asked if M'kar had to kill each husband to free herself to marry the next one in line. That was the kind of question he would ask. When M'kar watched the recording of the interview later, she wondered if her uncle hoped she might die fighting at least one of those husbands. Not that she would ever marry any of them, but it was the kind of nasty trouble that particular uncle would enjoy inflicting on her.

Be'dosho, Rokas, and Ashrock were triplets, but none of them looked like each other. Identical multiple births were considered a bad portent. Fraternal multiples either granted bragging rights to the parents' clans or were classed as bad omens, depending on the strength of the clan's enemies and allies. In the case of Ashrock and his brothers, a handful of prophets of doom took turns hammering on the doors of the clan house for a few years. The demands for sacrifice to protect Nisandros died away when they were outnumbered by the prophets who said the triplets were a gift from the Ancestors. Several of those original prophets had returned, not too decrepit to chant the equivalent of, "Told you so!" when M'kar was born, and new doomsayers invaded Ba'e'do'stra.

M'kar liked Rokas, but she thought Be'dosho had helped several failed assassins get past security into the clan house. He was probably the one who invited this prophet to come make his demands.

The stinky old man had first answered yes to Be'dosho's question. Then his eyes rolled back in his head, and he shuddered a few times. His voice rasped when he insisted that the Ancestors would allow M'kar to have eight husbands at the same time. They would give her power to enslave all the other clans for the benefit of her grandfather's clan.

Ba'shiq and his sons let him keep talking until he finally identified which Ancestors were giving him his instructions. They had all hated each other when they were alive, so their agreement in this matter was highly suspect. The clinching point was that they all were enemies of Ba'e'do'stra. Ba'shiq then declared the meeting ended, and ordered the crazy old man thrown out into the storm.

The prophet's visit had stirred the pot at home, so M'kar was glad to be entirely away from the clan house. During storms, when they were stranded at home, the high-ranking men only had two choices of entertainment: war games that resulted in bloody wounds, broken bones, and comas, or philosophical discussions. Their favorite topic for the last nine years was the impact of M'kar's birth on Nisandros. Too many agreed that she was a figure of prophecy. Most arguments were over whether she fulfilled prophecies of blessing or doom.

Some cousins and uncles had been advocating for her death since before her birth, insisting M'kar's existence threatened their world's survival. The only way Nisandros could eventually overcome all its enemies and rule a star empire was for her to die. None of the advocates for sacrifice could agree on what sort of ceremony the Ancestors required. Momentary allies turned into deadly enemies over petty details. Poisoned or bled out? What knives to use? What kind of altar? Which Ancestors would preside over the sacrifice?

Ashrock and Jeyn assured her the constant disagreements meant nothing would ever happen.

"Don't you worry, *mi'sho'ki*," her father had said on several occasions. "These idiots rely on the Ancestors for authority, and nobody can ever agree on what the Ancestors want, or what they are saying."

Finally, the storm died down enough to allow for safe travel. Ashrock and Jeyn came by land-cart to Rissor to fetch M'kar home. She would miss her new friends, but she looked forward to the long, bumpy trip down the storm-sodden roads and across the Barrens. This journey offered the three some real privacy and family time. Despite the vastness of the sprawling clan house, both were nearly impossible. Someone was always watching and listening and breaking in and interrupting. The first three hours of the journey from home, Ashrock and Jeyn had spent detecting and killing a handful of spying devices planted in the land-cart. Then there was sabotage to the communication equipment to overcome.

"Po'pa, this isn't really a game anymore, is it?" M'kar said, after her parents explained why they were half a day late arriving to fetch her.

"No." Ashrock tightened his arm around her. She waited for him to tease and move his hand up to circle her throat, but he didn't. That emphasized how serious everything was. "The game has gone too far. It isn't fun. It's time we grow up. Eh, my love?"

"Don't get me started. This drive is far too short for all the things I would need to say in a lecture on the infantile mindset of this entire planet." Jeyn's mouth twitched as she visibly fought not to smile. She took her gaze off the road in front of them long enough to nod to her husband and daughter sitting next to her on the wide bench seat.

She was driving the land-cart, being the better driver. Ashrock was proud of her skill, especially going over rough terrain and in bad weather. M'kar wondered if her parents planned on mishaps and delays, because they had come to fetch her in the second largest land-cart. It had plenty of room for the bench seats to fold down into beds, with spare clothes and food, survival gear and medical kits in the bins under the seats. It even had a sanitary facility, though it was little more than a tank with a lid and a seat. After the lavish hospitality of the Rissor Clan, a few days of roughing it, with just her parents for company, might just be fun.

"We had hoped not to have to leave for a few more years. There is so much more work we need to do, gathering your mother's data," Ashrock continued. "And I have delayed making my own arrangements, preparing a landing spot for us ... but we will still be comfortable. When the weather clears, in all the fuss of opening the passes and river crossings, our preparations won't be noticed."

"Where are we going?" M'kar asked, after choking back a dozen other questions. Ridiculous questions, with obvious answers. After all, her parents had talked often about fleeing Nisandros.

"Where would you like to go?" Dr. Jeyn asked. A sudden, hard gust of wind pushed the land-cart sideways. She turned the back of the vehicle to the lashing of the rain and hit the brakes. "I can go anywhere in the Alliance. A good dozen research and educational institutions would gladly take me on, just to have first rights to all the reports I'll probably spend the next five years churning out. Where you two will be happy is more important."

The rain roared down on them, loud enough M'kar thought she couldn't hear herself if she spoke. She felt her father's laughter, though she couldn't hear it. He wrapped his arm tighter around her, and scooted over a little on the bench seat, so she was pressed up against her mother now. M'kar sighed, happy to feel so small, wedged between her parents, and safe from spying eyes and critical voices and the impending threat of another honor scar if she made one wrong step.

She was proud of the lightning bolt on her temple, earned when she was four and poked out the eye of the first assassin to actually get his hands on her, but M'kar didn't like the thought of ending up with as many scars as her father had. She thought her mother, with her unmarked skin, was the most beautiful woman in the universe. Maybe she wouldn't be a famous scholar like her mother, but she wanted to look like her. Her mother's relatives were anthropologists and archeologists, searching for the Gatekeepers and other lost Human cultures. Some of them had to learn self-defense and fighting techniques. Why couldn't she be a warrior and a scientist at the same time?

M'kar had plenty of time to think while the rain and wind rocked and battered the land-cart. None of them were able to talk with so much noise. After a few minutes of the pounding, Dr. Jeyn checked the instruments and indicated with hand gestures that the heavy downpour would continue a while longer. The three moved to the back of the land-cart, with room to stretch out and get comfortable. While Ashrock fussed over the tiny heating coils, to make some emberwing tea and toast bread and cheese for them, M'kar pulled blankets and cushions out of the storage bins under the seats, making a cozy nest for them.

Dr. Jeyn settled down with her tablet. M'kar saw enough over her mother's shoulder to know she was working on another one of her discussions of Nisandrian culture that had already made her famous across the Alliance.

A red light flashed four times. She turned to find a warning on the screen in front of the driver's seat: water had risen enough to threaten the stability of the soil under the wheels. M'kar scrambled forward and hit the anchor control before the piloting computer asked if the anchors should be deployed. The land-cart shook four times as the telescoping anchor poles shot down from the frame, into the bedrock. If the rising water approached the bottom of the vehicle, another warning would sound, with time to either retract the wheels and anchors altogether so the land-cart would float, or telescope the anchors further, to raise them above the water. All depending on weather forecasts, current speed of the water, and their location and elevation.

By the time M'kar crawled the two meters back to the nest, Ashrock had brought their food over. They curled up on the cushions and wrapped blankets around themselves and M'kar happily settled between her parents again. She bit into the first slice of bread with melted cheese and hissed a little when she burned the roof of her mouth.

"I can hear myself."

"That didn't last long," Ashrock said. "What are our chances? Another storm will roll in without warning, as soon as we pull up the anchors and head out? Or if we sit and wait for an hour, nothing will happen?"

"Until we pull up anchors," M'kar added. That earned a chuckle.

"Let's wait a little while. At least until we finish eating." Dr. Jeyn took a sip, her eyes lit up, and she laughed as she lowered her mug. "Oh, I had a nasty idea."

"We stay out here and make them think we got drowned?" M'kar guessed.

"Close." Her mother nodded and tapped the end of her nose. "We need to test you for mind-reading, if you're going to keep eavesdropping like that."

Chapter Three

"Hah! Between your family's psionic heritage popping out when it's least expected, and all the knots my ancestors made in our genetics, we should be prepared for many surprises, with our *mi'sho'ki*," Ashrock said. "We should plan for trouble. Forget our plan to wander for a few years to shake the assassins off our tails. Settle right away on Le'anka. I want access to the best teachers, for whatever gifts surprise us. They'd be fools not to offer you a position at the Academy."

"Wouldn't that be nice?" Her voice softened, so the dying drumming of the rain almost muffled it.

"What was the rest of your idea, Mom?" M'kar asked.

"First, make contact with your father's oath-scar friends who owe him the biggest honor debts. We'll ask them to help us sneak off the planet." Jeyn grinned when Ashrock let out a bark of laughter louder than the rain banging on the roof. "Then, we leave this cart perched on the top of Etrusca's Wall, so it looks like we went inside to explore. After those stories the boys told, they'd expect me to be curious enough to take the chance. How desperate are the nitzickers to profit off M'kar, that they'd swallow their fear and stage a rescue?"

"Depends on how loudly our enemies crow. If they're loud enough, all the schemers will revolt, just to disappoint them." Ashrock nodded. He didn't look as amused as M'kar expected. "It's a lovely, nasty trick, my love, and I'm proud of you. And worried. I think I've become a bad influence on you."

"Don't brag too much, *ne'gu'shki'do*. I haven't told you the worst of the tricks we used to play when I was a student." Jeyn nodded twice for punctuation and took another sip of her tea.

"Don't you want to play a trick and make them think we're lost forever?" M'kar asked.

"Yes, it might be fun, but think about all your mother's research, all her files, all our books, the knife set I bought for your ninth birthday ..." He winked as he trailed off, clearly teasing.

"We could have fun sneaking into the clan house and stealing things without anybody knowing," she offered. "Great-grandfather showed me most of the secret passageways and assassins' spy-holes."

That got a more normal bark of laughter from her father, and a tight hug that nearly knocked her mug out of her hands. The three curled up together and talked and laughed and plotted, coming up with new ideas and tossing them aside in rapid-fire fashion, until the rain came back loud enough to make talking impossible. Despite the noise, M'kar fell asleep, curled up between her parents.

When she woke a little less than an hour later, the storm had passed. Her parents had settled her on cushions directly behind the bench seat, and the land-cart was moving again. She listened to them talking and was a little disappointed to hear that they wouldn't just disappear, no matter how fun that would be. There were matters of honor and ceremony to consider. Although Ashrock resented the power games being woven around his daughter, he didn't want to cut all ties with his family and homeworld. Someday, he might want to come home. The fewer hurt feelings and honor scores to settle, from how Ashrock and his wife and daughter left the planet, the safer they would all be, no matter what happened in the future.

~~~~~

When the land-cart grew close enough to the clan house, its identification beam triggered the first of the security sensors. A stream of messages for both Dr. Jeyn and Ashrock flashed on a screen in the control panel. He read them off, one by one, and they discussed how to deal with each request for information or an errand an elder in the clan needed them to perform. Then Ashrock groaned.

"What, Po'pa?" M'kar asked.

"Anguak has come to visit Grandfather." He sighed.

"Is he the one who always smells like he has wet diapers?"

That got a snort from Dr. Jeyn.

"That's a very kind description of the old lunatic." His next sigh turned into a weary chuckle. "He actually makes Grandfather look reasonable and balanced. The problem, my little warrior --"

"Besides his smell filling the entire clan house?" Dr. Jeyn said.

"Besides that. Anguak is very old-fashioned and devoted to the Ancestors. He gets nasty if you mention Enlo in front of him or you don't pray to his Ancestors when he does."

"He's easy enough to avoid. Especially since he's only got one leg, and he's too vain to use a wheelchair or hoverchair," she pointed out.

"You're right, my love, but you know we'll have to go through a ceremonial greeting when we return. Someone will make a fuss over M'kar surviving the crash. And staying with Rissor. Anguak will come with Grandfather, and he'll go into an unholy rage when he sees her new tattoos."

"Is he the one who thinks it's an abomination if girls have tattoos?" Dr. Jeyn asked.

"Not tattoos, but any sign of devotion to Enlo. Especially when Etrusca is involved."
~~~~~

"Oh." She nodded and pursed her lips in thought.

"What's wrong with Etrusca?" M'kar asked.

"Nothing, *mi'sho'ki*." He wrapped his arm tight around her. "Anguak hates Enlo, and he curses Etrusca for turning her back on the Ancestors."

"He's stupid to hate Enlo."

"I agree." He nodded and didn't laugh like she expected. "But Anguak is considered a very holy man because he's very crazy."

"And if he's holy, and he tries to hit me, I can't hit him back?"

"You'll be condemned as a blasphemer." Dr. Jeyn sighed. "Are you sure we can't just vanish on our way home?"

"They know we're coming. At least Grandfather warned me."

"I like Great-grandfather. Can he come with us when we go to Le'anka?" M'kar asked.

"No, I'm sorry. I think he would like it very much, but he's also crazy enough to be holy, so he isn't allowed to leave Nisandros."

M'kar didn't think that was fair, but she knew better than to say so.

Dr. Jeyn suggested they spend the remainder of the ride praying for Enlo to protect them and keep their enemies from coming to the greeting hall. M'kar prayed hard, until her head hurt.

She was nearly dizzy from the effort when she walked into the greeting hall two hours later with her parents. A deep sigh escaped her when she saw her grandfather, Chieftain Ba'shiq, sitting in his high seat at the far end of the greeting hall. Her great-uncles and uncles and cousins sat on their different levels around him. The aunts and great-aunts weren't blood members of the clan, so they sat on the long benches that ran down either side of the long hall. She tallied the faces that were missing and felt a little better when some of the worst of her cousins weren't there.

She looked for the seat tucked into the corner, as high as her grandfather's chair, where Great-grandfather Aquid always sat. M'kar almost stumbled. Aquid's seat was empty. If he wasn't there, then his guest couldn't come to the greeting.

Enlo had listened. Enlo had answered her prayers.

Everyone waited in silence, their faces set in ceremonial solemnity while Ashrock and Jeyn and M'kar walked down the center of the hall, between the two long fire trenches, until they stood before the high seat.

"Well done, Little Blade," Ba'shiq said, breaking the silence before it became a crushing weight. "You have strengthened the ties of friendship with Rissor." He chuckled, startling M'kar, and from the widening eyes, many in the hall. "And frustrated those fumbling attempts to trap you into a betrothal. Well done indeed."

Great-uncle Basqid tipped his head back and opened his mouth. Ba'shiq skewered him with his gaze, silencing him.

"Some will insist that our friendship can only be deepened further by marriage. I say the scramble to win your favor and my favor will be far more profitable. Make them wait until you're old enough to choose. I swear on your tattoos of Etrusca's vows, I will not force you to marry anyone in Rissor. I commend the vows you have taken." He cleared his throat. "Some here may think I betray the Ancestors, but in the end, all bow to Enlo. Even the Ancestors."

That got more widened eyes and choking sounds and whispers from around the long room. M'kar didn't know what to think. She doubted her grandfather prayed to the Ancestors, much less to Enlo. She couldn't figure out why he was talking like he respected them all. She had more questions by the end of the ceremonial welcome, which wasn't as long as she had feared it would take.

Other than her grandfather, nobody else talked to her during the ceremony. That was fine. She didn't want to talk to them, either. M'kar was glad to finally retreat to her parents' suite of rooms and close multiple doors to block out the rest of the house and the clan. For now, she was completely alone. The clan council had asked her parents to stay back for a few minutes for a private conversation.

She stepped into the common room, intending to look for a favorite book chip. A salty-metallic stink slammed into her nose. Movement to her right. She dropped to her knees and rolled away. A dark figure leaped at her from the open door of the storage room. Later, the assailant turned out to be a particularly stinky young acolyte of yet another self-proclaimed prophet. She only knew he was streaked with dirt, and skinny, and whipped thin cords at her. She somersaulted away, with the tip of one cord stinging the side of her neck. M'kar snatched up a boli stick, left out from her parents' morning sparring. It gave her enough reach to snag loops of the cords and whip them around, smacking the attacker in the face and neck.

Blood spurted. She was close enough to see the barbs embedded in the braided leather thongs. Poisoned barbs, judging by how the acolyte collapsed, shrieking and foaming at the mouth. Doors slammed open and her parents hurtled into the room. Ashrock sighed and shook his head and looked at Dr. Jeyn.

"Don't expect me to be your conscience this late in the game," she said, and went down on one knee to wrap an arm around M'kar. "I say let the *da'ook* suffer."

"Yes, but we won't know who sent him if he dies." Ashrock winked at M'kar and stepped over to the shelf by the door, where one of the many ever-present bottles of general antidote waited.

He poured the antidote on the young man until he sputtered and choked and nearly drowned. Then he caught M'kar under her arms, hoisted her up to sit on his shoulder, and went into the next room to call for household security. He worked out his and M'kar's frustration by castigating them. Either they had failed in their duty, or they had helped the assassin sneak into their quarters.

"It is most definitely time, *mi'sho'ki,* that we choose discretion over honor or valor, and find a more sensible world for you to grown up in." He snorted. "Your Po'pa is getting too old for this stupidity."

~~~~~

Ashrock and Jeyn put their plan to leave Nisandros into action as soon as they got up the next morning. There were dozens of little details and messages to handle, material to collect, loose ends in research projects to tie up, promises to fulfill, and private farewells to perform with friends who could be trusted to keep their secret. The winter storms in the northern hemisphere would end in three decs, and that wasn't nearly enough time to make all the arrangements to take the first shuttle that could go up to the Alliance's orbital station. The formal announcement of their departure had to be made at the right time and the right place, with the right witnesses, or the uproar could justify their family being detained. Hurt feelings and insult claims had to be prevented at all costs.

M'kar had her part to play, running errands for her parents, returning borrowed items, retrieving items that had been loaned or taken without permission. She returned to their family suite with a handful of book chips that had been borrowed from her mother's library over the years. M'kar was grinning in triumph, until her cheeks hurt. She had retrieved the chips with as much sneaky stealth as they had originally been taken by various cousins and aunts and uncles. Considering how dusty some chips were, and how deeply they had been buried among personal possessions, she doubted anyone would realize the books had been reclaimed until luns or even years after she and her parents had left.

Then she saw the shriveled old man sitting on the bench by the fire pit in their common room, and her grin fell off her face. M'kar immediately looked around for Anguak. She sniffed hard, trying to find him by his dirty wet clothes stink, since she couldn't see him in the shadows.

"Little Blade," Great-grandfather Aquid wheezed. "Right on time." He beckoned, holding out a bony, wrinkled arm covered in blurry red and black and green tattoos.

M'kar bit her tongue to keep from asking what "right on time" meant. The crazy old man would just say he had seen into the future, so he knew when she would be back in the suite.

Of course, he *was* waiting for her, so maybe he did have visions?

Her father would laugh and say that showed the old man's cleverness, constantly playing mind-tricks on people. They were very good tricks, M'kar had to admit. Especially when his voice got hollow and his eyes rolled back so all she could see were the whites. Many people
~~~~~

would say the Ancestors spoke through him when he talked like that.

"Tell your father, don't trust the one-eyed pilot, and don't trust the woman with the blue-tufted ahsnaq riding her shoulders. Trust the Ankuar," he finished on a whisper. "Wait until the Ankuar comes and then bargain with him for the ride up to the station."

M'kar wanted to ask, "What station?" but she was afraid to play games and pretend she didn't know what the old man was talking about.

How had Aquid figured out they were trying to find a shuttle ride up to the Alliance's orbital station, and from there arrange passage to Le'anka? Her mother had the best spy-killing equipment, straight from a friend in Fleet security. She regularly swept their suite for anything that would help the clan spy on them. There was no way her great-grandfather could have been spying on them, listening to their plans.

Yet he knew. How?

"You need to leave as soon as possible," Aquid said, his voice normal again. "You went to Etrusca's Wall." He patted the bench next to him. "Tell me about it. Did you see Etrusca? Is that why you wear her mark now?"

"Did I see Etrusca?" She settled on the bench. He smelled of tongue-stinging fire sweets, rather than the medicine-and-paper-skin smell of most old people. "Is she supposed to be there?"

"I don't know if she's *supposed* to be there." He chuckled and winked. "But I've seen her. Many times. I've talked to her. Contradictory woman won't tell me if she's dead or alive." Another chuckle. "Don't tell Yntriell, but I asked her to marry me a few times."

M'kar nodded. Yntriell wasn't her great-grandmother, but she was Aquid's third wife.

"Every time I asked, she laughed at me." He chuckled again. "She was right to laugh. Don't have the gift of being eternal, like she does." He sighed. "That was a long time ago."

His gaze focused on M'kar again and the humor faded slowly, like water draining from a basin. "You need to flee, Little Blade. To a kinder place. Where you will make many strong, brave, clever friends. You will need them when you come back. To anchor you." His voice took on that hollow tone that made her shiver. "A good place where you don't need honor scars. Always more and more honor scars, until you're erased, buried under them. Come back when you don't want to. Make sure the *boostifaks* don't get what they want. Make sure you do get what you want. When you come back, the surbda craters will be safe hiding places. Understand? The safest places on the planet. Even though they need to be taken apart once and for all. Hear me?"

"Yes," she whispered, and nodded hard, when he gripped her shoulder with a bony hand and looked deeper into her eyes.

"Safe for you. Maybe you'll see Etrusca. But remember this, child. You can only go in and out safely a few times. After that, you leave pieces of yourself behind. You'll get eaten. Bit by bit." The intensity shattered off his face, and he was only a frail, crackle-voiced old man again. "But who knows? Maybe you're the one who can fix the broken pieces. Pull the rotted tooth before the whole body is poisoned." His fingers tightened on her shoulder again. "This is important. Take the broken pieces away. Off the planet. Where their power won't pull at us and keep trying to shred us. Promise me, Little Blade."

"I promise."

"Good." His eyes filled with tears and he shuddered and exhaled, then gulped in air like he had tried to run a race up the highest tower steps. "Etrusca's marks protect you." A snort escaped him, turning into a snicker. "Old Anguak would have a brain-spark, if he got a look at you. Proud of you," he added, as the door swung open and Ashrock walked in.

"Grandfather?" The tension in her father's voice seemed to lift M'kar off the bench.

"He says we have to leave. He says not to trust anyone but the Ankuar," she hurried to tell him.

"Does he now?"

"Take the little one to safety, boy," Aquid said as he struggled to his feet. "She's worth more than the entire clan combined. This one is going to fix things. She's going to remove the poison from the craters. You are leaving, aren't you? It's not just an old man's daydreams? I dreamed this one right, for once?"

"Yes, Grandfather." Ashrock held out his hand and M'kar ran to him. He took tight hold of her hand.

"Good boy. Always knew you were the smartest one out of them all." He nodded and tottered out of the room, muttering, "Good boy," several times, until he moved out of earshot.

Ashrock slowly went to the door and closed it, then sat down on the same bench Aquid had used. He had M'kar repeat back for him everything the old man had said. Her father never told her if he talked to the one-eyed man or the woman with the ahsnaq, but she shivered when she glimpsed the pilot of the shuttle they took early in the morning, two decs and eight days later, as the last of the winter storms sputtered out. He was a typical Ankuar, with white hair and cocoa-dark skin, and silvery-blue eyes.

~~~~~

A package was waiting for M'kar when she and her parents reached Le'anka. They took a roundabout route, to confuse any hopeful assassins or kidnappers their clan or enemy clans might have sent after them. M'kar was nine Standard years old by the time Master Reydon and Healer Thean and their fourteen-year-old son, Thyal, welcomed the little family to their
~~~~~

home near the Academy grounds on Le'anka.

The package was from Desra, with small gifts from the women of the Rissor clan for her and her parents. It also had a long letter in the code used by the women who took Etrusca's marks and vows. M'kar grinned in anticipation of the challenge of decoding the message. She had been practicing, sending messages to Desra during their travels. She didn't think she would break her vows to the sisterhood if she asked her parents for help. Those vows had specified hiding information about Etrusca and the sisterhood from the men of Nisandros, especially clan leaders, but M'kar reasoned they didn't apply to her father any longer.

Decoding the letter, and then checking it against the key, only took four hours. M'kar was proud of herself for remembering so much and so accurately. Desra's report on the status of the various clans was nearly a year old now, with a note to pass that information on to Ashrock. However, M'kar didn't tell her parents about the scientific data Desra included, gathered from the surbda craters spread across Nisandros. Her vows specified never to speak about the craters or their recluse friend who lived in them, until the right moment in history. She had no idea what to do with that information, and what the right moment was. Yet the leaders of the sisterhood sent her the information, wanting to take advantage of her living on Le'anka now, the center of scientific advancement in the Alliance.

The letter listed a number of changes in the environment of the surbda craters, how the zones of interference with equipment had been expanding slowly over the decades. Those who went into the craters reported that the pillars in the center of each crater didn't shake and wobble as much as they had. If that was a reduction in the power that created illusions and filled the water in each crater with healing energy, the leaders of the sisterhood were worried. Could M'kar send any Alliance sensor equipment to help them more accurately track the changes? It would have to be specially designed and shielded, so the interference didn't render the equipment useless.

M'kar had no idea how she could get her hands on sophisticated equipment like that, and she told Desra so, when she wrote her letter in response. Then she added the important words: *Right now.*

If she told her parents, or any adult, they would get all sorts of specialists on Le'anka and maybe in the Fleet involved in investigating. That would be good for finding the answers the sisterhood wanted, but bad for the secrecy that had been requested decades ago by "our friend, the recluse." M'kar promised Desra and the sisterhood she would investigate and ask questions and find someone with the right scientific knowledge, but warned that task could take a long time. Maybe even a whole year. Maybe two. After all, she hadn't registered yet for primary level classes at the Academy. She hadn't even had a tour of the Academy grounds. How could she find the right people to investigate the mystery of the changes in the craters when she didn't yet know where to look?

Two days later, M'kar was entirely alone with Thyal for the first time. Master Reydon and Healer Thean were busy with duties at the Academy. Dr. Jeyn and Ashrock were interviewing to determine what academic courses they could teach, and which scholars they would work with to expand the Alliance's understanding of Nisandros.

A message arrived shortly before the noon meal, with information on a home nearby that had become available, if Ashrock and Jeyn were interested in viewing it. M'kar had been alone all morning, working on her lessons and testing to determine what course of studies she would join at the Academy. She was in one of the house's formal gardens, practicing her physical disciplines when Thyal arrived home from his morning lessons and accepted the message. He came out to the garden and watched her until she completed a complicated lunge-twist-kick-somersault maneuver that brought her back nearly to the same position she had been in when she started.

His applause startled her, and she immediately dropped into a crouch, one arm raised to protect her head, the other hand reaching for her belt knife. Which she had left in her bedroom, since she was supposed to be safe on Le'anka.

"That's incredible." Thyal stepped down into the sunken garden where she had been practicing. "Could you teach me to do that?"

M'kar's first reaction was to respond with a nasty remark, but she caught herself in time. He wasn't one of her crude, homicidal cousins. Thyal looked like he meant the compliment, rather than using it to disarm her before he attacked. Her parents had promised her that most of the people on Le'anka wouldn't be looking for a chance to hurt or kill or kidnap her.

"I don't know. I've never tried to teach anyone," she finally said.

"Well, I'm supposed to be a teacher someday, so I can teach you to be a teacher, and you can teach me to ..." He grinned and gestured, his hands approximating the moves she had made.

"All right." M'kar surprised herself by grinning back.

"Are you hungry? We have to get our own lunch today. Oh, here, this came." He handed her the sealed packet and waited until she read it before he turned to lead the way out of the garden.

"I need to tell my parents," she said, and explained the message.

Thyal took her to the household communication station and showed her how to locate someone on the Academy grounds and determine if they were free to speak. Her parents were together, preparing to share a meal with some of Dr. Jeyn's school friends. They wouldn't be able to go look at the available house until they were done with all their meetings. Perhaps not until that evening.

"I could show M'kar where it is," Thyal said. "I don't have classes until third hour this afternoon, and Father suggested I show her around, and let her get out of the house for a while."

"Please?" M'kar thought she would choke on the yelp of excitement. She liked Thyal's house very much, so full of light and quiet, and no nasty cousins lurking around every corner. Still, exercising in the gardens wasn't enough anymore. There was so much Academy to explore.

In moments it was settled, and Dr. Jeyn promised to contact Security, to notify them the two children would be stopping by to look at the house. Thyal called up one of the household carts to drive them to the house, with a slight detour along the way.

"This is my favorite place to eat," he told M'kar, when they were heading down the paved pathway through the residential district. "Father says if we plan carefully, we can eat our way around the entire Alliance in two luns, just visiting the restaurants at the Academy." He frowned and studied the map displayed on the screen of the control panel of the cart as the guidance program drove them. "I don't know if we have any Nisandrian food here yet. I'm sorry. I didn't think maybe you were homesick for it."

"No, never." The next moment, she almost blurted that she did like shriek beast stew. M'kar knew she had spoken too soon. She wondered if she would ever eat it again. Would her father be able to find the right ingredients to make it here, so far from Nisandros?

The restaurant Thyal took her to specialized in packaged food for Academy students to take with them and eat on the run between classes. It sat on a rise in the rolling landscape of the Academy grounds, with a half-moon-shaped paved courtyard on one side, full of two- and four-seater tables. The L-shaped building was open on the inner side, displaying the many shelves full of packaged food and drinks, and a bank of heating units and eating utensils on the side that opened into the eating courtyard.

Four young men in the dark gray uniforms of Fleet cadets stepped into the serving line just ahead of Thyal and M'kar. One turned around and nodded greeting to Thyal, who nodded back. Then his gaze drifted down to M'kar. He nodded to her, started to turn away, then frowned and looked back. M'kar got a prickle of warning down her back.

Chapter Four

M'kar met the cadet's gaze and tried to put on that neutral expression her father insisted was far more frightening than a glare or frown or baring her teeth. He stared at the sharp dip where her eyebrows met between her eyes. She had laughed when her father joked about disguising themselves by shaving that little bit of their eyebrows, but now M'kar felt sick. It was such a small thing, this telltale, so why did she hate the way his gaze seemed to snag on her face like that?

"Don't tell me you're courting already," the cadet said, turning back to Thyal.

M'kar muffled a snort of laughter at the wide-eyed look Thyal gave the cadet, then her, then him again. He shook his head. "M'kar is a guest in my parents' home."

"Is that real?" He gestured at the white lines paralleling the long, thin scars on her right arm, then upward to the lightning bolt at her temple. "I got to tell you, playing around like that could get her in big trouble."

"With who?" Thyal asked, his tone going quiet. Just like Master Reydon's voice had become when dealing with a very rude Ankuaran who had intruded on their dinner in the garden the night M'kar's family arrived on Le'anka. That was the quiet her father wanted her to try for, when dealing with troublesome people and animals.

"Oh, hello." Another of the cadets turned around, glanced at M'kar, then back to Thyal. "Two *baqwaks*, pretending to be Nisandrians. Came through the plaza this morning, saying they were looking for their little sister." He glanced at M'kar again, gray eyes narrowing. "Described her tattoos pretty accurately."

"I don't have any brothers," M'kar said. "They're liars."

She caught her breath, positive that frown on Thyal's face meant he was going to contradict her. Yes, she had three half-brothers, but they wouldn't come to Le'anka to look for her, and they wouldn't go around telling people she was their sister.

"We should go back," Thyal said, and reached for her hand.

M'kar held on and ran, keeping pace with Thyal all the way to their cart. He didn't let go until they were seated, and he needed that hand to program the commands to head back home. When the cart jolted forward, he contacted Academy security, then asked them to contact Dr. Jeyn and Ashrock and Master Reydon.

"I'm sorry." M'kar looked behind them. No one had followed them from the restaurant. She gripped the edges of the bench seat and willed the cart to move faster. She couldn't remember any of the landmarks they had passed, and that was stupid. How could she find her way back to Thyal's house if something went wrong and they were separated?

"It's not your fault." Thyal patted her hand. "They're not very good hunters, making a stupid mistake like that. What do they want?"

"Kill me or marry me, it's all bad for me."

That made him laugh, though he did manage to smother the sound into a snort. Security responded, asking for more information. Thyal gave the officer the names of the cadets who had been talking to them.

"Be careful," the woman said. "The only Nisandrians we have on record currently on Academy grounds are Dr. Jeyn Fleetwind, Ashrock of Ba'e'do'stra, and M'kar Fleetwind-Ba'e'do'stra. Please take shelter quickly and stay there, until we locate the intruders."

"Understood." Thyal frowned at the control panel as the connection died. "Maybe someone is pretending to be Nisandrian to cause trouble?"

M'kar didn't have any answer for that. She flinched as the path the cart followed dipped down and they headed for a short tunnel, passing from one section of the Academy grounds to another. Muffled thuds echoed out at them, then shadows erupted from the tunnel, turning into birds. She caught her breath and ducked down, even though the clear panel at the front of the cart, and the curving roof protected them from collision.

For a heartbeat, she thought she saw herself. Multiple images of herself. Crouching down in the front seat with her arms raised as a shield. Her head throbbed like something sharp wanted to erupt from her temples and through her eyes.

The moment passed and the cart darted into the tunnel. M'kar sat upright. The sharp sensations faded but her head still throbbed. She thought she heard birds calling inside her head. The frightened and angry squeaks of little furry, sharp-toothed creatures joined them. She didn't know their species. The voices grew louder with every heartbeat. She yelped when the cart emerged back into the sunlight and pressed her hands over her eyes.

"What's wrong?" Thyal said.

M'kar tried to say she didn't know, but her throat felt stiff and hard. She couldn't force the words out. She shook her head and held on tighter to the edges of the bench.

"Are you sick?"

She nodded.

"Take deep, slow breaths and close your eyes and listen to your heart. Tell it to slow down. That helps."

M'kar didn't think it would, but she tried it anyway. She closed her eyes and listened to the rattle-hum of her heartbeats. The gasping hiss of her indrawn breath.

The cart stopped, startling a yelp out of her. She opened her eyes, expecting to see the door of the cart shelter at Thyal's house. Instead, the cart had stopped a dozen meters from the path to the house. She looked at Thyal, then turned to look where he looked, with a frown darkening his sharp-boned, tanned face.

Two men stood on the pathway to the front steps and main door of the house. One faced the cart. The other turned around from the door and looked at the children in the cart.

"Go, go, go," Thyal snarled, and slapped the controls for the cart. "Security. The intruders are at our house!"

The men yelled and raced after them. The cart seemed to crawl as it moved forward. M'kar wanted to jump out of the cart and run, but she knew it went faster than she could run. The smart move was to save her energy. She turned to look as the men ran and shouted, cursing Thyal and the cart and her.

M'kar understood those words. The language. They were speaking Nisandrian. She hadn't heard Nisandrian since leaving Nisandros. She wanted to laugh at how strange the words sounded, but she couldn't breathe. Everything felt wrong. She should be able to fight and defend herself, but her head pounded and her limbs had frozen. What was wrong with her? Had they already shot her with a tranquilizer, and she didn't feel the dart?

Go away. Go away! Leave me alone! I'm not going back.

The bird cries and squeaks and pips and creaks of all the creatures filling her head to the point of bursting exploded into fury.

A dark cloud swirled down out of the sky and enclosed the two men. They screamed and cursed and waved their arms and spun around, trying to break through the cloud. It grew thicker. A matching cloud of darkness snaked across the ground. The animal sounds erupted out of M'kar's head and into her ears. The darkness reared up like a wave and engulfed the men. They went down, lumpy shapes that writhed and screamed.

M'kar tumbled out of the cart and landed in the lavender and rose-streaked moss lining the side of the pathway, retching. Thyal shouted something and suddenly he was there, kneeling over her, holding her as she shuddered and fought to breathe. He was still holding her when Security found them and used stunner wands to drive away the swarms of birds and small ground-dwelling creatures that covered the shivering, weeping, ragged, bleeding, smothered men. He didn't let go of her until a small, pink-faced woman with a crown of white braids wrapped around her head knelt and put her arms around M'kar and patted her back.

M'kar didn't know how she knew it, but the little woman made the angry, confused cries of all the creatures go away. Shuddering with relief at the quiet inside her head, she burst into tears.

By the time Security found her parents, and Thyal's parents, and dealt with the two failed murderers, M'kar and Thyal had been taken to the closest healer station. The little woman introduced herself as Master Maenta. M'kar had calmed down enough to notice how everyone hurried to do obey her, and they didn't ask questions. Maenta held M'kar's hand the whole time, and that was even more comforting than Thyal holding her hand. She asked for a room where the three of them could be alone, and quiet, and asked for a drink that was all creamy pink and lavender and mint green swirls. M'kar didn't think she could swallow anything, but she tried. All the shivering and throbbing and brief sharp stabs in her head quieted, and she felt the humming in Maenta's hand holding hers.

"Ah, better already? Very interesting," Maenta said with a smile and a nod. "You can let go now. You don't need me shielding you."

M'kar didn't understand.

"Master Maenta has been shielding your mind," Thyal said. "You have a Talent and it woke up, and you weren't able to turn it off."

"Because you didn't know how you turned it on," Maenta added, nodding. "Yes, young Thyal, I understand now why your parents insisted you be given advanced classes. You will be a great asset to the Academy, when you have finished your training. As for you, little one ..." She sighed. "You're confused, aren't you?"

"I have a Talent?" M'kar couldn't yank her thoughts off what Thyal had said. "I'm not old enough."

Thanks to the psionic heritage of Dr. Jeyn's family, and the genetic manipulation that had been done to the ruling families of Nisandros centuries ago, there was no way to be sure if the emergence of M'kar's psionic Talent was too soon or right on time. Everyone agreed, as they talked over dinner and into the evening, that the combination of so many drastic changes in her life and environment, combined with the trauma of the attack, had awakened her animal-focused Talent rapidly and with some violence. Her course of studies would now have to include mental and physical disciplines to help her harness this newly awakened ability and avoid the physical shock and draining she had endured today.

Master Reydon insisted on taking M'kar as his student. He specialized in dealing with anomalous Talents. He was currently taking a period of rest while preparing to assemble his next group of students. Maenta was part of the dinner discussion, and she agreed to be in charge of M'kar's foundational teaching before handing her over to Reydon in three luns. M'kar would be the youngest student he had ever taken, and the youngest member of the class.

Thyal had felt the energy and psionic resonance as M'kar's Talent awoke. His instincts guided him in trying to shield her as she called all the animals for nearly a full kilometer in all directions, to defend her against the would-be murderers. He kept her shielded from possible physical damage, until Maenta felt the disturbance in the mental atmosphere and came to investigate and help. Reydon and Thean made no effort to hide their deep pride in their son. Thyal would be like his father, with an over-arching Talent that would allow him to touch on and interact with and even control other Talents, when necessary.

Because of that, Thyal would be part of this new class. M'kar thought he looked happy, but even more he looked stunned. Had she made trouble for him? Many classes he had planned for the next few years at the Academy would have to be canceled or delayed.

"I'm sorry," she said, as they walked down the hallway to the bedroom wing of the house, after their parents sent them to bed.

The five adults were still talking in the common room behind them, their voices muffled with seriousness and the lateness of the hour.

"For what?" Thyal frowned.

"Everything's all changed. You can't take the classes with your friends that you wanted to."

"I suppose." He shrugged, then grinned. "You've got nothing to be sorry about. Think about what you did today."

She couldn't help thinking about any of it. Especially the part when the two men calmed down once the animals left them alone, and they got angry and cursed her, and kept cursing her until Security hit them with stunner wands to shut them up. They spoke in the war tongue of Nisandros, and M'kar wished she had never teased her father to teach it to her. Those men vowed they would find her and kill her no matter what it cost them. She had embarrassed them. They were trained, dedicated killers, sent on an honor vendetta decreed by the Ancestors. Not that she cared about the Ancestors. But those men should have been able to find her and shred her before anyone realized what was happening. She was just a little girl, nine years old, and she had defeated them. Not only that, but she had made them scream like frightened little girls. She had commanded all the animals to come in her defense. They had shredded the men's clothes and scratched and bit them and defecated all over them. That was the worst part of the embarrassment. The smell.

"We both learned to do new things today, that we didn't know we could do," Thyal said. "People come from all over the Alliance to ask my father to be their teacher, and he *wants* to teach us. Do you know how special we are? And that's because of you, because I wouldn't have figured out what I could do if I didn't have to help you."

"Listen to your fellow warrior, *mi'sho'ki*," Ashrock said, his voice coming from the shadows of the hallway. A moment later he came around the corner. He scowled at them, brow furrowed. "Didn't we tell you both to find your beds? You have had a long, draining day, and the days ahead will be even more so. Go!" He made a shooing gesture down the hall.

M'kar laughed. "Tell me a bedtime story, Po'pa?"

"Ah, there, you see?" He sighed gustily and crossed his arms and leaned against the wall, still scowling, teasing, at the two children. "You win one small battle, and you think you know better." He lunged, catching M'kar around the waist with his massive hands. She squealed as he tumbled her upside down and hung her over his shoulder. He held her ankles with one hand and swatted her bottom hard with the other. "You will obey as long as I can spank you!"

M'kar could hardly breathe for giggling. Thyal's wide-eyed expression melted into a grin.

"I have an idea, my fine young warriors." Ashrock nodded as he lumbered down the hall to M'kar's room, three doors down from Thyal's, on the other side of the hall. "In the morning, we will have the hearth-kin ceremony. You fought together and for each other. That is something to celebrate. Even if you did not, sadly, shed any blood."

That created a dilemma for M'kar. A hearth-kin ceremony was a solemn occasion, and she needed to find a suitable present for her new hearth-brother. She lay awake long after her father tossed her into her bed and tucked the blankets in so tight around her she could hardly move. The answer came to her in the early morning hours, after she had wriggled free of the tight cocoon and could sit up in bed and watch the sunrise.

Her most valuable possession was the data on the surbda crater entrusted to her by the leaders of the sisterhood. She would share it with Thyal, and make him part of the secret and the quest.

~~~~~

Thyal was fascinated as much by the legend of Etrusca and her marks and the vows of the sisterhood as he was by the data from the surbda crater. He compared Etrusca to Neoma, the visionary who had awakened Le'anka to the truth of Enlo and initiated the quest to reunite the Human worlds and races.

"Except everyone finally gave up trying to kill Neoma," M'kar had to point out. "Etrusca vanished into the crater, hiding from three clans who joined forces to silence her."

"True. Maybe she'll come back someday and scare the clan leaders into some brains. I know I'd be scared if someone who should have died centuries ago sat down in front of me."

That mental image made her laugh.

They didn't talk about the surbda crater data, but once in a while, Thyal had an idea for research they could do, to help them understand what was there. Then, a dec before they were to meet their classmates, he
~~~~~

had an idea. He had been trying to do some research into physics, Tyers Chutes, jump gate technology, and time warping, without attracting the attention of the Masters who specialized in such areas. He nearly pulled M'kar out of the dining room to tell her, when he got his idea in the middle of dinner. Explaining the people and the back story behind the idea took some time.

Nearly twenty years before, Fleet found a derelict ship with a group of abandoned children barely surviving in the darkness and cold inside. The most intensive searching couldn't track the children by their genetic markers or the bits of data about the ship itself. Those children were raised on Le'anka, and one of them was the leader of a group of Academy students referred to by their teachers as "the insane geniuses." The saying was that they would either crack the code of the Gates and the Gatekeepers, or they would recreate the disaster that prompted the Gatekeepers to scatter the Human races among the stars.

Thyal wanted her to meet Jasper Lore, an engineering student in his first year of Basic, preparing to join the Fleet. He was already making waves with his instructors and the Fleet designers and engineers. Thyal proposed showing Jasper the data, and let him simply run with it, and keep giving him whatever new data Desra sent M'kar. Whatever theories or answers Jasper came up with were almost guaranteed to be world-shaking and history-making, no matter how many years it took to get there.

M'kar agreed. She liked Jasper from the moment they met, even though he spoke very little to her and spent most of the first meeting looking through the data files she gave him. His gaze lingered on her tattoos and the dip in her eyebrows long enough to prove he saw them, but he didn't react with any of the fear or that "barbarians at the gate" type of revulsion many people displayed when they realized M'kar or her father were Nisandrians.

She gave Jasper an abbreviated version of the warping of time and senses when she was in the surbda crater, then had to explain what they were. Jasper expressed some exasperation that Nisandros made the craters forbidden territory, but he was fascinated by the energy drain and the sensor blackout. Some things he said didn't make any sense to her, but then, Jasper was twenty and she wasn't yet ten. He talked about Chute theory, the possibility of anchoring a Chute to a planet, and awakening a Gate once they understood Chutes better. The time and perception warping while in the crater got him excited, and he referenced more than a dozen theoretical papers that meant nothing to her.

He didn't seem irritated or even surprised by M'kar's request that he keep his research and what he discovered secret from any authority figures. He shrugged as if none of it mattered when she explained that his work could turn into a diplomatic problem between the Alliance and Nisandros.

"Politics and politicians." He snorted, then turned to the next page of data she had given him. That calm pronouncement matched how she felt about politicians and diplomats. If they left her alone and didn't complicate her life, she wouldn't call out a blood vendetta against them.

~~~~

Over the next three years, Desra sent four more letters full of sensor readings and descriptions of what others saw when they spent time in the surbda craters. Jasper cobbled together three prototype sensors and finagled help from friends in the Diplomatic Corps to deliver the equipment to Desra and the sisterhood. The response and any proof that the sensors did any good took luns to get back to them, because the up-and-down of diplomatic relations between Nisandros and the Alliance sometimes created blockades to communication and travel. If not for her growing interest in what the surbda craters contained and her haphazard lessons in physics, Chutes, and Gates from Jasper, M'kar would have been happy if Nisandros never joined the Alliance. If that happened, the clans might demand that she and her father be returned to Nisandros.

That was the last thing she wanted. She had big plans, once she had graduated from her class with Master Reydon, which had been named Infrenx, for the fire-born healing bird of legend. She would join the Fleet and explore the universe on an E&D ship.

Five attempts were made to kidnap her, and two to assassinate her, along with three attempts on her father's life. Ashrock seemed not to care about the danger to himself, but he was an awe- and terror-inspiring juggernaut when it came to attempts on his daughter. The second failed assassin found out too late that the Ancestors had no authority or influence on Le'anka, and crying out to them for assistance and vengeance was a waste of breath when Ashrock got hold of him.

M'kar focused on her lessons with Infrenx and learning every variety of self-defense skill offered by the many cultures of the teachers on Le'anka. She tried not to have to depend on her Talent to call every animal within psionic hearing range to defend her. Every time she used her Talent in public, the chances grew that Nisandros would learn about her animal-focused Talent. That knowledge would increase the efforts to drag her back to Nisandros to use her in a diplomatic marriage, turn her into a high priestess to rule the planet, or have her slaughtered as an abomination. The reasons and the end results didn't matter to her, when she spared time to think about them. What mattered was ensuring that Academy security didn't allow that one lucky kidnapper or assassin to reach her.

Master Reydon and other authorities at the Academy had already registered strongly worded recommendations that when M'kar joined the
~~~~

Fleet, she would never be sent to Nisandros. Her life depended on it. There was no guarantee that diplomatic exigencies wouldn't require the sacrifice of sending her back to the planet of her birth, but high-ranking officers and authorities had promised to give her adequate warning. M'kar was confident she would have enough time to break and run and vanish before they came for her.

The year M'kar turned fifteen, her fears came closer to reality, with a sudden surge in positive developments between Nisandros and the Alliance.

"We have completely lost all the protection that being a half-blood gave you," Ashrock had announced at dinner, after reading through the latest official communication from the Diplomatic Corps. "We have embarrassed enough kidnappers and assassins, I thought we had finally earned some peace. Nearly a year of it. How quickly that time has flown by. Now, with the barriers coming down and those *boostifak* diplomats on both sides offering information no one has any right to ..." He sighed heavily. "Once the visionaries hear about your gift, it won't matter that it comes from your mother's bloodline or you're not pure Nisandrian. They will insist on having you under their power and so-called protection."

"Can they force us to return?" M'kar wished she was still small enough to curl up between both her parents. Granted, she still could, but she would look ridiculous.

"They can make all the noise and threats they want," Dr. Jeyn said, glancing up from her copy of the communication on her tablet. "But knowing how long it takes for a planet to apply for and receive membership in the Alliance, so they have the right and the power to enforce such demands, you'll not only be a full adult by then, but you'll be an officer in the Fleet. If that's what you still want to do."

"I still do."

"And if the diplomats lose all their intelligence and sense of justice by then," Ashrock growled, "and agree to turn you over to people who intend to sacrifice you, one way or another, then you can steal your ship and flee past the known edges of the universe." He winked at her. "You can find your brothers and adventure with them. Take me with you, *mi'sho'ki.*"

"Promise."

M'kar doubted her half-brothers would be easy to find, forget about persuading them to include her in their crew. Ashrock corresponded with his three sons, but they never included her or her mother. She knew they were successful and their services as explorers were in demand throughout the Alliance. Other than that, there wasn't much she knew about Ashar, Bannar and Shauq. Although sometimes she did wonder how much they looked like their father, and if she would recognize them if she ever met them.

She held out both her hands, palms up, for Ashrock to cross with his hands, palms down, to seal the vow. When he withdrew his hands, he left a sealed, clear packet, enclosing a thick sheaf of what looked like paper, heavily inked with all sorts of glyphs.

M'kar caught her breath when she recognized the glyphs and the message they carried. Most important was the marking of an eye, with multiple thin blue lines radiating from it. A letter from Desra.

Ashrock chuckled and gestured for her to leave the dinner table. M'kar clutched the letter packet to her chest and ran. This was the only reason to be glad that diplomatic relations had opened up again: a message from Desra and resumed communication with her vow sisters.

It contained the usual reports on the status of the various clans, to pass on to Ashrock and his friends in the Diplomatic Corps. Desra reported that Ke'Jor was even more impossible to deal with, now that he was approaching his manhood test in the wilderness and spending most of every day assisting his father and grandfather. Ke'Niq had been caught sneaking out of the clan house to meet with rebel forces, earning long lectures from his father and grandfather. He had fled altogether on his sixteenth birthday. The sisterhood had a good idea of where the rebel forces had set up headquarters, and Desra indicated that they generally supported the rebels' goals and ideals against the Upper and Lower Halls of the clan leaders. The rebels wanted to join the Alliance -- which meant many clans dug their heels in, resisting joining, even if they believed it was a good idea.

M'kar didn't know whether to be glad or worried about that bit of news. Neither was Ashrock when she shared it with him.

The sisterhood leaders reported that the latest of Jasper's devices planted in a southern hemisphere surbda crater had been discovered by the Dagoo'ni'craf Clan's scouts, and destroyed. Could she send another? Something perhaps with defensive programming? Something that would either shoot any would-be attackers, or allow it to fly to safety?

Chapter Five

M'kar supposed Jasper would see the challenge in the request, rather than be exasperated that his latest prototype and proof of his genius had been destroyed. Nisandros in general was rough on equipment, and the surbda craters were especially destructive. She had no idea how long it would take for Jasper to create something new, since he was always busy with engineering projects and competitions at the Academy, and consulting with Fleet engineers. Plus there was the chance when the new equipment was built and functioning, diplomatic relations would deteriorate and a new blockade would halt shipments. Several years could go by before the equipment reached the sisterhood. She told Desra so, when she finally sat down to write her letter in response.

M'kar hadn't had time to write to Desra with the last shipment of equipment, because Jasper's diplomat corps friend was working against a deadline to get the package onto the next courier ship going out. She needed to update Desra on changes that would probably delay the new equipment even more than a blockade.

Jasper was in love, as much as a man who worshipped engineering and engines could be. M'kar thought she knew him well enough, after six years of friendship, to know Treinna Jammeson was "the one." Treinna was a linguist, in her second year of Basic, and so adept at learning new languages, she was already in high demand as a translator.

M'kar thought about what she wanted to say, what she needed to tell her friend, and prove to the leaders of the sisterhood that she was fulfilling the promise they had seen in her. She grinned and didn't care how ridiculous she looked, in the shelter of one of the many sunken gardens of the Academy, where she had come to write her letter. Surrounded by friendly birds and flying serpents who kept watch in the thick bushes surrounding the garden, she had utter privacy. No one could sneak up on her, no one could interrupt.

I am two years ahead of schedule at the Academy now. My psionic Talent inherited from my mother, and as she puts it, "aggravated" by all the genetic tweaking of my father's ancestors continues to grow in strength, and show odd little blips off of the ordinary animal-focused psionic range. My teachers say that between my Nisandrian training and the advanced classes necessitated by my Talent, I will be able to enter Basic to join the Fleet ahead of schedule.

Perhaps when I am seventeen, rather than twenty. Ask for prayers to Enlo that I will be in contact with the right teachers and with more engineering specialists who can give me the equipment you need.

She then went on to describe the members of Infrenx class, whom she hadn't been able to introduce to Desra yet, thanks to the protective secrecy she and her family had to maintain. Such precautions had become superfluous, with the current diplomatic changes. Besides, who would Desra tell who would betray their vows to the sisterhood and endanger her?

For the first few luns, I was afraid I was the main reason for Infrenx. Because my Talent is extremely anomalous. Hard to measure. Meaning the possibilities for disasters are hard to measure as well, even this far along in my training. As our Master has said many times, Talents are proof that Enlo has a nasty sense of humor.

The most important task is to develop our relationship as a family. We need a strong mind-circle as our foundation to grow and gain discipline. We need it as a weapon and a defense. Master says there must be a reason for why so many anomalous Talents have shown up at this time, but in the same breath he warns us not to become vain or consider ourselves important to the fate of the Alliance. He likes to remind us of many tales from Neoma's teachings and other holy writ, where Enlo worked through insects and weak or even ridiculous animals.

There are nine of us, including Master Reydon's son, Thyal. He will be an overarching Talent like our Master when his training is finished. He is our anchor point in forming the mind-circle. There are only three girls in our class, including me.

Taila is little, like a doll. Her Talent is generating fire out of thin air. She can even start fires in vacuum, but they don't last. Master says her goal is to create fire under water and keep the flame alive. Then she will have perfect control.

Survis is from an extra-gravity world. You'd think he would be extra strong, and he is, but he's a telekinetic, and just like he had to learn to be much more gentle when he left his planet, so he wouldn't break everything, he needs to focus on fine control of his telekinesis, so he doesn't crush things or fling them too far.

Nolan is an empath, and doesn't just sense others' emotions, but he can influence them. He's the oldest member of our class. He had the basic training his world offered, and used his Talent in peacekeeping, until he panicked and lost control when he spread peace over a mob starting to riot. He put everyone asleep so deeply that they didn't awaken until three days later.

Garion is a lifeform sensor. He tells races or breeds apart, but his impressions come as smells and colors. He needs volume control when he receives, so he doesn't get sick.

Kelli is a variant of broadcaster, so she picks up the thoughts of others and can share them. She needs to learn fine control, so she can be a communication node that doesn't depend on equipment, to work security or diplomacy.

Aryk is a touch healer. He was captured and enslaved as a child. His owners used him up and tossed him aside when they thought he was dead. He's older than me -- everyone is older than me -- but in a lot of ways he's hurt so badly he seems a lot younger than me.

She went on to describe some training exercises, and how their class learned from and helped each other. Master Reydon had told them on their first day as a class that they would become a family, because they needed each other to grow and learn and survive. Their Talents had been given to them for a purpose, and chances were good that they might be asked to put their lives on the line for the Academy, for the Alliance, but most important of all, for each other.

Only Thyal and M'kar were residents of Le'anka. They shared their families and homes with their classmates. Thean took Aryk under her wing and taught him ways of healing he could use that didn't require him to touch and share the discomfort of his patients and drain himself dry. Ashrock delighted in taking the class out into the wilderness on the far side of Le'anka to teach them survival techniques and hand-to-hand combat.

Reydon gave them their name, their focal image, and had a contemplation house built for them, so they would always have an anchor on Le'anka and the Academy. They were Infrenx, the bird of fire and healing, with the power to rescue souls from the clutches of death.

~~~~~

Eight days after M'kar sent off her letter to Desra, with no real hope the packet would get through all the diplomatic and cultural barriers in less than half a planetary year, Taila reached a new milestone in her fire-wielding Talent. Ever since Master Reydon had named their class Infrenx, she had felt challenged and duty-bound to create an infrenx out of fire. This became even more important to her after their class graduated from spending the entire day together, to only mornings. In the afternoons, they studied under Masters who specialized in their future occupations. Taila was determined to create an infrenx as a signal that could be seen anywhere on Academy grounds, so they could come together in an emergency.

That day, they had met after their afternoon classes were done to share dinner outdoors and plan their next training outing, in the preserve
~~~~~

lands. Ashrock and Master Reydon designed tests that would strengthen their mind-circle and teach them how to work together using their Talents. They needed to pass certain tests to earn shelter and food and bedding, which was crucial during cold or stormy weather.

Their meeting place was one of the sunken gardens just a few steps away from the main plaza where the grounds of the Academy, the Alliance Council complex, and the main spaceport of Le'anka intersected. M'kar was third to arrive, and she felt the electric tingle of excitement in the air before Taila and Nolan saw her stepping down into the garden.

"What happened?" she asked, as her two classmates turned around.

"Watch!" Taila flung her hands up and kept them raised over her head. She tipped her head back so her long cascade of black curls spilled down past her belt. Sparks danced between her fingertips, then spun together in a globe. In a few heartbeats, the globe warped and flattened and spread out, into the shape of an infrenx outlined in flickering flames. She grinned so widely, M'kar's jaw hurt in sympathy.

"Impressive." M'kar reached the long stone table already holding two covered dishes. She put down a long basket of mezipa and an insulated bag full of shriek beast stew. Everyone expected her to bring those two items whenever they ate together. The fat and sugar of the mezipa counteracted and soothed the incendiary qualities of the stew.

"You think so?" She bubbled with delighted laughter and took a few steps backward, arms still raised.

The infrenx dove several meters, the flames nearly skimming the tops of the heavy, green-black bushes that sheltered the sunken garden and created a privacy screen. Then it arched upward, twice as high as before. She swirled one hand. The construct of flames rose higher and slowly circled the garden. Voices came from the plaza, cries of excitement and questions and what could have been fear.

"What do we do if Security shows up?" M'kar asked.

"Oh, why do you have to be the most grown up of us all?" Taila tried to pout, but her lips kept stretching into a delighted grin.

With a toss of her head, she lowered her hands and the infrenx dove toward the garden again. The flaming outline disintegrated, so it was nothing but a cloud of sparks that settled around them. M'kar held her breath, fighting to look relaxed. She trusted Taila, but she had learned to be cautious around her friend's fire Talent.

Survis arrived just a few moments later, with Kelli and two Security officers nearly on her heels. Fortunately, or perhaps not, one of them was Taila and Survis's instructor. They were learning to use their Talents in crowd control and emergency situations. He shook his head, his mouth drooping into a stern expression. Then he said something to his associate. She left, and he crossed the pavement of the garden with his hands clasped behind his back.

"Did we panic anyone?" Survis asked. He had no reason for concern since he hadn't been there when the infrenx was flying. M'kar admired that about him, always stepping up and taking responsibility and shielding the smaller, younger, or weaker members of the class.

"Not quite. A lot of people stopped and stared." The officer snorted loudly, and a crooked grin wiped away the official scowl. "That's not easy to do around here. We had a few collisions. Most of what I heard on my way in here was speculation on what kind of holographic field generator was being used, if it was portable, what the power source was, and why you chose that particular image." He glanced over his shoulder at one of the three entrances into the garden. The opening was shielded by a hedge two meters wide and two meters tall. The sun was at just the right angle for M'kar to see the shadow of someone in the opening, blocking others from entering. She suspected that little bit of protection wasn't going to last much longer.

"We should probably move to another location," Thyal said, from the second entrance. This led to a path through a spiraling hedge maze. M'kar wondered how long he had been there, nearly invisible in his ability to stand perfectly still in the shadows.

"Quickly. I'll run a delaying action," the instructor said. He gave Taila and Survis that look M'kar hoped to never get from her teachers -- the one that said they were going to have a serious talk, very soon.

Some people were coming up the path through the spiral maze. By their excited voices, they were seeking the source of the infrenx in the sky. Using the slave finger language Aryk had taught them, Thyal said to walk slowly and pretend they didn't know what was going on. They broke up into twos and threes and headed down a branching path, avoiding the one that went straight through the spiral. M'kar walked with Thyal and Garion and stopped twice when other people approached them through the maze, to look back the way they had come, searching the sky.

The passage through the spiral maze took maybe five minutes. As Kelli remarked later, that was six minutes too long. They clustered together once they were out in open landscape again and picked up speed. Behind them, they heard raised voices.

"They don't sound angry or alarmed," Thyal said. He tapped his ear and nodded to M'kar.

She understood. He wanted her to link with animals and check the situation back in the garden. Kelli and Taila stepped up to link their arms with hers. That way she could keep walking while her focus was through the birds and two skitters that had nested in the hedges surrounding the garden. The furry little tree rodents were upset over the noise and numbers of people coming into the garden, but the general impression she received was that people were more curious than angry or worried.

"We're going to get a name for ourselves, if you keep that up," Kelli said, after M'kar reported what her animals showed her.

Taila stuck her tongue out and wrinkled up her nose. Kelli sighed, but she joined in the laughter with the rest of their class.

"Amazing," Aryk offered. "Any change back there?"

M'kar muffled a sigh and regained contact with the birds. The skitters didn't appreciate having their senses "borrowed." An odd sensation washed over her, like a single, thick string had been plucked and thrummed, inaudible but felt in her marrow.

Her gut tightened as the instinct for trouble, learned in the clan house, rose up to alertness. She took a deep breath and slammed down her mental shields, cutting off the contact. She hoped she had cut off that string of uninvited psionic contact hard enough to give the intruder a headache. She needed to report what had happened, to understand it. Since Master Reydon wasn't there to dive into her mind, she needed to tell Thyal. He would be a Master someday, after all. Might as well start now. She tugged her arms free of Kelli and Taila, thanked them with a smile and a nod, and picked up her pace.

"I felt something." Thyal slowed to let her catch up with him.

"I think someone tried to hitch a ride." She rubbed her temples.

"Up ahead there's an alcove. It's not private, but we can do it quickly and hopefully not attract any attention." He gestured to where the path ahead of them branched. On the right, a paved seating area was tucked under some low-hanging branches of a shamble tree. They picked up the pace and reached the seats just a few steps ahead of a group of people M'kar automatically labeled tourists. People who wandered the Academy grounds as if students were on display to entertain them.

She turned around to see how far behind the rest of Infrenx was, and nearly came nose-to-nose with one of the women in the group of ten. The thick cloud of heavy perfume enfolding her was nearly visible. M'kar's nose itched, and she fought not to sneeze. The woman's mouth dropped open. She went pale under her heavy cheek and eye paint. Then her startled look shifted to a scowl.

"That's not funny, little girl!"

"Excuse me?" Thyal stepped up, tucking his arms into the wide sleeves of his tan student robe. M'kar choked on the need to laugh, seeing how closely he mimicked one of their teachers as he prepared to freeze a troublemaker with disapproval.

"Playing around like that," the woman snapped. She flapped her hand at M'kar. "Filthy Nisandrians. Bad enough they're allowed on Le'anka now, but you stupid little children ought to have better taste than to paint yourselves like them."

M'kar snapped out, in Nisandrian, the first three lines of a proverb about blind people pretending they could see. The woman went pale again, then flushed dark red, so her face paint looked pale in comparison.

"Wipe off that makeup and speak Standard like a civilized Human!"

"We've got trouble on the prowl," Nolan announced, stepping into the shade under the trees. "Someone is focusing on M'kar, so tight they're broadcasting. Really strong minds. No discipline pattern I recognize."

M'kar was glad they hadn't been able to eat yet. The thrumming sensation made sense now. "I think I just got pinged by a mind-hunter. They caught my psi when I was checking behind us through the birds."

"You can't go home," Thyal said. "They'll be watching your parents, expecting you to go there for support. My house. Infrenx, mind-circle and defensive circle."

"Excuse me?" the woman said, clearly offended that no one was paying attention to her.

"There's no excuse for you," Survis growled, pitching his voice low so the pavement tiles under their feet seemed to vibrate.

Their class formed a circle and clasped hands. Someday, they wouldn't need physical contact to establish their mind-circle. Right now, M'kar was grateful for Thyal's grasp on her left hand, and Kelli on her right. In moments, the gentle humming sensation of the circle filled her blood. They couldn't borrow each other's Talents yet, but they could see through each other's eyes, hear through their ears, and share strength. Thyal let go of her hand and turned to take up point. M'kar fell into step behind him as he clasped his tool wristband and pressed the sequence to signal Security. She did the same with her own wristband and fought down a growl of exasperation. When would her enemies learn they could never take her back to Nisandros against her will?

The rest of Infrenx class fell into defensive formation around her. With the growing shadows as afternoon turned to evening, she could fade into the background. Establishing their mind-circle should have thrown up a mental baffle and cut off her psionic "scent," so the mind-hunters couldn't follow her. Nisandros had bred for psionic Talent in the centuries of isolation after the dispersal of the Human races by the Gatekeepers. Fortunately for the rest of the universe, the genetic tinkering had produced mostly physical superiority, such as speedy healing and sharper senses. The few psionic gifts were limited to mind-hunters, who could follow the mental signature of their quarry.

Fortunately for M'kar, pride crippled them. They refused to accept psionic training help from the Academy. While mind-hunters were strong, they didn't have the training that would make them a truly formidable enemy and give them a chance to catch her.

The tourists muttered, and M'kar caught a few comments about how rude they were, but the loud woman who led the group didn't say anything more or draw attention to them. Infrenx moved out of the shelter and headed down the pathway. Ordinarily, M'kar would mind-touch the birds swirling overhead to watch around them. Not this time. The mind-hunters would sense that psionic activity. She would be foolish to send up a signal and help them follow her to shelter.

"Can you get a passive reading on them?" she asked Nolan.

"Enough to know they're looking, but I'd have to turn up the juice to do any locating." He grimaced. "Sorry."

"Being warned is half the battle," Thyal said.

M'kar was sure she heard the tapping of boots on the pavement behind them, catching up with them, then diverting down one of the intersecting pathways. That was the problem with the spiral maze. It incorporated three spirals, and the pathways intertwined so there was no guarantee that speed would put them ahead of their pursuers.

"Excuse me? You're a Master, aren't you?" a man called from ahead of them. He stepped out from an intersecting pathway to block their way.

M'kar's first impression of him was an overabundance of purple in his clothes, such a deep shade it vibrated. Then when Thyal stopped, making everyone else stop, she got a better look. The man's clothes looked like a uniform. She saw the emblem on his right shoulder, a long block with a stylized planet and an unfamiliar star formation, that reached halfway down his chest. She couldn't remember the name of the planet, but she had seen the emblem in a packet of information her father had been studying.

Diplomat, or bodyguard for one, some newly discovered planet, or one that wants to be considered for membership, she sent through the mind-circle.

Qahngress, Thyal returned, while he responded to the man, politely correcting him. No, his long robe merely meant he was an advanced student in the Academy.

Oh, run away! Aryk's mental voice was filled with laughter. *We got invaded in the middle of a lecture on parasitic attacks on the blood-brain barrier yesterday. Royal twins who claim their twin bond makes them high-level Talents. They want to skip testing and jump right into classes. Forget that we're halfway through the term.*

Hush, Kelli told them, breaking off any comments about to swirl through their mind-circle. *We might need to hear this.*

More people dressed in the same violent shade of purple stepped from the shadows of the overhanging trees. The man bombarded Thyal with questions, giving him no time to answer. M'kar caught a glimpse of the twins, with petulant sculpted faces and gold chains around their necks and wrists. They were too obvious in their twinship, she decided, with their matching clothes and matching golden-blond caps of tight curls. That was fine for ten-year-old twin girls, but these two could be twenty, the boy a good ten centimeters taller than his sister.

A shiver raced up her back to meet that thrumming sensation pulsing at the base of her skull. The mind-hunters were close.

"Break and shield," she snapped, and spread her arms, shoving her classmates away from her.

The Qahngress leader exclaimed, sounding offended. Probably because she had interrupted him. M'kar didn't care. She turned, and there they were. Mind-hunters, badly disguised in red- and gray-striped Security uniforms. One pointed at her. The other pulled a stunner wand from his holster as they picked up their pace.

"That's not standard issue," Survis growled, and stepped up next to M'kar. "Let me block."

"Don't risk it." Aryk gestured for everyone on the path to get out of the way. "Could be lethal --"

M'kar called on all the birds and skitters and tree-slithers and every creature she could reach with her mind. Amazing, how much energy she had when she was furious. Amazing how the effort hurt for only a heartbeat, before a cloud of furious animals darted down at the men.

They didn't see the animals coming, from above and below and behind them until suddenly there were small furry creatures leaping at their legs and arms and birds dive-bombing to peck and beat at their faces. M'kar went to one knee with a sudden, sharp pulse of strain pain behind her eyes. She would have a bloody nose, at the very least. The pain vanished under a cold, sharp, exultant burst of glee as she guided all those furious animal minds, driving her two attackers backward and away.

"Dunk!" Taila cried, pointing at the fountain tucked into the curve where three paths intersected.

M'kar choked on a burst of laughter as she shoved with her mind. The cloud of attacking animals lunged, sending the men, cursing and howling, stumbling backward over the lip of the fountain into the pool. The animals dispersed, seeming to evaporate. Survis and Thyal got to the men first and snatched away the stunner wands as they struggled up out of the meter-deep water.

Creamy brown dripped off their faces, revealing the tattoos they had hidden under a thick layer of makeup. One of the men wiped the mess out of his eyes and his gaze landed on M'kar. He bared his teeth in a fierce grin as he lunged to his feet.

M'kar leaped, slapping her right hand on the lip of the fountain, pivoting to hit the man in his right cheek with her knee. He went down with a broken curse and knocked his partner back into the water. Two coalwings came to rest on her shoulders. The flame-colored birds reared back, skewering the men with their beady stares.

"Just try something. I dare you," she growled. The coalwings screeched, sounding eerily like they echoed her words.

"She has Talent," the smaller one, who had mostly blue tattoos on his face, whispered to the other. "Why didn't they tell us?"

M'kar thought she would heave right there.

In her fury, she hadn't intended to show off, just terrify them into messing their pants. Once these two got word back to Nisandros ... the assassins and kidnappers would be even more determined.

Security arrived before the onlookers could start asking questions. M'kar wanted to run all the way home to her parents. She wanted to pound those men unconscious, but that would be stupid, giving them a chance to touch her. Who knew what other weapons they had on them?

"On my father Reydon's authority." Thyal stepped up to grip M'kar's shoulder. "I want these men fully restrained. Sedate them if you must. I charge them with intent to kill."

The second mind-hunter leaped to his feet and took two steps before Survis whipped the stunner wand across his chest. The man shrieked, two octaves higher than he should have, and went down in the water with poison-green sparks of energy sizzling all over his body. His partner howled and arched up out of the water, covered in green sparks, to splash down and thrash for a few seconds.

"I think that's proof," Survis said, handing the stunner wand over to the closest Security officer. "Set to lethal levels."

Security took Infrenx class to Reydon and Thean's home before recording their side of the incident. Jeyn and Ashrock arrived just moments after Infrenx. M'kar didn't care about Nisandrian dignity. She ran to her parents. Ashrock's face was a twisted mass of scars and tattoos and fury that made his eyes glow.

Thean led them to a private room and left them alone, to hold each other and make bad jokes, and cry a little now that the danger had passed. But only temporarily. Who knew how much the kidnapping and murder attempts would increase, once the clans learned M'kar had strong psionic Talent?

Chapter Six

B'keerimo had become something of an ally recently, thanks to his courtship with Desra. He wrote with reports on what the prophets were saying now, the political maneuvering, and how M'kar fit or didn't fit into prophecies written in a tongue so ancient no one could agree on the translations. One of his letters had a long list of superhuman abilities she would have to develop to be considered the prophesied one, which ones required her death, and which ones automatically made her the supreme ruler over all the clans.

M'kar told her parents everything that had happened by the time Thean knocked on the door. Could they talk to Security now? The rest of Infrenx had already given their statements.

Very little needed to be added, after everyone else gave their descriptions, and Nolan and Taila drew sketches of the layout of the site of the attack. Telling her story again seemed rather anti-climactic, and M'kar was surprised to find she was hungry, by the time Security thanked them and took their leave.

Infrenx was just settling down to eat in the garden closest to the house when visitors arrived. The Qahngress delegation had found them, led by the man who had accosted Thyal.

"You know, we wouldn't have had that whole ugly mess out there, if he had just left us alone," Garion murmured. "All those questions he asked, he seemed to think Thyal was lying to him, or hiding something."

Their class clustered together under the dining pavilion, watching the purple-clothed man approach Master Reydon. He introduced himself as the guardian of Nyx and Nyssa of the royal house of Qahngress. The twins stood on either side of him. The girl's lip curled with discontent as she studied the surroundings. The boy pouted and looked at the ground about a meter in front of his feet. Their escort rested a hand on either of their shoulders and smiled and talked.

Master Reydon shook his head. Several times. The man just kept talking and smiling wider.

"Can you hear what they're saying?" Nolan whispered.

Master Reydon and the intruders stood a good ten meters away. The burbling of water trickling down the support posts of the pavilion created enough white noise to mask the low-voiced conversation. That was the whole point of the running water, but M'kar resented it now. The man wanted something. Master Reydon kept refusing, but he kept pushing.

"What are you getting from them?" Thyal whispered back.

Thean left their group and crossed the pavement to join her husband.

"The Master is fighting some frustration, irritation ... and he's got a headache. The other man is ..." Nolan shook his head. "He's all glossy, and kind of ringing." He shrugged. "Sorry, that's all I'm getting."

"M'kar, if I boost you, can you spy?" Aryk held out his hand, clearly offering his healing ability.

"I don't think you should, after what you just did," Thyal said. "Father wouldn't want you to risk hurting yourself."

She stuck her tongue out at him and clasped Aryk's hand. Several of their classmates laughed. Quietly. A rumble of approving laughter from her father encouraged her even more.

A bayha was hiding in the bushes just beyond where the three intruders had stopped on the path. M'kar latched onto a mind just as furry and sleepy as its round, waddling body. She prodded it to move out and circle the group of five. Bayhas were used to augment security around private residences because they were easily tamed and highly loyal. They didn't so much attack invaders as they made a nuisance of themselves with high-pitched squeals and tangling themselves among the legs of attackers.

"He's trying to persuade Master to take on the twins as students. Now that he's seen us in action, he insists we have a duty to defend them," she reported, after listening to the man.

"That doesn't make sense," Kelli muttered.

"It sounds like he's said this several times already, maybe with different words, because Master keeps telling him, 'As I said already, no, that is not possible.' What's wrong with the *nisduik*?"

M'kar fought not to rub at her temples, because that would be admitting the strain she fought against.

"Infrenx class has been in existence for five years now," Master Reydon said.

She reported the conversation in whispers as it continued.

"It is not the custom of the Academy to interfere with the bond the students have established. It is a unity of soul as much as mind."

"But these are royal twins," the man said, and smiled wider. "Twins are rare, and their twin bond enhances their healing abilities. You will make an exception for them, of course."

"There is no 'of course' about the matter. I will not. Infrenx is far ahead of these novices. I will not slow or alter their course of study for your convenience or disrupt the bonds and patterns of energy flow."

"But these are royal twins. Everyone makes an exception for them."

M'kar nearly cheered, seeing the man's assured smile finally flicker and fail, just for a few moments.

"Perhaps on Qahngress that is so, but this is Le'anka." Reydon turned to the twins, who were looking at him now. Perhaps for the first time. "This class has progressed far beyond you. Even if you have the Talent to join a mind-circle, you will not be grafted into the mind-circle of *this* class. The matter is closed."

"Reydon is too polite and civilized," Ashrock rumbled when M'kar reported those words. "Perhaps I should do my duty as hearth-brother and pick up the interloper by his ankles and toss him over the wall."

That earned some chuckles from her classmates. Jeyn smiled and shook her head, but said nothing in reproof.

"They smell bad. The bayha doesn't like it. There's something wrong. It's ..." M'kar frowned and closed her eyes in concentration. The aroma coming off the three intruders was thick and sweet, but in another breath turned rancid, then musky, and other impressions she couldn't sort out. It had a natural base, yet something wrong with the smell made her instincts shout it was no longer natural. She had never borrowed a bayha's senses before, so how could she be sure what she was smelling?

"What?" Thyal said. "Initiate circle. Show us."

She complied without thinking, opening her mind to her classmates.

"Pheromones," Aryk said after only a few seconds. "All three of them are loaded with ... they're strongest on the girl. We've just started studying mind-control techniques using natural substances to escape detection by scanners looking for toxins or synthetics."

He barely finished saying "mind-control." Thyal snatched up a pitcher of iced water and launched himself from the pavilion. He doused the girl with most of the water, then splashed the rest in Master Reydon's face, while shouting what Aryk had said.

The twins' guardian fled, dragging them after him. Taila and Kelli tackled the girl, Nyssa. Nyx broke free and darted to the left, heading deeper into the garden. M'kar went after him, bringing him down with one leap. Hitting him raised a cloud of what she could only describe as very old, concentrated, bad perfume. The smell clung to her even after two hot showers and scrubbing her skin raw. Nyx was starry-eyed and wobbly, staring at her as Security hauled him away.

The man who had brought the twins there got away, able to outrun the rest of Infrenx class. Thean was busy with Master Reydon, who had gone to his knees, retching.

<center>~~~~~</center>

By morning, the Qahngress embassy was in chaos, and all sorts of contradictory rumors spilled across the Alliance ambassadorial quarter. Qahngress had been in turmoil for several decades now, making it slow to initiate relations with the Alliance. There were six political parties, all working against each other. The twins' alleged guardian served

53

opposition forces who had taken members of the vast royal family to use as hostages and pawns in the struggle for power.

The girl, Nyssa, was sent to enslave Master Reydon by generating a false soul-bond with him and put him in thrall to her. The goal was to establish a powerful ally in the Alliance and the Academy to support that party's goals and work for their best interests. Master Reydon needed two doses of a strong blood purgative to treat the negative effects of the pheromone cloud that baffled the most talented healers at the Academy. There were elements that threatened psychotropic alterations to his brain chemistry and affected his hormones. The twins were both ill from the pheromone clouds that had enveloped them. The healers charged with analyzing and dismantling the chemical time bomb declared it a sloppy recipe. It could very easily have killed both of the delivery vectors. The healing aspect of their twin bond wasn't strong enough to protect them from the poison they wore. Nyssa's healing Talent was supposed to work with the pheromone cocktail to seal the supposed bond.

"The people of Qahngress have a very slippery grasp on what psionic Talents can do, and how powerful a twin bond is. Or isn't," Master Stayar, the lead investigator, reported to Reydon and his family just four days later. "The twins have been told from the cradle that they are special and powerful, because twins are so rare, and mixed-gender twins even more so. They do have a very low-level healing ability, but only within their twin bond. They have convinced themselves, and everyone around them, that their twin bond is a sign of great psionic power. Their handler believed that sexual attraction mixed with her overestimated psionic strength would be enough to enslave you."

"Overestimated indeed," Thean said, her voice heavy with disgust.

Nearly five decades ago, the Academy had agreed that a twin bond was a threshold Talent, limited in range and usefulness. The ability to share thoughts, even over long distances, did not equal psionic Talent if it did not extend beyond the bond. While they could heal each other, it wasn't psionic-based if they couldn't heal other people. The twins' healing Talent was only strong enough to let them diagnose, not initiate healing.

Most of the Qahngress delegation requested asylum on Le'anka. The twins repeatedly filed petitions for psionic Talent training at the Academy. They were repeatedly denied and offered standard medical training.

~~~~~

The failed mind-hunters refused to cooperate and reveal who had sent them after M'kar. Ashrock called in many diplomatic favors to ensure those men were unable to communicate with anyone who could send the news back to Nisandros that M'kar had Talent. In her next letter to Desra, M'kar gave all the information she could obtain about the men, to help the
~~~~~

sisterhood try to identify the instigators on Nisandros. Desra's return letter, which took nearly a year to reach her, vowed that no one would ever betray her secret.

In the same letter, M'kar sent a large data file Jasper and his friends had assembled, experiments and tests to perform at various distances from the surbda craters, and various depths within the craters. None of them were ready to discuss their theories because there were so many possibilities. The energy fields and resonances the sisterhood had recorded over the years and sent to M'kar excited them and provided plenty of fodder for more theories. Jasper warned that this research could take decades. He promised that he and his friends would stick with the investigation until they came up with a theory. Or until Alliance scientists were allowed to explore all the surbda craters.

M'kar doubted that would ever happen. It would require Nisandros becoming a member of the Alliance, and even then, the more recalcitrant and obstinate clans would refuse to allow any off-worlders to invade the surbda craters. For the foreseeable future, all data would have to be gathered by the sisterhood, for as long as their friend the recluse protected them from the warping of time and senses.

~~~~~

The next test of Infrenx's unity and teamwork came as a relief, a valid excuse to get away from the Academy and regular confrontations with the twins' supporters. They met at the Academy's private landing field once their classes were done for the day, and took a hoversled to the edge of a nature preserve an hour away. They took podboats and paddled as far as they could go until evening grew too dark for safe navigation in unfamiliar territory. Then M'kar led the way, borrowing the senses of the local nighttime creatures. They hiked inland, heading toward the river that would take them back to their starting point, portaging their small, light craft. They reached their intended camping spot a full forty minutes ahead of schedule. A sealed crate waited for them, with rewards released to them based on how well they met their goals. The crate had food for a feast, heavy on their favorite foods to celebrate. A portable pavilion waited inside a storage shed, with cushions and mats, promising them a comfortable evening. They had brought tents, to sleep two and three each, if they reached camp after the deadline. Better shelter was part of their reward for working together so well and saving time.

They were all in a festive mood, laughing and teasing Taila that the test of her skills cooking over an open fire hadn't been canceled, just delayed. M'kar and Garion had indulged in some spearfishing during their time on the water, and they had plenty of fish and bottomcreepers to add to tomorrow's breakfast.

The class had just finished setting up their camp when they heard
~~~~~

voices calling from the darkness down the slope to the east. M'kar and Thyal went to investigate. They didn't take handlights. If this unexpected interruption was part of their test exercise, they weren't going to make it easy for the newcomers to find them.

The voices came from a group of men and women in muddy clothes, looking worn and sweaty and scratched by underbrush. The carried handlights, revealing clothes in a familiar shade of purple.

"We have a problem," Thyal said, after they listened long enough to make out the names of Nyx and Nyssa in the unfamiliar language. Judging by the harsh tones used, the people were cursing the twins.

"You mean besides identifying who let them into the preserve? They couldn't have permission, otherwise we would have been warned. They're hunting for the twins, aren't they?" M'kar whispered.

"I've seen most of them at one time or another over the last lun, getting the twins out of trouble. They go wherever they're told they shouldn't be, just to prove they can do whatever they want." He shuddered. "I had a bad dream the other night, about what our lives would be like if that scheme had succeeded and established a bond, however temporary, between Nyssa and Father. If either of them didn't die from pheromone poisoning."

They kept walking, following the search party. The six people were making so much noise, Thyal and M'kar could talk at nearly normal volume without being heard.

"You go back to the others," she said. "I'll follow them, see what I can learn, so we can figure out what to do. It's not part of our testing, but ..."

"The Masters will make it part, once they hear." Thyal grinned, a snort of laughter escaping him.

He returned to camp. She stayed still, letting the searchers get a little farther ahead of her. When she looked back, up the slope, she caught a glimmer of the light from the fire pit where her class had gathered. The pavilion contained most of the light, so it hadn't attracted the attention of the search party. She visualized the map of the local terrain, trying to plan how she would lead the search party away if they got too close to Infrenx's campsite. Her first impression of the Qahngress twins made her inclined to leave them lost, and hopefully miserable. However, she heard her father in the back of her head, laughing and scolding her that she was being unkind to the wild animals of the preserve, inflicting Nyx and Nyssa on them. How could she get the intruders out of the preserve without any damage to them or the preserve, or discovering Infrenx's location?

The search party came into a clearing filled with moonlight. M'kar climbed a tree tall enough to let her look down on them. The leader pulled a tablet from a deep pocket in his jacket. He tapped it and it lit. He spoke into it and waited. No response. He spoke again, and a third time, growing more impatient. Did he honestly expect the twins to respond?

M'kar moved out along a limb that let her look down on the tablet. It was a tracker. She made out two pink blinking triangles, marking the location of their quarry. Did the twins know they had been tagged? The simulation of the landscape helped her calculate their position in relation to the search party.

The searchers were off by maybe twenty degrees. M'kar waited until they moved out of sight and hearing, then climbed down. She made no effort to be quiet, and mentally cast ahead, searching for night-roaming creatures. A flock of fang-gliders were perfect for her plan. Their wings were membranes that glowed in the moonlight from a bio-luminescent spore that grew on the undersides. She lightly touched the minds of three of the flock and asked them to locate the twins. In less than ten minutes, a squeal from Nyssa signaled a successful hunt. The squeal turned into a shriek, and then a spill of more of Qahngress's indecipherable language that only Jasper's sweetheart, Treinna, seemed to enjoy conquering. M'kar followed her ears and watched through the eyes of the gliders to guide her. She came out of the trees at the top of a steep drop.

In the moonlight, the twins were easy to spot ahead of and below her. Their purple clothes were ridiculous for a hike through the forest, with flowing sleeves and flaring cuffs on their trousers. Nyssa struggled in the middle of a clasp-thorn patch. On her right, her brother smacked at the trailing vines with a long branch, vainly trying to hold down the tangle of thorns and vines and exploding fruit to let her stumble clear. Her hair was long and loose, caught in dozens of thorns. M'kar muffled laughter. When the twins invaded Master Reydon's home, they had short, curly hair. Now their hair was long. Were they wearing wigs then, or now?

The clasp-thorn got its name from the two-part thorns that snapped closed when something foreign touched them. M'kar anticipated half an hour to cut all those thorns out of Nyssa's hair. Another stream of squeals and furious words erupted. She grinned at the thought of telling Nyssa all her hair had to get cut off.

The air rippled around her, and for a few seconds she couldn't tell up from down. Not very comfortable, since she stood on the edge of a sheer drop. M'kar took a staggering step backward. At least, she hoped it was backward. Then everything cleared, and she felt the presence of the rest of Infrenx.

You could have warned me, she said as their mind-circle enclosed her. Following the energy trail, she found them approaching a few hundred meters behind her.

Taila giggled, and M'kar caught a whisper of the sound with her ears and mind. The two down in the clasp-thorn patch didn't hear.

In moments, she showed her classmates what she had done and

discovered. Everyone agreed, if they made contact, the twins would latch onto them. For all they knew, the siblings had learned about their outing and had come out here to force themselves on Infrenx.

Wisdom said to keep the twins and the search party from knowing other people were nearby. While it would have been satisfying to leave both groups of intruders to keep struggling, they knew they couldn't indulge in childish or petty nasty tricks. Their teachers would be disappointed, and yes, this incident could be included in their test, which they would then fail.

I could try to break the vines, Survis offered. *Maybe Taila can singe the thorns so they break and let her go, and more don't catch her.*

But are they alert enough to realize when she gets free? Aryk countered.

Garion laughed. The sound echoed through the darkness, drowned out when Nyssa squealed louder and then snarled something at her brother. M'kar almost felt sorry for Nyx.

What's so funny? Nolan asked.

M'kar's already linked with some fang-gliders. Why not have them dive-bomb and scare the twitterhead into running? She might even think she got herself free, Garion offered. In moments, they had their plan.

Taila created tiny pockets of fire in the thorn patch, sending up puffs of smoke visible in the moonlight. Nyx stood up several times and looked around, but every time he said something his sister snarled, and he returned to trying to free her hair. Nyssa shrieked fury when he ducked and fled under the first diving sweep of the fang-gliders. She laughed at him when he tripped into a dent in the landscape, hidden by the tall grasses. Then a fang-glider swept close enough to catch at her hair. She shrieked and thrashed and broke free and kept shrieking as the fang-gliders dove down again, and again, herding them to the right, away from the ridge where Infrenx watched. And laughed, muffling the sound with their hands.

Garion helped M'kar guide the fang-gliders to keep up with the twins and drive them toward their search party.

When Infrenx returned to their campsite, they discussed the situation and agreed: the eight outsiders who had illegally entered the nature preserve, now wandering in the dark forest, justified using the communications equipment meant for emergencies. Thyal sent a short message to the patrol team for the preserve, giving the coordinates of the twins and the search party, and where M'kar estimated the two would meet up.

Then Infrenx could finally relax and make their delayed dinner and enjoy their time together.

~~~~~

During those nights around the campfire in the preserve, their class
~~~~~

had developed a tradition of sharing important secrets and sensitive bits of their lives, problems they were facing, questions they had. Infrenx knew about the sisterhood on Nisandros and the quest to understand the dimensional warping within the surbda craters. M'kar had brought Desra's latest letter on this outing. She waited to share it with her classmates until they had finished eating, and after the retrieval craft flew by, taking the search party and the twins back to civilization.

> *Vow Sister:*
>
> *Our Elders have become concerned. Our recluse friend has not met them during their last four visits to Etrusca's Wall. They asked our sisters in the clans by the other surbda craters, and she has not appeared there. They fear that the Ankuar and Gatesh scientists did more than take energy readings before they were caught by the patrols. We know of five teams of so-called scientists who have been caught and ejected from our world. Who knows how many more avoided detection? They all claim to be searching for Nisandros's Gate. We fear they have equipment that drains the energy within the craters, or they are experimenting, perhaps trying to bend the time-warping qualities of the craters for their own use.*
>
> *We are in defensive mode, to interfere with future intrusions. Some of our sisters stole the data chips from the most recent invaders. We refuse to call the Ankuar or the Gatesh scientists. Certainly not on the same level of honor of the scientists in your Alliance. I will try to send copies of the data chips to you in the future, but I here enclose some of the data that was downloaded, if you can make any sense of it. Our elders beg you to be careful in your quest to make sense of this information. You are not to put yourself into danger, compromising your father's honor. If this will cause trouble and block Nisandros joining the Alliance, then you are to feel no guilt if you obtain no help for us.*
>
> *However, our elders would be grateful for some answers, some theories. Our recluse friend shows her face so rarely, and speaks so cryptically, yet we trust her and live in readiness for the day she leaves the safe haven of the craters and walks among us again. We will rise up in rebellion and havoc, if we discover that outsiders with no honor have endangered her, and perhaps have ended the mission Enlo entrusted to her, long before its appointed time.*

M'kar stopped there. The rest of the letter was personal information, messages passed to her parents, news of the clan. Infrenx discussed the letter, the news, and if it was worth the risk to go beyond Jasper Lore and his group of genius students with the new data. The wrong person brought into the secret could initiate a chain reaction of inquiries and just the sort of investigation that would create diplomatic havoc. The current peaceful communication with Nisandros had lasted longer than anyone expected. The news that Gatesh and Ankuar scientists had landed on Nisandros to do studies would cause negative reactions in the Alliance. Mostly because no Alliance scientists had been allowed to do any studies, other than further anthropological studies of the culture. No physical science. And no searches for the Gate that had brought the people of Nisandros to their world. The Gates were always quiet, impossible to analyze or take samples for study. No Gate had been found on Nisandros, even though there were plenty of legends that indicated there had been a Gate at one time.

Before they ended the discussion, Infrenx agreed that the search for understanding of the surbda craters would stay with Jasper and his team. The less the instructors at the Academy and within the Fleet knew, the smaller the chances that some advancement-hungry diplomat would hear about the newest developments and cause trouble.

~~~~~

Infrenx left their camp at dawn the second morning, riding the river to where air-cars waited to take them to meet with Master Reydon in his home. After morning prayers, they had their traditional celebration breakfast and reported on the events of the two days in the preserve. This report had more laughter than usual.

"I wonder how long it took to get the thorns out of all that curly hair," Taila said. "And I have to ask, is that a natural shade of gold?"

"You, hush," Kelli said, and the two leaned close and giggled.

"Please don't make me turn this into a formal report," Reydon said.

"Sorry, Master," M'kar said. Her face warmed when she realized how amused she sounded, meaning she was not at all sorry. She bowed and spread her hands in silent apology.

The others muttered apology and followed suit. Garion stepped forward and clasped his hands behind his back, taking the recitation posture. He quickly covered the journey through the preserve, but stumbled when he got to how Infrenx dealt with the twins and their search party. "We ... herded them in the right direction to meet the search party. M'kar found fang-gliders, and used them to ... ah ..."

"Frighten them," M'kar offered. "And make them move. We didn't want to break the non-communication rules of our retreat, even if they approached us rather than us approaching them."

"And we didn't want them to know we were there," Thyal said, standing up to take over from Garion. "I was certain they would find an excuse to stay the entire time with us."
~~~~~

Chapter Seven

Once they finished the tale, which took longer than the herding effort had taken, their teacher praised the new depths of their mind-circle and teamwork and commended them for being responsible and careful. He passed on thanks from the Diplomatic Corps and several members of the Qahngress embassy. Replacements had arrived yesterday, sent by the newly stabilized government of Qahngress. The new ambassador was granddaughter of the empress. She had personally apologized to the Academy in general, Master Reydon in particular, and promised Nyssa and Nyx would be closely monitored and controlled. She also sent thanks to Infrenx for the steps they had taken to locate and look after the twins.

"No one should have known we were there. Who told them that we called in the retrieval team?" M'kar said.

"That needs to be investigated. Everyone with whom I have discussed this matter agrees that security was violated, and perhaps reveals to what depths those royal twins will sink to get what they want." Reydon shook his head. "I fear we have not seen the last of them, despite the promises of the ambassador."

~~~~~

Several days later, the teacher of M'kar's afternoon sociological structures class asked her to wear full Nisandrian dress, for the benefit of her classmates. She rarely wore Nisandrian-style clothes or jewelry to classes. They were saved for family time, or when her parents had guests in their home who would consider the cuisine and clothing and traditions of Nisandros interesting, and feel honored by the display. At the same time, M'kar never made any effort to hide her tattoos.

That afternoon, she wore a browband with the shriek beast emblem of her clan, which held back her hair and made her facial tattoos more visible. She chose a sleeveless shirt, the shoulders pulled up with gathered stitches, to reveal her starflower sisterhood tattoo on her shoulder, and the multitude of long, thin scars on her arm from that air-car crash when she was eight, ice-white against her deep tan.

On her way to her first afternoon class, with ten minutes to spare, M'kar caught a glimpse of a particular shade of purple she had grown to loathe. She kept walking, but mentally reached for the closest animal mind -- a bird. She didn't even check what species it was as she sent it back the way she had come. Sure enough, she spotted Nyx trotting along, craning his neck and very obviously watching her. She considered sending the
~~~~~

bird to dive bomb him, but she refused to give him the satisfaction of knowing she knew he was there. She settled into her usual seat in the lecture hall, maintaining a light touch on the bird's mind to keep it watching Nyx, but only checked on his activities four times during the two-hour period. She shuddered when the second and third checks showed he hadn't moved from the bench that gave him a good view of the door of the lecture hall. On her fourth check he still hadn't moved. She muttered a Nisandrian oath, but soft enough the classmates on either side of her didn't react.

When the class ended, she called up four more birds and a handful of skitters and sent them to circle Nyx and distract him. Then she went out the back entrance of the lecture hall and the building and took the skyway path across four buildings to her sociological structures class. Survival instincts learned in her cradle prompted her to look through the eyes of another bird, even though she was effectively on stage nearly the entire time and couldn't afford to be distracted while her classmates asked questions. She shuddered when she found Nyx waiting outside the door once more. Her irritation grew because she couldn't enjoy the discussion with her classmates as much as she would have liked. Some of their ideas and conceptions about Nisandrian culture were so wrong as to be hilarious. Even her teacher laughed with her and her classmates as she corrected one wrong idea and impression after another.

Nyx was more than a nuisance, this time. How did he find out her schedule? If someone gave it to him, even more security protocols for the Academy had been violated. If he had been asking through proper channels, they should have notified her that someone was asking how to find her, without being polite and leaving a message at her home.

Someone had to be following her to get the information for Nyx. He certainly had no stealth skills. Why had he targeted her? What kind of idiot thought he could irritate his way to acceptance in a group that didn't want him?

She couldn't take the same evasion tactics after this class. Thyal would be waiting in the plaza outside the lecture hall, to meet with Jasper and Treinna for an update on the surbda crater research. Yet Nyx now sat in that plaza with a drink. Maybe she could send some birds to drive him away?

Finally, the class time ended. M'kar responded to last-minute questions tossed at her from all sides, laughing with her classmates when different people asked the same question nearly at the same time. She thought she answered all the questions, but couldn't be sure, because she had a hard time keeping her mind off Nyx and what he could want. She barely heard their teacher's closing prayer for Enlo's blessing on them.

An awful idea nearly earned a gasp from her. Nyx wasn't going to try a variation of his sister's attempt on Master Reydon, was he? She remembered the awful smell of him, musk and something sickening sweet and bitter, when she tackled him during that incident in the garden. Would he try to overwhelm her with pheromone poisoning? Did he think she was so weak-willed she could be swayed by artificially induced sexual attraction?

She muffled a bubble of laughter into a cough, mercifully drowned by the sounds of her classmates getting up from their seats and shoving tablets into packs and calling to each other about meeting up to study, to exercise, to eat together. M'kar took her time leaving the lecture hall, letting the crowd dissipate. If Nyx confronted her, the fewer bystanders to be hurt, the better. She would surround Nyx in a whirlwind of fur and feathers, claws and wings, and hold him in place until Thyal could summon Security.

"We have an intruder," Thyal said, stepping from the shadows to fall into step with her as soon as she emerged outside.

"Nyx. I couldn't lose him after my last class."

"That is serious." He tipped his head to the right and linked his arm with hers. As soon as they went around the corner of the building, they picked up speed.

A wail filtered through the voices and footsteps as students headed back to their dormitories or to the dining halls or another class. M'kar muffled a chuckle as she directed the skitters to create a diversion. Just long enough for her and Thyal to cut through a classroom building. He laughed with her, but his smile faded as she shared what she had been thinking. Then they reached the Academy garden where Treinna and Jasper were meeting them.

"I think it's good our families are eating together tonight," he said, as they stepped down into the garden, surrounded by hedges for privacy.

"What do you wager my father won't find it amusing?"

"I don't take wagers I know I will lose." He managed a crooked smile, then he nodded to the two people waiting on a low bench in the shadows.

Treinna waved to them, then stood and executed a perfect bow, Nisandrian-style, arms folded tight to her chest, chin at just the right angle, to indicate she was honored by the meeting. If she wanted to serve as linguist on an E&D ship, Treinna had to know the cultural signals of the known worlds, pick up the signals on new worlds, and put them together into a pattern she could easily pass on to her captain. M'kar responded with arms spread as she bowed, putting her head lower than Treinna's had been, offering full friendship and trust. And to let Treinna know she had executed the bow perfectly.

Jasper stayed on the bench, all his attention on the tablet in his hands. M'kar didn't mind. He was always like that, his brain handling multiple exercises and equations and formulas at the same time. He didn't seem to be paying any attention to the exchange as Treinna took the task of relaying the latest theories woven together by the insane geniuses. That was typical for their meetings. Sometimes M'kar wondered if Treinna and Jasper had a psionic bond that let him talk through her. He came out of his engineering haze, as Treinna called it, the moment she used the wrong term in explaining something to M'kar and Thyal. Again, typical for their times together.

When they separated, Jasper and Treinna shared one of those glances that sent a sharp pang through M'kar's chest. It was the same deeply communicating, affectionate look her parents shared. While she was glad for Treinna and Jasper, M'kar tasted a bitterness she could only describe as envy and longing. Thanks to all the stupidity with Ke'Jor and all those attempts to kidnap her and drug her into agreeing to a betrothal with one clan leader or another or his son, she hated the general idea of marriage. She wouldn't marry, unless she could be sure she would have the same laughing, teasing, passionate oneness her parents shared.

Thyal was quiet as they walked through the Academy gardens, heading for the residential section. M'kar caught glimpses of him studying her face, and the awful suspicion grew that Thyal knew exactly what she was thinking. There could be nothing more humiliating, if she was right.

Except maybe her father guessing what was bothering her. After the last kidnap-into-marriage attempt, he had suggested she call on Thyal's hearth-brother vows and ask him to protect her with a betrothal. After all, he had said, in some cultures, their hearth-kin vows could be taken as a prelude to betrothal.

Sometimes she wanted to just pound her father until he stopped laughing or lost consciousness. It didn't matter which happened first.

Then a whiff of aroma reached her on the warm, late afternoon breeze, coming from behind them. Musky and powdery, sweet and bitter, with a hint of sweat smelling of anger and a little bit of fear and blood. And the dusty aroma of feathers and ... was that skitter dung?

M'kar muffled a grin.

"My shadow has caught up with us," she whispered.

"It is undignified for a future Master to run," Thyal said with a hint of groan in his voice that didn't match the mischief in his eyes.

That didn't mean they couldn't take long-legged strides, ducking between buildings, using shortcuts, and generally making it as hard as possible for Nyx to keep up with them. The problem with trying to keep track of Nyx as they dodged and turned was that they paid more attention behind than ahead.

Another figure in the same purple outfit stepped out of the long shadows just before they crossed from the academic side of the Academy grounds to the residential side. Nyssa clasped her hands demurely at her waist, fluttered her eyelashes and tipped her head slightly to the right, as she stood in the exact middle of the path before them.

"You are not allowed to be here." Thyal sounded tired rather than angry. M'kar envied his self-control. She would have snapped out a demand to know how Nyssa could justify disobeying the order not to come within two hundred meters of Master Reydon, his lecture hall at the Academy, his office, and his home.

The distancing agreement with the Qahngressian embassy should have included Reydon's *family*. M'kar mentally tripled the required distance, when they got close enough to see the adoring, sickening sweet look of suffering Nyssa fastened on Thyal.

"You haven't figured it out yet? You haven't been suffering as I have all these long, lonely days?" Nyssa's voice somehow managed to be a croon and a whimper and a song at the same time.

"Don't ask her," M'kar said. "That'll just give her an opening." Testing her theory, she reached for Thyal's hand and interwove their fingers.

Nyssa let out a wail almost exactly like her brother's and pressed the back of her hand to her forehead as her knees folded.

Thyal had the sense not to leap forward to catch her.

Nyx appeared from behind them, racing to catch his twin. She clutched at her brother as she struggled upright again. The fury in her eyes made a lie of her delicate, traumatic wilting.

"Give up," she snapped. "He's mine. That's the whole reason that stupid trap of Tarangar's didn't work. There was a stronger bond, a real bond, that overruled the pheromone overload."

"A bond?" Thyal shuddered, faintly, just enough for M'kar to feel in their joined hands.

"That explains everything." Nyx grinned and he spread his arms as he stepped forward. M'kar had the awful feeling he was going to try to hug her. "It's all a great big mix-up. You're getting conflicting signals. You and me, M'kar, we're meant to be. And Nyssa is soul-bonded with Thyal. It's perfect."

"It's insane," M'kar snapped.

"But it's the truth. I'm soul-bonded with Thyal. That's why the pheromone trap didn't work on his father." Nyssa clasped her hands under her chin and fluttered her eyelashes. "It's wonderful. I've never been so happy."

"You have never been so thoroughly self-deluded before, either," Thyal said in a calm, almost bored tone of voice. "I suggest you submit to the healers and undergo a thorough examination, as well as having your blood purged. You are suffering the after-effects of the pheromone poisoning and imagining something that does not exist."

"Soul bonds are real!" She stomped both feet, several times. "Our soul bond stopped me from trapping your father. We belong to each other!"

M'kar couldn't speak for all the Nisandrian curses clogging her tongue. She did manage the chittering sound of the fang-gliders. Nyssa's head snapped around to stare at her, moving so fast she knocked herself halfway off her feet. Her face was pale and her eyes wide with terror. A moment later, that dissolved into fury, her face flushing a shade of purple-red that made M'kar wonder if her hair was naturally that pale gold, and maybe her skin tones were chemically controlled. No one of her pale coloring could burn so dark.

"You --" Nyssa pointed at M'kar. "You --"

"My hearth-sister and I are late for an important meeting," Thyal said, when Nyssa struggled for words. "Please excuse us."

"What does that matter?" Nyx finally lowered his arms, as M'kar hadn't run into them.

She would rather hold hands with the nose-picker, Ke'Jor, thanks very much.

"We're meant for each other. We're bonded, and that means we can join Infrenx class, and everything will be perfect," he finished.

"No," Thyal said.

"But --" Nyssa began.

"No. Submit to a thorough psychological and medical examination and have your blood analyzed and purged. If you do not, then I must report you to Academy security, to ensure that in your delusion you do not cause harm to yourself and others."

He stepped around them and tugged M'kar along behind him. His face turned resolutely away from Nyssa and Nyx. The Qahngress twins stood there, mouths dropping open further with every heartbeat, and watched them hurry away.

M'kar mimicked the fang-glider's chittering, earning a long, harsh shriek from Nyssa.

"They are insane," she muttered.

"Let's hope so. Insanity is easier to heal than self-induced delusion." Thyal let go of her hand, gathered up his long outer robe to tuck into his belt, met her gaze, and then leaped forward into a run. They were safely in the residential district, and it didn't matter who saw them running.

M'kar needed to run, to work off the shock and confusion and exasperation. She wondered if insanity was a communicable disease, and how much exposure she needed before she was infected. Then again, she was genetically disposed to insanity, since the ailment certainly ran in her father's bloodline.

Thyal notified his parents of the incident, and Reydon filed a formal report. Both sets of parents shared M'kar's concern: someone in the

Academy administration was selling information about students. Thean added her authority as Premier Healer to the recommendation that the twins be examined and tested. Likely, they were suffering delusions as delayed reactions to the pheromone poisoning.

When Thyal's parents joined them at M'kar's home for dinner with her parents, they brought a formal apology from the Qahngress ambassador. She promised the twins would be kept under house arrest until a diagnosis had been made and treatment had commenced.

Ashrock groaned and turned to M'kar. "What sort of trouble have you gotten into now, *mi'sho'ki*? You didn't give us all the lovely, grimy details, did you?"

"I told you what was necessary," M'kar grumbled.

"But not the vicious, deliciously wicked details." He wrapped an arm tight around her shoulders, crushing her to his side. "Tell me, delight-of-my-old-age."

"Po'pa ..." M'kar tried to twist free of his grip, but he just dug his fingers in harder. She considered demonstrating the new flip move she had learned in self-defense class, but chose instead to laugh.

The full story, and stories of other members of the Academy who had embarrassing or confusing encounters with the royal twins, took the six of them through dinner. Ashrock recommended they warn other members of Infrenx, in case the twins tried similar tricks with the rest of the class, to gain admission to their ranks.

The first reports from the authorities dealing directly with the twins were discouraging. Clearing up the ugly mess might have been easier if they both truly had been suffering lingering effects of pheromone poisoning. But they weren't. The proof of soul bonds with Thyal and M'kar was all in the twins' heads.

Nyx proclaimed himself heartbroken and sent a formal request to Ashrock for permission to court M'kar. The request was denied. Further investigation revealed that his sister had encouraged him to pursue the relationship.

Nyssa claimed her Talent had grown exponentially since meeting Thyal, using that as proof of their soul bond. Master healers labeled the growth a figment of her imagination. Nyssa went into hysterics, insisting her life was endangered if anyone came between her and Thyal. She created so much trouble, the ambassador had Nyssa put into medical hibernation, until she could send her back home to Qahngress.

Her hibernation affected Nyx. He went through the day in a constant drowsy state, and alarmed friends by falling asleep in the middle of conversations. This resulted in Nyssa being brought out of hibernation and the twins staying on Le'anka for nearly two luns, to investigate this anomalous aspect of their twin bond.

Nyssa had some faint, uncontrolled power of persuasion, which seemed to come out strongest when she employed it for healing purposes. She gained herself a large cadre of admirers and supporters, some of whom thought Thyal was being entirely unreasonable by refusing to accept her soul bond with him. After the twins were put under constant scientific monitoring to understand their bond, Nyssa's supporters began a campaign to publicly shame him into accepting the soul bond.

Infrenx class focused so much on protecting Thyal, they forgot the constant threat to M'kar. The next Nisandrian team waiting for its chance to attack apparently realized this.

Survis and Garion were meeting M'kar to go to one of the courtyards set aside for group exercises. They saw the attacker leap from a tree just outside the tall hedge surrounding the courtyard. Survis mentally snagged the man and held him aloft, upside down, while Garion and M'kar searched him. They found an old-fashioned injector, a wand with a hollow core and tipped with a ball covered with dozens of hollow needles. The purpose was to slap the victim and inject the substance, usually a poison, with enough force to penetrate blood vessels and speed the reaction time.

M'kar recognized the salty-moldy scent of the drug, used to make its victim vulnerable to any command. She had no compunction about slapping her attacker in the arm. Garion said later she should have slapped the man's face with it.

The drug worked quickly, and by the time Security arrived, they had a confession from the prisoner. He willingly handed over the equipment he planned to use on M'kar. Starting with a bridal fetter for her wrist. It had the same genetic lock as the dyes used for honor tattoos, to bond it to her flesh. The ancient design, which would deliver more of the drug whenever she tried to resist, was proof enough of which clan had decided to capture her as an alliance bride. They didn't fear the consequences of taking an unwilling bride. That clan had a history of keeping brides drugged just enough to be no threat to their unwanted husbands. Which, Ashrock remarked later that evening, explained the mental defects in the clan for the last five centuries.

M'kar was just furious and frightened enough to listen when Ashrock and Master Reydon approached her with an idea. It would not only protect her from the most superstitious and tradition-shackled Nisandrians, but help protect Thyal.

The answer lay in a simple tattoo for both of them, settled prominently in the dip of the collar bone. It was a glyph representing the heart, settled in the middle of a gate. In essence, from the moment Thyal and M'kar took the tattoos, they would be considered in the first of ten steps to a traditional betrothal.

M'kar nearly leaped on her father to give him that threatened, well-earned pounding. She restrained herself because Master Reydon, Thean, and Thyal were right there in the room, and visibly approved of the plan. Thyal didn't even flinch when Ashrock said that dangerous word, *betrothal*.

"It's nothing but ink, *mi'sho'ki*," Ashrock said, after she took several loud, deep breaths to calm herself.

"Yes, but the tradition --"

"Exactly. We are depending on tradition to defend you. Anyone who comes after you is already a superstitious idiot, obeying the lunatic commands of even more superstitious idiots. They will see the mark and flee in terror of the dark spirits and Ancestors who will devour their souls if they violate the betrothal created by the mark. You do not believe in the power of the dark spirits or the Ancestors. Thyal does not believe. And this is just the first step. There is no curse, there is no sin, when the day comes that one of you finds your true soul-mate and asks the other to free you from the betrothal that isn't even official, because after all, it is just ink. No ceremony. No vows. You see?" Ashrock nodded slowly, visibly willing her with the intensity of his gaze to accept the ridiculous plan.

M'kar did see, despite the haze filling her eyes that she was afraid would be anger, or at the very least hurt feelings, if she examined it too closely.

"How will this protect Thyal, exactly?"

"When the next person lectures him on his cruelty to that deluded girl," Master Reydon said, "he will tug down his collar to show him the tattoo and ask how he could be soul-bonded with her when he is already pledged in ancient ritual to another." He shrugged, as if it were obviously simple. M'kar didn't miss the glint in his eyes that hinted at mischief.

"I don't have to tell anyone that you have the matching mark," Thyal added.

"Unless that person has a screaming temper tantrum in the middle of the Academy grounds and brings Security running," she muttered. Then suddenly, she saw the humor in the whole idea.

Still, there was that niggling bit of uncertainty at the back of her mind as she agreed to the idea, and she and Thyal sat still for the application of the multiple layers of colors. The artist Thean brought to the house didn't use Nisandrian dyes, made specifically to bond with the genetic structure so it always stayed bright and strong and could never be removed. Except by removing enough layers of skin and flesh to cause a great deal of damage and pain.

~~~~~

Three days later, M'kar and Thyal were to meet with Treinna's friend from back home, Genys Arroyan, who was in her third year of Basic and
~~~~~

on the Fleet command track. Genys had gone to Jasper for some help in understanding Gate theory and Chute mechanics, and he had been distracted with a new packet of data from the sisterhood. Jasper hadn't intended to tell Genys anything, but he slipped up enough to admit that he and Treinna were friends with someone from Nisandros, the source of the data. Genys offered to help M'kar prepare for her early entrance exams for Basic if she would help her with Nisandrian vocabulary beyond the general trade language. A friendship was quickly developing, and today would be the fourth study session. Thyal was joining them, to guide M'kar in her role as teacher. Several instructors at the Fleet Academy had already indicated they would be asking her to help teach some courses because of her background.

M'kar was late arriving at their meeting place, a small alcove off one of the study gardens. She had sensed someone following her and took several detours to lose her unwanted shadow. Genys hadn't arrived either, which surprised her. She hadn't even decided whether she should go look for her when the communication link in her student identification wristband chirped. Genys had left a voice message. Someone was following her, and she was trying to identify who it was before meeting M'kar.

A few moments of thought, to weigh her options and come up with a plan, and M'kar left the alcove to go find Genys and help her. She saw Thyal coming down one of the many intersecting paths through this portion of the Academy gardens and decided not to wave to get his attention. She might get the wrong attention. When she got closer, she was surprised and then worried by the scowl wrinkling his face. He straightened his hunched shoulders when he saw her. She flashed him a quick message in the finger language Infrenx had devised for their own use. He nodded. They both turned down paths that intersected a dozen steps later.

"Someone following you, too?" she asked, pitching her voice low.

"Several. I'm worried that I can actually feel the animosity powering those eyes focused on me."

"Genys is trying --" She flinched when her bracelet chirped again. The message was clear despite its brevity.

"Nisandrian pest," Thyal read aloud, when she showed him. One corner of his mouth quirked up. "Not referring to you?"

Chapter Eight

M'kar laughed and tried to nudge him hard in the side with her elbow. Thyal must have anticipated it. He neatly skipped sideways, out of her reach for two steps, then moved back in close enough to make her stumble. She laughed at a few wide-eyed glances he earned. Chances were good people didn't even notice her in their shock at seeing a high-ranking student in the telltale light brown robes, acting silly.

Up ahead, the traffic parted as students and cadets headed down different paths leading to lecture halls and study gardens. M'kar spotted the glossy black rope of Genys's hair, with silver cord woven into the thick braid. She gestured at Genys, who was walking away from them. Her raised hand created the perfect line of sight to a man wearing an Anokian acolyte's silver robes, contrasting sharply with the red and green hashmarks of tattoos on his left cheek. She could almost laugh at the arrogant foolishness and mistakes of the hunters sent after her.

"I see him," Thyal said, before she could say anything.

"Meet up with Genys. The *a'goo'si* is so focused on her, he won't see me coming."

"I will notify Security." He nodded to her and picked up his pace just slightly, as M'kar darted down a path to the right. It branched in another five meters and would allow her to come up from behind the badly disguised Nisandrian hunter.

The confrontation was almost too easy. She ducked low, pivoting on one hand, and swept his legs out from under him with a hard, fast swing of both her legs. M'kar wanted to laugh when she was kneeling on the hunter's chest, pressing his own restraint bracelets against his throat. His eyes widened far enough to threaten to pop out of his head and he went pale under the ugly smears of multiple scars and tattoos covering him from hairline to the deep V of the collar of his borrowed robes. He gasped for breath and finally yelped in fractured tones.

"No one told me you were given!"

The fresh tattoo seemed to burn in the dip of her collarbone for a moment, as if his frightened gaze ignited it.

M'kar hated it when her father was proven right. Ashrock would laugh and remind her of this moment for the next several luns. Maybe years.

Then Security arrived and took custody of the man, who shivered and whimpered and kept ducking to avoid meeting her gaze. M'kar couldn't even laugh at how she didn't have to say anything for Security personnel to know what to put in the report. Enough incidents had occurred in the last few years, she knew some of their names.

Before the onlookers started to drift away, M'kar was free to hurry down the pathway to catch up with Thyal and Genys.

In that short time when she was distracted, one of Nyssa's supporters had caught up with Thyal. She lectured him, waving a finger at him, scowling, and generating a fine spray of spit in her fury. Thyal glanced away from her just long enough to meet M'kar's gaze. She grinned and tugged down the collar of her shirt to touch her tattoo. Thyal frowned for a second, then he burst out laughing.

That shocked the venomous young woman into silence for a few seconds. Long enough for Thyal to tug open his robe enough to reveal the tattoo. M'kar wasn't close enough to hear the exact words, but the young woman's reaction was loud and shrill. She jumped up and down, waving her arms, shrieking, mostly consisting of "No," and "You traitor," and "Impossible."

Lyrian, a Security guard, had followed M'kar, in case there were more attackers waiting for their chance. She stepped up and took custody of the young woman, silencing her with the threat of a stunner wand in her face. Genys linked arms with Thyal and they hurried away down a path branching to the left. M'kar kept walking, past Lyrian struggling with Nyssa's friend, then took another branching path to catch up with them. The three spent most of what remained of Genys's free hour trying to decide how to avoid reporting this incident to their parents.

Within three days, the newest rumor spreading through the Fleet dormitories claimed that a certain command candidate was betrothed to the youngest Master at the Academy. Ashrock laughed loudest at all the wrong details in the rumors. Genys very truthfully responded to every questioning look and comment: there was nothing to the rumor, and whoever spread it had some mental or emotional problems. Everyone was relieved when Nyssa and Nyx were finally sent home to Qahngress, and her supporters found something else to be righteously indignant about.

Ashrock and Jeyn invited Genys to dinner, to get all the juicy details, and soon she was an adopted member of the family, just like Treinna and other cadets M'kar had befriended and brought home. Genys promised to help her prepare for her entrance exams for Basic. She warned her that people would assume M'kar would go into Security.

"As far from the diplomacy side of the mission as possible, you mean?" M'kar shrugged and gave her a lopsided grin. "I intend to use my Talents," she said, tapping her temple, "rather than my fists and feet."

M'kar was pleased to learn that her advanced classes at the Academy allowed her to skip many required courses in Basic. If she entered several years early, skipped enough courses, and applied enough experience points, she might become one of the youngest officers in the Fleet.

Around that time, Nisandros and Gatesh fell into another cold war where most of the weapons were insults and accusations. Nisandros instituted a new blockade, refusing to allow any shipments or visitors from off-world. The cessation of the bits of sometimes unintelligible scientific data Desra smuggled off Nisandros didn't worry Jasper. He had more than enough to work on and decode and untangle for years to come.

"By the time they're ready to play nice, we might have something to offer them. Theories, at least. And maybe we'll have some sensor packs devised that are shielded from whatever those interfering energy fields are." He offered M'kar a distracted smile and turned back to his tablet full of calculations.

~~~~~

Three days before her seventeenth birthday, M'kar attended a lecture on new theories and discoveries related to a theoretical broken Gate found on a Hiver-devastated planet. Jasper had asked her to attend. He knew everything the scientists were going to say about the pile of rocks in a ring of warping energy fields, but he wanted M'kar's input. She didn't know whether to be flattered or worried that Jasper thought she could offer a new perspective on their ongoing project.

At the end of the lecture, her head was spinning around a disturbing, vague idea sitting in a dark corner of her mind. How could she ask Jasper questions, to understand what she had been hearing, if she couldn't put those questions into words? The new information had made her less confident about traversing Chutes. How Humans had ever learned to navigate Chutes without smearing themselves an atom thick across the universe was a testament to Enlo's undeserved grace and mercy.

She wasn't paying attention to her surroundings as she got up from her seat in the auditorium and followed other students out of the building. Her eyes didn't focus right away on the three men blocking her path just outside the door. She started to go around them, then her brain registered their matching jumpsuits in eye-bleeding orange and poison blue. Ba'e'do'stra clan colors. She twisted aside, anticipating weapons to appear out of thin air, knives aiming for her neck or gut, tangle-stones wrapping around her ankles and wrists.

The tallest and widest of the three men grinned as she dropped into a defensive crouch. He had unusually white teeth in his space-tanned face. Odd that she could actually see his skin. None of the three had much in the way of scars and tattoos hiding their features. As if they had left Nisandros early in their lives and didn't follow the ancient traditions. The dip in their eyebrows was easy to see. The last Nisandrian who had smiled at her, who wasn't her father, had been trying to kill her. As usual.
~~~~~

"A little slow," the shortest of the three said, "but what do you expect of the academic life? You have to do better than that, little sister, if you're going to represent the clan in the Fleet."

M'kar choked out a long string of Nisandrian oaths, the particularly acidic ones Treinna would enjoy learning. Her hobby was collecting profanity from every language she mastered. Treinna and Jasper were getting married in another lun, and M'kar was giving her a compendium of curses her father had collected for years, as a wedding present.

"That sounds like our father. How is the old *qascraq*?" the tallest one said.

"How did you find me?" she spat.

"With great difficulty." The middle one stepped forward and dropped into a crouch mirroring hers, so they were eye-to-eye, but with two meters between them. M'kar didn't doubt he could leap that gap if he had to. So could she.

Had her half-brothers finally given in to the nastier members of the clan, and come to cleanse Ba'e'do'stra's honor by slaughtering her?

"You've been getting into a lot of trouble." Ashar, the oldest brother chuckled. He sounded like Ashrock. "The steps we had to take, convincing Security we weren't here to skin you alive ... it's worse than Father let us know, isn't it?"

Bannar was the middle brother, and Shauq the youngest. They were nineteen, sixteen, and twelve when Ashrock had married Jeyn, and had fled off-world after a particularly nasty brawl with most of their cousins when M'kar was six. She had always hoped that her brothers had been fighting to defend her, but nobody would ever tell her the truth about that battle that had left rooms on three floors of the clan house in ruins.

"I'm alive and the Academy hasn't been melted into glass by a nuclear blast, so no, not that bad."

That earned laughter from Ashar and Shauq.

Laughter filled most of M'kar's memories of the five-day visit from her brothers. She didn't see them much, and that was fine. They were strangers to her, and it was only right that her three brothers spent most of their visit catching up with Ashrock. Ideas she had rarely entertained gnawed at her for luns afterward.

Just how much had her father sacrificed to marry Jeyn and leave Nisandros so she could survive to grow up? Ashrock always insisted that he enjoyed his life. Nothing worth having could be had without sacrifice, and he believed this was the life Enlo had designed for him. But she had to wonder and feel some guilt. Ashrock would scold her if she tried to talk to him about it. How much had her father lost, simply by being her father, her hero and defender? Ashrock was proud of her, but now she felt inadequate. Her father needed his sons, and he had sacrificed them to prove so many of Nisandros's beliefs were wrong.

Her brothers had maintained sporadic contact with Ashrock, and generally ignored Jeyn and M'kar. She had been fine with that. Better to be ignored than to know her half-brothers agreed with those who wanted her dead. Then they appeared on her home territory, friendly and interesting. They had their own ship and traveled the universe exploring, providing security for scientific expeditions and investigating planets for the colonization arm of the Alliance.

M'kar thought she liked her brothers. She wondered if maybe they liked her a little. And maybe someday they could be friends.

Their visit was over quickly, and she was relieved and disappointed. How could all those years of separation be made up for in just five days?

They couldn't, but she comforted herself that maybe a wound her father would never acknowledge had started to heal.

~~~~~

Nisandros's blockade didn't prevent spies, mind-hunters, hopeful assassins, and kidnappers leaving the planet. The persistence of her clan, and her clan's enemies, complicated the process for M'kar as she entered Basic at age seventeen. Three years early.

One hundred incoming cadets gathered in the Fleet's main assembly plaza for an orientation meeting and speech. Everyone was in cadet uniforms. It never occurred to M'kar to use makeup to cover her tattoos or alter her eyebrows. The stares and wide-eyed doubletakes had stopped years ago. She was a known, accepted presence at the Academy.

No one thought to warn the incoming class of cadets.

A gregarious young woman giggled after the fourth instructor reminded the cadets that everyone was to be quiet. She turned around, grinned at M'kar who was standing directly behind her, and started to say something. Then her gaze landed on M'kar's tattoos, visibly traced the lightning bolt by her ear, followed it to the blue lines around her eyes, and from there to the dip in her eyebrows. She flung out her arms as if to ward off a blow, shrieked, and kept shrieking as she backed away. After five steps, her incoherent shrieks became coherent.

"It's a Nisandrian! How can you let a Nisandrian in here? I was promised I would be safe from those filthy Nisandrians!"

M'kar later learned the hysterical young cadet was Nacy Camola, daughter of two reclusive and obscure research scientists, raised in an isolated biological research station. Her brother was Arys Camola, a rising star in the Diplomatic Corps. He had convinced Nacy to join Fleet, see the universe, and make her mark. On the journey to Le'anka, Nacy had run afoul of a band of Nisandrians who lived down to the worst stereotypes of their race. They harassed her into hysterics, requiring tranquilizers to continue her hopscotch journey from her parents' very remote research
~~~~~

station to the Academy.

Nacy's screams and pointing hands and other cadets scattering away from M'kar made her a visible target for the waiting assassins from the Be'har'vu Clan.

Ashrock had given M'kar a new set of knives, made to be concealed in her clothing, as a birthday present and to celebrate her entrance into Basic. Ordinarily, those knives would have been forbidden, but the years of attacks had persuaded the Academy officials, and now the Fleet, to make a special circumstances exception for her.

The assassins came from three angles, including swinging down from the top of the ornamental façade of a five-story-tall classroom building on the west side of the plaza. An instant prickle of warning in her scalp had M'kar pivoting and ducking in a low sweep, to survey her surroundings. She caught movement from the corner of her eye, whipped off her uniform cap, and pulled the first stilleto from her braids, which had been holding them tightly in place. Other knives were tucked up her sleeves, in the ankle-high sides of her boots and down the front of her jacket. Before the first of the instructors on the platform realized what was happening, M'kar leaped and met the assassin on his downward swing, climbed up his body, slashed at the cord he hung from, and twisted them both around in mid-air. When they hit the ground, she was on top. He landed head-first on the pavement tiles.

The other two assassins struck with magma-bolt guns. One streamer of liquid metal grazed M'kar's leg, ruining her cadet uniform and leaving a burn scar down her calf that she later decorated with a tattoo of five infrenx winding around it. Six young men and women, all headed for the Security track, dove into the fray. They never got a hand on the two remaining assassins, but they did distract them long enough for Security to respond to the alarms and surround the plaza. M'kar took down one of the two, and in the process highly impressed several instructors who saw her in action, managing to maneuver on her one uninjured leg as she leaped and spun and slashed and flung her knives.

The Be'har'vu clan had paid ridiculous fees for the information that M'kar was entering Basic, the orientation schedule and map, and the location of her parents' home. Their assassins were foolish enough to document their plans and the identity of the racist idiot in Security who didn't like Nisandrians, didn't want Nisandros in the Alliance, and sold them the information. He had learned about Nacy's terror of Nisandrians and arranged for her to be placed close to M'kar in the plaza.

Academy officials dealt with the greedy traitor. The spaceport officials dealt with another opportunist who cleared the Be'har'vu to bring forbidden weapons onto the planet.

More important, M'kar impressed Fleet Commodore Engray, who

led the entrance examination committee she faced the next day, on crutches. The commodore defended M'kar when several members of the committee, including Arys Camola's sponsor and distant cousin, wanted to deny her entrance into Basic because of the inherent danger that followed her with the ongoing assassination and kidnapping attempts. Engray growled and scolded them for their fears and their refusal to grant M'kar the shelter and community she had certainly earned. Then he finished by requesting she lead a personal defense class. The policy of the Academy, especially the Fleet side, was to take advantage of all the cultural teachings of the many worlds whose students came to them. Nisandrian defensive skills were clearly necessary, for the good of future officers of the Fleet.

Arys Camola and his sister filed claims against M'kar, insisting she was only playing at being Nisandrian and had done it specifically to terrify Nacy. They couldn't come up with any reason why M'kar, who didn't even know the girl existed, would put in so much effort to masquerade as a Nisandrian. When the assassination attempt was fully investigated, the Camolas didn't have a fragment of a stump to stand on, much less a leg. They still tried to put all the blame on M'kar for Nacy's disgraceful public fit, which led to her being denied entrance into Basic.

In the end, M'kar was only delayed by two hours from moving into the dormitories, with Genys Arroyan, in her final year of Basic, as her roommate and cadet mentor.

<div align="center">~~~~~</div>

By this time, Infrenx only met every four days. Everyone else in the class had moved on to various service functions in the Academy and were preparing to head out across the Alliance in their planned careers, using their Talents. Thyal was now a junior Master at the Academy, with a demonstrated aptitude for working with new students and helping them to adapt to Academy life. M'kar's class in Nisandrian self-defense techniques, mixed with glimpses of Nisandrian culture, was highly popular from the first day of the new term. Ashrock pretended to be jealous that her classes had more people attending than the celebration for the release of his newest book of children's fables.

M'kar dared to hope she had finally come into her own. She was surrounded by people whose faces lit up with interest when they got close enough to see her tattoos and scars, rather than going pale with fear or wrinkling with apprehension when they realized she was one of the few Nisandrians who lived on Le'anka.

Two decs into the first term of Basic, she decided she had jinxed herself.

Nyssa and Nyx seemed to rise out of the pavement of the plaza, aiming straight at M'kar on her way to her morning class. At first, she didn't recognize them because they wore the uniforms of cadets, just like nine-tenths of the people in the crowded plaza that morning. The twins stood out because they had an escort. Even though they didn't wear the ubiquitous purple of Qahngress, the two men and two women were identifiable by that particular non-uniform of civilian personnel all over the universe in the service of very important people.

M'kar firmly believed that people who required escorts just to cross the central plaza had no business joining the Fleet.

Just ten meters away was the sloping path to the sunken courtyard where her students would be assembling in another ten minutes. M'kar slowed, trying to calculate just where the twins' path would intersect with hers. She didn't care how it looked, the moment Nyx's attention focused on her, she would run. It didn't matter what direction she ran. Common sense said not to let herself be cornered.

Four meters before that dreaded meeting, the twins and their escort crossed paths with a group of cadets standing in a lopsided circle, having a discussion. The man leading the escort walked up to the cadets, pulled his shoulders back so he stood taller, and he glared down at them for a full five seconds -- M'kar counted. The cadets moved aside, as if telekinetically pushed by the force of the man's glare.

Had the twins returned with psionic backup to renew their campaign to join Infrenx? They would be disappointed, as most of Infrenx had graduated to service positions. There were no classes for them to infiltrate. Perhaps they would demand private lessons with Master Reydon? Or maybe they wanted something new?

Please, please, Enlo, be merciful. Protect Thyal if you don't protect me.

A flicker of fire snapped across the bridge of her nose. M'kar let out a yelp and automatically reached up to check her eyebrows. Taila had scorched the eyebrows and hair of everyone in Infrenx before she got her control refined. She had even offered to singe the dip in M'kar's eyebrows to remove that little telltale identification.

M'kar turned and saw Taila and Survis leisurely strolling from the other side of the plaza. Today, they were to help her teach. They had had great fun over the last few days planning how to use his bulk and telekinetic power and her ability to shoot thin streamers of flame to test M'kar's students and throw them off balance. They gestured for her to wait for them. She grinned and silently thanked Enlo for this answer, sent before she had even prayed. Taila's sharp tongue and Survis's bulk would help intimidate those people who were clearly there to enforce Nyssa and Nyx's every wish.

"Recognize them?" she asked as they met up. She gestured with a twist of her head at the six who were coming closer now.

"Forefathers, have mercy," Taila said with a groan. "I completely forgot. I was going to warn you. Ramming speed!" She caught hold of M'kar's hand and ran, heading for the archway into the courtyard where people were streaming inside ahead of them. Survis hurried after them. He was remarkably light on his feet, for all his massive size.

"Warn me?" M'kar blurted.

"I ran into them in the infirmary yesterday. I'm helping Master Sopeesia with the pyro class, and one of the little ones set herself on fire." Taila looked back as they reached the archway. "They're actually good healers, more's the pity, and already taking infirmary duty, but ..." She slowed and turned, walking backward.

"But what?"

"I saw them on my way from the embassy quarter. We're late because I stopped to warn Master Reydon on my way to meet Tai," Survis said. "Should have warned the rest of the class." He groaned and gestured at the archway behind them.

M'kar turned to look, even knowing she would see the twins. A chime shimmered through the air overhead, warning that the exercise period was about to start. She gratefully turned her back on the six intruders and headed for the raised platform at the far end of the courtyard, where she could be seen by all her students.

Who had been foolish enough, or intimidated enough, or maybe even nasty enough to allow those self-important twits back on Le'anka? Maybe someone on Qahngress had come up with a magic potion guaranteed to grant them psionic Talent?

Scary thought.

No attack took place before the exercise period began. She slid out of her shoes and peeled out of her jacket and spread her legs for steadiness before covering her upturned face with her hands for prayer. No one asked her, and she wasn't about to admit that prayer wasn't a Nisandrian morning ritual. M'kar prayed every day, dedicating her mind and body and heart to Enlo. Her mother had taught her that taking good care of her body was just as much worship of the All-Maker as any song or hours of discussion of holy teachings or reading the words of the prophets.

Just before she covered her eyes, a flicker of movement caught her attention. Survis and Taila nodded to each other, then Taila fled the garden. When M'kar finished her prayers and uncovered her eyes, she looked to Survis. He nodded to her, and with a few flicks of Infrenx's finger language, told her Taila had gone to warn the rest of their class.

Nyssa and Nyx hadn't closed their eyes, although two members of their escort had. Nyx was looking around, studying everyone in the courtyard and the high walls hung with years of vine growth. Nyssa wasn't really looking at anyone, as far as M'kar could see. The twins and their escort stood about ten meters away, by the archway entrance, so

M'kar couldn't read anyone's expression. Deliberate?

The twins didn't interrupt the session. M'kar avoided looking at Nyx, so she had no idea if he was staring at her with that same brainless look of adoration he had used before. Couldn't that be blamed on the pheromone poisoning? If not ... she thought she might feel sorry for him. And despise Nyssa more for continuing to insist her twin was soul-bonded to M'kar.

She closed the exercise period with prayer, bracing herself for attack, but when she opened her eyes, the six intruders were gone. She gestured at the empty spot and Survis turned to look.

"Why am I not relieved?" he murmured.

"Because you're smart."

"Paranoid," he said, punctuated with a snort and a grin.

Perhaps the Qahngress twins had learned strategy, or even courtesy during their years banned from Le'anka? Perhaps they really had been cured of the pheromone poisoning? Or as Taila and Kelli hoped, someone had finally got it through their stubborn royal heads that no, they didn't deserve to have everything they wanted?

Maybe they were telling the truth when they applied to enter Basic and join the Fleet? They wanted to increase their medical knowledge and serve in the Fleet as a gesture of good will from their world, to help Qahngress to be accepted as a member of the Alliance.

For the next three luns, Infrenx lived on alert, ready to leap to Thyal and M'kar's defense. The need never arose, other than nearly daily sightings of the twins as they went about their heavy schedule of classes and service hours.

Chapter Nine

Then the day came for the oldest members of their class to leave on their first off-world assignments. They met for a farewell breakfast at Ashrock and Jeyn's home. He insisted on feeding them as warriors, and as adopted sons and daughters of his household. Reydon and Thean joined them, and they had a good time, laughing and reminiscing, and warning each other about people who had been troublesome and might strike again, once Infrenx class was no longer there to race to each other's rescue.

This included the Qahngress twins, whom everyone agreed had been too well-behaved recently. Masters in the medical division reported the twins were good healers. They needed to stay together so their twin bond would facilitate their healing gift. Friends throughout the Academy and the Alliance Council's many levels reported that the twins had been very busy charming their way through the embassies and levels of the government. Those who knew the history of their problems with Infrenx, and with Thyal and M'kar in particular, feared long-term problems when they took advantage of all that goodwill they generated.

Despite their suspicions, the members of Infrenx were all in a good mood when they left Jeyn and Ashrock's home and went to the spaceport to make their goodbyes before Nolan, Survis, and Taila boarded the shuttle for the orbital station, to meet their ships. Master Reydon had done his job well, and they all vowed to make their teacher proud, and return with amazing stories.

~~~~~

Arys Camola regularly aired his grievances against M'kar and tried to convince newly appointed officials to support him. He never got far enough in his campaign for anyone to learn what exactly he wanted done to her. He had great success irritating officials who respected and admired Ashrock. After notations were put in his records about his "unreasonable obsession with punishing all Nisandrians in general" for his sister's continuing mental and emotional problems, he made another, bigger mistake. He approached first Dr. Jeyn, then Ashrock, requesting special tutoring in Nisandrian culture. His vague explanation that he thought Nisandros would be the next "major frontier" in diplomatic activity didn't sit well with either of them. He approached Ashrock three times, each time less polite and more demanding. The third time, he informed Ashrock that it was a "matter of honor," and he owed Camola for the damage done to his sister.
~~~~~

That also went on Camola's record. Along with reports from several concerned witnesses that Camola was biding his time until he could "make those barbarians pay, once and for all," as he had threatened multiple times in multiple situations.

Camola never approached M'kar. He never gave her any reason to file complaints against him. She itched to do so, especially when she realized how he tainted her opinion of diplomats. Many of her parents' friends were diplomats. She couldn't just dismiss the entire breed as arrogant, opportunistic, and self-righteous. Yet she found it all too easy to agree with classmates who chafed against the D portion of E&D ship assignments. They were all of the old-school mindset that if a new world reacted foolishly when a ship appeared unexpectedly in their solar system, such as lobbing a missile at the ship, that ship should go in blasting, put the entire planet under military rule, and teach those savages what real civilization meant.

Cadets with such attitudes were identified during Basic. Their careers were guided so they never had a chance to be in the position of overruling their captains and starting an interstellar incident that would give the Ankuar or Gatesh or other troublesome races an excuse to ignite a war.

Until he attacked her in front of witnesses, all M'kar could do was be alert, but not to the point of fraying her nerves. She had to present an outward appearance of forgetting that Arys Camola existed. And hope that frustrated him to the point of tearing out his own hair.

She applied the same "wait and ignore" tactics to the young men among her classmates who had started making romantic gestures. She calculated that they were only interested in proving themselves brave enough to risk Nisandrian anger or insanity, rather than interested in *her*. Too bad they didn't let her disinterest and seeming inability to remember their names from one day to the next discourage them.

Finally, Genys and Treinna gave her valuable advice for testing suitors' motives and frightening away the ambitious egotists: introduce them to her parents. Jeyn tangled their brains with highly intense sociological discussions. Ashrock terrified them with questions such as their familiarity with Nisandrian courtship rituals and battle requirements. Did they know how quickly they could heal from knife wounds, broken bones, or how long they could navigate after losing at least a quarter of their total blood capacity?

That worked moderately well, so that by the end of the first term of Basic, M'kar no longer feared encountering yet another cadet who decided his career was better served through romance than through hard work.

The Qahngress twins never approached Thyal or M'kar for conversation, but they regularly encountered them in their daily travels between classes. That regularity could only come with the help of an entire staff of personnel to watch at doorways and from rooftops, and even employ the aide of tiny spying drones. Jasper and his crew of insane geniuses had great fun tracking the command frequencies of the drones. First they blocked them, then they inverted the commands, so whatever the drones were commanded, they did the opposite. Finally Nyssa and Nyx gave up on technological spying.

In the second term of Basic, the Qahngress twins changed their tactics. They missed classes and scheduled work periods in healing clinics or stints on Medical Station Anwesta, to sit in the lecture halls where M'kar was taking classes or Thyal was teaching. Or sit by the doors, waiting for their targets to see them. As Treinna put it several times, "see their suffering and give in under a massive weight of guilt."

When the twins missed the scheduled shuttle departure for their learning unit assignment to a colony battling viridian plague, they were called up before a disciplinary council and put on probation. On the advice of Thean, the twins were confined to a regimented route between their dormitories, their classrooms, and their work assignments. They were required to wear monitoring bracelets to ensure they did not deviate or go near their targets. For six luns.

After the disciplinary council met, Genys shared a story from her and Treinna's homeworld, Gaea. There was a malevolent spirit so powerful, it needed to inhabit two minds and bodies. Otherwise, the heat and weight of its presence drove the possessed person to insanity and death within hours. The spirit took to possessing twins, because they shared bodies and souls, according to Gaean belief. They were known through folklore as Mirror Monsters, and could rampage for years, driving their victims insane through twisted, convoluted reasoning that knocked them off their spiritual and moral foundations.

The Qahngress twins were quickly dubbed the Mirror Monsters by a small circle of cadets who had witnessed them stalking M'kar and Thyal and earned their antipathy. The label was quickly picked up by people who had other reasons for disliking Nyx and Nyssa.

M'kar could think of several dozen worse labels than Mirror Monsters, but she didn't tell anyone. That would require explaining Nisandrian culture, and she did far too much of that in class. She used the label, but sparingly. The less she thought of the twins, the better.

Nyx refused to cooperate with her wish to forget him. He managed to get enough sympathy from classmates to sneak three letters to M'kar, when the communication system at the Academy blocked him from contacting her. They consisted of repetitions of the same plaint: why wouldn't she admit there was a bond between them? Why wouldn't she admit they belonged together? Who was threatening her, blackmailing her, holding her prisoner so she was afraid to seize the happiness and completion that waited for her?

M'kar might have felt sorry for him, but Nyx was clearly being manipulated by his sister in all this. His style of writing changed drastically, going from whiny adolescent to lyrical poetry whenever he mentioned his sister's suffering passion for Thyal. She insisted someone was performing evil psionic experiments on him to block the oneness of their minds and souls. Clearly, Nyssa was dictating some of his letters.

Each letter went to the administration of the Academy. After three warnings and the fourth letter, the Qahngress twins were shipped to a remote Academy facility for the remainder of their medical training. Orders were put in their files that they were never to be assigned to any planet within four jump gates and ten solar systems of Le'anka.

M'kar had barely sent off long celebratory letters to the other members of Infrenx, when Arys Camola made his final miscalculation.

It started simply enough, by irritating, then threatening the wrong low-level assistant. His younger sister had fallen prey to Camola's charms in his quest to gather information he could use to further his career. He insulted the girl, rather than cutting off all communication with her. His name and face were already known to the assistant when Camola found him, gave him orders he had no authority to give, and then threatened the assistant's career if he didn't perform the desired task.

That assistant checked with friends in higher positions, determined Camola didn't have the connections or influence to pull the power cable on his career, and set about to return the favor. He programmed checks on every communication Camola sent and received, watched his daily routine, and noted changes. He tracked how often Camola used data terminals that weren't assigned to him, to access information in security levels he wasn't cleared to use.

Then the assistant struck gold. He intercepted a communication between Camola and the head of the Be'har'vu Clan. Camola sent them travel clearances, false identities, and prototype personal shield generators that never should have left the Fleet research lab. Those shields were intended to keep Security from detecting weapons on their person or in their gear. The data Camola sent included M'kar, Ashrock and Jeyn's daily schedules and their images, to aid in identifying them.

Camola was watched carefully by Alliance Council security, Academy security, and Fleet security. The Be'har'vu assassins were allowed to get as far as the orbital station, but not permitted to land on Le'anka. Then Camola was brought up on charges. No defender was willing to speak for him in the short court hearing, because of the overwhelming evidence against him. His diplomatic career was incinerated and he was sent away for ten years of counseling and hard labor on the prison station orbiting Baytony Bot.

Note: the remainder of this story takes place in the middle of the mission related in **Here There Were Dragons**, *AFV Defender Book 2, the glossed-over portion referred to by M'kar as the "All the Boys I've Loathed Before Incident."*

The Present
On course from Mendax, currently in probationary status as a member of the Alliance, to Le'anka

Every time the *Defender* went through a jump gate and picked up a communications packet from a transmission buoy, the command crew held their collective breaths. The vindictive nature of the Maniterri culture made it difficult to predict when the backlash from the *Defender*'s precipitous departure from Mendax would hit. Officially, the *Defender* had been on shore leave, but unofficially they were there to "test the waters," if the planet was safe for Fleet crews to relax and unwind on shore leave. Genys and Maora had labored and sweated for hours over the report, trying to be clear and simple with their reasoning and justification for fleeing the planet, accepting blame for any diplomatic fallout without volunteering to put their heads on the metaphorical chopping block. Various officials and liaisons seemed to be in agreement that the *Defender* was wise to leave immediately after the first unpleasant encounter with Vitiarre, former ambassador from Maniterr to the Alliance. The entire culture of Maniterr was known for its litigious nature. The easiest course of action when the Maniterri had their itty bitty feelings hurt was simply to run for it. Any attempt to reason with them or meet them halfway just encouraged their litigious actions and increased their certainty that they had been wronged. Even if they had committed the crime.

Vittiare wanted dracs. The *Defender* had dracs. He was going to do whatever it took, including lying and manipulating the laws of other planets, to get his way. In this case, that meant filing claims with Mendax that the crew of the *Defender* had stolen their dracs from Vitiarre's party. Mendax's officials were fed up with the Maniterri by that time, and deliberately delayed responding until the *Defender* had left orbit.

M'kar was still fuming about it, four days out from Mendax. She wasn't above using the ship's complement of dracs to spy on her captain and get a foretaste of whatever had come on the latest communication burst from Fleet. They were either going to celebrate having escaped with their careers intact, or prepare to stand before a tribunal on enough trumped up charges to choke a dozen dymcrait.

An hour after the *Defender* had picked up the latest communication burst, all she could get from Battleaxe was that Genys was busy filling out forms and responding to all sorts of documents. Official work consumed Genys's attention and concentration enough that her emotions weren't affecting her drac.

So was that good news, or should she worry?

"I can't take it anymore," M'kar announced, stepping into the linguistics lab, where Treinna and her team were hard at work on the latest batch of data to come from Draxonis and the newest discovered cache of ceramic plates.

Whatever their faults, and however they had destroyed their civilization, the lost inhabitants of Draxonis were a talkative bunch. They had recorded everything that could possibly help them restart their civilization. In triplicate. M'kar wondered how many times they tried to relaunch and recreate technology, only to have those dratted nanites show up and tear everything down again. The *Defender* and the various survey teams exploring Draxonis certainly had been blessed and protected by Enlo, that they hadn't brought a couple self-replicating nanites up to the ship, and accidentally spread them to the Alliance.

"Whatever has Genys so busy, it can't be anything like we fear." Treinna tapped a dark tablet lying on the far end of the long table where she was working. The entire table surface was a display screen, showing the ceramic plates, with spots of color marking the current section she was translating and comparing to previous plates.

The tablet screen lit up. M'kar wasn't close enough to see the details, but it looked like a list. Treinna leaned sideways to read it and nodded.

"The first person she contacted was E'bett. Then they brought Maenta in and had a chat for maybe twenty minutes."

"I'm surprised at you." M'kar shook her head and didn't even try to hold onto her mask of false dismay. "Spying on your captain?"

"Is it my fault she didn't put up privacy screens once she accepted the contents of the burst?" Treinna fluttered her eyelashes and got back to work. "Besides, I have Moonrise keeping watch with Battleaxe. If she was upset, I'd know before anyone else."

M'kar laughed. She couldn't get away with having her drac spy on the captain, but obviously Treinna could. Then the sound cut off in her throat as the words registered.

"She talked to both E'bett and Maenta?" M'kar sent a mental call for Barroo. She snagged a slip of plas-sheet and a stylus from the bin on the wall next to Treinna's workstation and scribbled, *Teacher? Who? When?* on it. She folded it in half when her little brown drac popped in, gave it to him, and told him to take it to Genys.

"Obviously that means something to you." Treinna stuck out her foot to block M'kar from getting past her, to reach the door.

"I'm hoping that's a response to our request for a teacher to focus on the developing Talents among our children." She nodded when Treinna sat up and a smile brightened her weary face.

Treinna's daughter, Tress, was at the top of the list of children needing special attention. The potential for Talent she had inherited from Jasper's unknown genetic heritage was waking up. M'kar was good at sensing psionic potential and awakening Talent, and she could teach the basics, but wisdom said to prepare for special needs and circumstances before they arrived. A little girl who inadvertently eavesdropped on adult thoughts and was immune to hoople emissions at age nine was likely only starting to unload surprises on her parents and teachers. With the misfit luck of the *Defender*, more children would soon display unexpected Talents.

Moonrise popped into the linguistics lab, crooning happily, and landed on Treinna's shoulder. The tablet shifted from displaying the list of Genys's activities to Captain Genys Arroyan's face.

"You know, you two could just ask, instead of spying and making me tell Battleaxe to keep Moonrise under control," Genys said, before Treinna or M'kar could respond.

"What's the fun in that?" M'kar grinned. "Good news?"

"Either there are a lot of spies at Fleet who need to be dug out and exposed to the light of day, or a lot of weak-willed idiots in positions of authority who haven't learned to say no."

"Why doesn't that sound good?" Treinna said.

"The first part is good, but I'm afraid it triggered the second part, which is bad. I'm off shift in half an hour. Meet me in the observation deck. Bring lots of mezipa."

"Something in your tone tells me my last two boxes won't be enough for the three of us," M'kar said.

"Then I suggest we grab all the comfort food we can find, because we're going to be griping and doing some preventative scheming. I don't think the remainder of our voyage to Le'anka is going to be long enough to figure out this one."

~~~~~

The good news was very good. Fleet and the Academy had granted the request for a special teacher. Because of his history with the Chief of Talents on the *Defender*, and for the good of his own drac's mental and emotional health, Master Thyal of the Academy had been assigned to the *Defender*.

Genys gestured at the box of mezipa, made by M'kar's father, with a fresh supply sent at regular intervals, because of the Nisandrian need to gorge under stressful situations. The many varieties of mezipa satisfied all the moods of comfort eating, with bread, sweet, salty, crunchy, chewy,
~~~~~

spicy, meaty, and savory, in different combinations. M'kar's favorite mezipa had a hard, savory flatbread base, covered in layers of crunchy nut-butter, crystalized sugar, bitter chocolate, smoked, fatty meat cooked to brittleness and then crumbled to dust.

M'kar opened the box and held it out to her two friends. They each took a large piece. She put it down on the floor of the observation deck, between their feet, and sat back.

"What's the bad news?" The thick chocolate chunky layer started to melt under the pressure of her fingertips.

"Two words." Genys took a bite and closed her eyes, chewing only twice before shifting the mouthful to her cheek. "Mirror Monsters."

"No." M'kar tried to take a bite of her mezipa, but the aroma suddenly made her gag.

"I spent the last three hours filing every protest with every authority I could, and even contacting our instructors at the Academy who were there at the time. We're heading for disaster that even our misfit luck can't neutralize." Genys shook her head and contemplated the uneaten portion in her hand. "I'm not a fatalist, and I don't subscribe to the galactic balance theory, where you pay for everything good with an equal amount of bad, but … well, face it, our history makes me pretty sure that this is one of those times we aren't going to have the pendulum swing in our favor."

"Especially if Thyal is coming on board," Treinna said. "That's their impetus for coming. If Nyx knew M'kar was here, he would have showed up years ago."

"Nyssa is the dominant twin. I can't ever see her calling in a couple hundred favors and pulling strings to help her twin make another romantic attack on me." M'kar nibbled her mezipa, encouraged when it didn't catch in her throat.

"What?" Genys asked, when Treinna snorted and nearly choked on her mouthful.

"Just had this awful, wonderful idea. Have a betrothal ceremony with Thyal as soon as we get to Le'anka."

"That is not funny." M'kar flinched, positive that betrothal tattoo at the base of her throat was hot. Obviously, Treinna had forgotten about that little gambit of her father's. What were the chances Nyssa had researched that tattoo, and realized it had no meaning because the other steps in the betrothal process had never taken place? If she knew it was a trick … she could be on a vengeance warpath.

"Nyssa would probably explode," Genys said. "I would pay good money to see it happen." She sighed and reached for the mezipa box. "You know Nyx is going to hound you again. We need to assemble our strategy now to protect you and Thyal."

M'kar hoped they could come up with some answers before she had to contact Thyal through their bond.

Genys had taken the first defensive step: calling on the aid of those who knew the whole embarrassing mess created by the twins during their Academy days. The bio-sheet on the twins indicated they didn't have much in the way of friendships with anyone on their many assignments. They had bounced from one ship or station to another, always requesting transfers at the earliest possible opportunity. Getting what she wanted at long last and thumbing her nose at those who had blocked her had to be Nyssa's motivation.

There was something wrong with someone who held onto one goal for so long that she had gutted the rest of her life. Had Thyal become her goal, since Infrenx no longer existed as a class, meaning she couldn't force them to accept her? Did she know about Infrenx's battle with the dymcrait? If the soul-bond had been real, no matter how weak, Nyssa would have felt Thyal's brush with death and come running to be with him. Logic said there was no bond and she didn't know. What would her reaction be when she saw Thyal and his hover chair? M'kar could almost look forward to her shock. Maybe she would finally give up on Thyal?

Genys hadn't received responses to her requests to cancel the transfer of the Qahngress twins to the *Defender*, so there was still hope. If the last resort failed, defending the sanity of the crew would rest largely on Tahl. She was the ultimate authority in Medical. She could put the twins in living quarters as far from Thyal and M'kar as possible, and make sure their work and leisure schedules never matched their targets'.

M'kar left the meeting to inform E'bett and Maenta about the good news and enlist their help in protecting Thyal. Maenta had witnessed the havoc the twins had created. M'kar had good reason to believe she would find great joy in frustrating Nyssa in small ways.

Far too soon, M'kar returned to the observation dome with Barroo crooning comfort, to have privacy and quiet to open up her link with Thyal. She had been trying to plan her words while she talked with Maenta and E'bett, and now in the quiet and shadows and chill of the observation dome, she realized it was now very late in the ship's day.

"What time is it on Le'anka?" she murmured, as she settled down against the empty equipment pedestal.

Barroo settled on her thigh. A mental image of sunrise over the tops of the Shadwala Mountains flashed from his mind to hers.

"Oh, you think so, do you?" M'kar laughed when he bobbed his head and chirped complacently. Some of the tightness in her throat and her chest loosened. "Troublemaker, what would I do without you?" He tipped his head to one side and crooned smugly. She had to laugh, then silently scolded herself to get on with the unpleasant task. Get it over with as quickly as possible.

She asked the ship's system what time it was currently on Le'anka, in the time zone of the core of the Academy. The response confirmed Barroo's mental image. He chortled and climbed up the front of her jacket to stare into her eyes.

"All right, smart-alec, tell me what I should tell Thyal about the nasty girl who wants to force him to marry her?"

Barroo's eyes got big and the happy, smug sparkles dimmed. He leaned back and blinked slowly. The colors shifted toward the yellows and dull greens of sorrow. Then an image unfurled in her mind, showing her and Thyal flying together, without wings, with his drac, Infrenx and Barroo flying escort for them, and lots of little creatures that looked like a mix of Human and drac.

"I don't even want to know what you think that is. Are you telling us to turn into dracs to escape her?"

Barroo chittered, clacking sharply at the back of his throat. What M'kar had come to interpret as his *Are you insane?* response. She laughed and cuddled him.

"All right. We'll leave it to you and Infrenx to protect us, will that make you happy?"

He crooned and snuggled down in her arms. She sighed and admitted, yes, she was delaying.

I assume you got the official notification? Thyal responded, the moment their minds touched.

And I assume you didn't get everything, or maybe nobody knows yet, otherwise you wouldn't sound so happy.

You're not happy?

I was, until the other dozen boots dropped!

We are talking about my joining the Defender *to be a teacher, aren't we?* Thyal's mental voice sounded uncertain. M'kar's chest ached at the realization that she had ruined what was probably a moment of triumph for him. He had physically recovered enough to leave the care of the doctors on Le'anka. He was strong enough, had regained enough mobility to tend to his own daily needs. The rest of his recovery could be trusted to a starship doctor and her team. They should have been metaphorically bouncing all over the room, celebrating together.

Chapter Ten

I'm sorry, M'kar said. Someone has fallen under the spell of the Mirror Monsters. It can't be an unlucky coincidence that they got themselves transferred onto my ship just when you're well enough to join us.

If this is a nasty joke, it will never be funny. Thyal sighed. Maybe Nyx is coming for you, and they don't know I'm coming aboard?

Oh, now you're getting nasty. She tried to put some laughter in her mental tone, but just like in the mind-circle, they could not lie to each other within the link. *I almost hope that's true, though, because if they don't know you're coming with us, and Genys runs out of strings to pull and higher-ups to blackmail ...* She hated saying it, but this was the last option she and Genys and Treinna had come up with, before they ran out of mezipa. *Well, maybe you should back out. Claim mental and emotional stress, or just plain tell the truth, you're fleeing a bride on the hunt. You could always go into preparatory retreat for taking your vows of life-service.*

There is no blessing in dedicating myself to celibacy and scholarship and contemplation as a means of hiding from danger.

I'm sure Enlo understands.

Lupi ... He sighed. *I know you're trying to protect me, and I love you dearly for it, but for my own spiritual and mental health, I need to face that threat. Although I will not ask your captain to stop trying to put up all the barriers she can, to keep those two off your ship.*

Genys is your captain, and the Defender is your ship now.

True. Well, what do you think I should do, until we know for sure how imminent the danger is?

They're transferring in from Ellamagorca. M'kar was relieved she had something positive for him to do. Genys estimates they'll arrive on Le'anka in three days at the earliest. Get up to Anwesta, and erase your tracks, so they waste time looking for you. We're not due for eight more days. We're making a lot of drops and pickups on the way.

In the meantime, Infrenx and I can enlist the help of the station's dracs to defend me.

Exactly. Oh, and contact my parents, ask for a triple shipment of mezipa, when I get home.

That made Thyal laugh.

~~~~~

Four days later, Ashrock sent M'kar a message reporting that Nyx showed up at their family home, looking for her and carrying the
~~~~~

traditional courting presents prescribed by Nisandrian culture. Her father had bluntly told the young man he wasn't good enough for his daughter, he never would be, and if he wanted to avoid broken bones and permanent disability, he should leave M'kar alone.

The ninny responded quite bravely, so I almost felt sorry for him, Ashrock wrote. *He said he would take the risk to prove his love for you and win your heart and my approval. Then he added that he didn't think I was that kind of brute. I had great fun agreeing with him, and then adding that the risk of injury wouldn't come from me at all. He went quite pale, so I believe he understands I meant the damage you would do him. Do live up to my hard work of preparation,* mi'sho'ki?

Reydon and Thean reported that Nyssa had come to their home, looking for Thyal. She was in hysterics because she had just found out about Thyal's "accident," as she referred to it. Whoever told her about his paralysis hadn't given her the details of the battle with the dymcrait. Nyssa claimed to be heartbroken that no one had sent for her, to heal her "beloved" with the strength of their soul-bond.

Mother narrowly escaped being wept all over, Thyal told her, after receiving the message and warning from his parents. *Nyssa rotated between grieving for my suffering, all alone, without the strength of her love to bring me back from the brink of death --*

She actually said that? M'kar didn't know if she should laugh or be ill. She was glad she was in the habit of going up to the observation dome for privacy when she communicated with Thyal. No one would see if she couldn't control her reactions to the latest strange news.

And quite a lot more nonsense. Mother wishes she had thought to tell Nyssa that you *brought me back from the brink of death. She might have swallowed her tongue, just denying the possibility.*

That might mean telling her about our unbreakable link. Of course, that is further proof she doesn't have a soul-bond with you, because then we would sense each other through the bond. M'kar snorted. *I think I just made myself ill.*

Wretched child. Thyal laughed, and that made her feel a little better.

I wish I had been there to see that. What else did she do and say?

I'll show you. Mother sent me a copy from the security recordings. Nyssa should give up medicine and become an actress.

You're cruel. She snickered. *I'm proud of you.*

She quite smoothly switches back and forth between suffering sorrow and outrage that no one told her I needed her. Mother pointed out that if we truly had a soul-bond, Nyssa would have known what happened to me. That shocked her into that icy calm that frightens me more than pheromone poisoning.

You should *be worried.* M'kar shudded. She had earned a few of Nyssa's icy glares. They came close to doing actual physical damage. *So, did she go away once she was shot down?*

No. She still insists jealous idiots have schemed to keep us apart and interfered with our bond.

I hope Lady Thean told her no one had to scheme because she had no right to know.

Almost in those words. Thyal's weary chuckle came clearly through their link.

I love your mother so very much. How she manages to be so incomparably gracious, and yet speak the truth … She is amazing.

Agreed. But Mother was tested to the limits with Nyssa. She did rattle her enough to admit she requested the transfer to the Defender *as soon as she learned about my assignment.*

We need to find her informants and send all our dracs to visit them.

~~~~~

Two days before the *Defender* reached Le'anka, Ashrock sent a report of the twins' activities. Nyssa had a public meltdown when she tried to access Thyal's medical records and was denied. She insisted she needed them to prepare to correct what had to be mistakes made by inadequate medical personnel.

Master Pocrates confronted her with an interrogation regarding what she knew of Thyal's injury, his treatment, and current condition. Most of the details of the dymcrait attack and Thyal's injury were locked away under multiple levels of security. What the general public knew was little more than rumor. Master Pocrates calmly and gently led her to admit, repeatedly, that she knew nothing. Therefore, how could she claim that the personnel treating Thyal had been inadequate?

Nyssa's next tactic was to inflict her treatment plan for Thyal on Tahl. She had specific plans for an intensive treatment regimen under her supervision alone. Tahl copied her response to Nyssa to her duty records, saying she did not approve of her underlings shirking their duties to pursue outside activities for personal gratification.

Genys continued pulling every string to try to block the transfer of the twins, even as they were packing their gear and boarding the shuttle to take them up to Haven Station, the hub of the Fleet, where they would officially transfer over to the *Defender*.

~~~~~

I see you, Thyal said, when the *Defender* had come within visual range of Anwesta Medical Station.

Where are you? M'kar reached up to tap the control for the screen in Genys's ready room. She was alone for the moment, waiting for contact with him.

Infrenx sees you, and I see through her. Is it safe to come over? She's rather eager to be among friends again.

That's fine. Have her come to me. She grinned when Barroo chirped happily at the mental image she showed him, of Infrenx joining them. *Why does that sound ominous, being among friends again?*

Granny has decided to inflict the silent treatment on both of us, since she's finally figured out that we're going away with the Defender, *and she can't come along.*

Well, that's fifty Decker owes me. She flinched when Infrenx popped into the ready room, then held out her arm for the little gold, orange, and brown drac to land.

What were you betting on?

Our dracs aren't nearly as twitchy as they were the last time we came back to the station. I say it's because Granny is still having a snit and giving us the silent treatment, instead of interrogating all our dracs to find out what we've been doing. Decker claims she's finally learned her lesson or some patience. I swear he said that because Spitfire has been scolding him about his attitude toward Granny.

She needs to learn to be loyal to her ship, not to her gender.

Agreed! A mental ripple warned her, just before the rest of the ship's young dracs popped into the room to greet Infrenx. *We should be settling into orbit soon, and we'll be shuttling over. The children are excited.*

I am eager to meet them.

Then M'kar pulled out of the link, because all the dracs wanted to include her in their celebration.

When the *Defender* settled into orbit around Anwesta, Infrenx returned to Thyal, and took the ship's six young dracs with her. Just before he popped out, Barroo let M'kar know that the twelve teacher dracs had already gone over to report to Granny. He seemed a little upset at their rudeness. Granny had put M'kar in charge of all the adult dracs, so in his mind that meant they had to at least say goodbye, if not ask permission to all leave the ship at once.

"Interesting," Genys said, when M'kar reported this. "Our six are getting the silent treatment, but the teacher dracs aren't. Makes you wonder what Granny is up to, doesn't it?"

"I've got more important things to think about than a miniature silver tyrant having another temper tantrum."

The group taking the first shuttle to Anwesta was small: Genys, E'bett, Maenta and M'kar. They would officially greet the newest member of the crew and transport him and his belongings back to the ship. Dinner with the command crew would follow a tour of the ship and settling him in his quarters.

All seven dracs were waiting with Thyal in the lounge area off the shuttle docking area. He had better color in his face, and some gauntness had filled in around his mouth. His cheekbones and chin didn't look so sharp. He sat upright in his hoverchair, instead of partially reclining like the last time she had seen him. She could almost convince herself that he would swing his legs over the side of his chair and stand up on his own two feet. Almost.

Maenta and E'bett both knew Thyal, and they didn't hesitate to greet him with hugs. M'kar envied them. Which struck her as somewhat silly, because she had never had that kind of relationship with Thyal.

His gaze met hers as Maenta stepped back, and Thyal gave her a thoroughly wicked grin. M'kar braced herself for something embarrassing. No, wait, that was something her father would do, not Thyal. She stepped up and pressed her hands flat together, palm-to-palm, and bowed in greeting.

"Hearth-brother."

"Hearth-sister." He gave an abbreviated, sitting bow, which displayed how much control over his trunk muscles he had regained. No need for the torso brace. *Thank you for not getting sloppy on me.*

M'kar crossed her eyes at him. Barroo and Infrenx trilled laughter, and a moment later the other five dracs joined in.

Since Thyal was meeting them on Anwesta, rather than at the Academy, Genys made audio contact with Master Seyshell to formally accept Thyal as a member of her crew, transferring him from the Academy's authority. When the link with Le'anka closed, all the dracs let out trills and swooped around the room, celebrating.

"Well, now that we have their approval ..." Genys gestured back toward the docking arm for the shuttles. "Shall we?"

Tahl met them when the shuttle reached the *Defender* and the five disembarked. She ran the medical sensor over Thyal, recording his bio-stats for entry into the ship's monitoring system. Then she gave him his crew wristband. Tahl met M'kar's gaze and tipped her head, gesturing behind Thyal's hoverchair. They walked together behind him as their group headed through the ship. Genys led the way, with E'bett and Maenta on either side of him.

"Problem?" M'kar murmured.

"I just got a communication from my incoming crew. It's been transferred to your databanks." Tahl rolled her eyes.

"Bad?"

"The girl does not know how to do humble. She knows she's operating on missing information, and she's offended I didn't think to share that information with her already."

Ha'ess settled on Tahl's shoulder and added a few chirps and clicks of agreement.

"You haven't shared any, have you?"

"I'm not going to. I confronted her with her lie that Thyal wanted her to have all his medical information. Oh, and she's being very forgiving of my lack of sensitivity in a very tender situation."

"Only in her imagination." Thyal stunned M'kar with how far he could turn his neck to look over his shoulder at them. Her reaction must have been clear on her face, because he grinned evilly.

"Have I mentioned how sharp Le'ankan ears are?" M'kar felt free to stick her tongue out at him.

"Sorry," Tahl said. "I just thought M'kar should be warned, and she could warn you."

"And now we are warned." He glanced ahead of them, where Genys, E'bett, and Maenta had slowed and turned to look back at the three of them. "Has there been any action on Nyx's part toward M'kar?"

"Not a chirp, no attempts to find her cabin or link code."

"Hopefully that means they don't know she's on board," Genys said.

"I don't suppose we can jump to the head of the line for missions, and forget to stop at Haven?" Maenta widened her eyes, projecting a look of innocence with her rosy cheeks and crown of white hair.

"I wish," Genys said. "Sorry. A third of the crew is on shore leave, starting two hours ago. We are scheduled to replenish supplies starting tomorrow evening. Only an emergency equivalent with Gatesh and Ankuar teaming up to attack from two fronts could get us permission to leave before everyone is back on board and our stores are full."

"Fear not, my children." She tucked her hands inside the generous sleeves of her robe. "We shall survive."

"And if we don't, there's still a good chance we'll look back on this someday and laugh," E'bett added.

~~~~~

Granny sulked when M'kar met with Dulit and Flinders and Aeola, the liaisons between the dracs and Anwesta personnel. Not all the station's dracs avoided M'kar, but their greetings were restrained. They waited until Granny was busy elsewhere to approach her and share images of their lives and their efforts to contact the sleeping minds of the cocooned Hiver victims. Several had good news for her, once again increasing her knowledge of the drac "facts of life."

"You're going to need to request a strong animal-focused Talent," she warned the trio of drac parents and Commodore Roop, when she made her report. "There are four drac pairs in different stages of reproduction. One is about to lay their trio of eggs any day now … and I can see I was right. You didn't notice any change in the female's behavior when she went into heat."

"We still have a great deal to learn about dracs," the Commodore said with a great deal more calm and a lot less resignation than M'kar knew she would be feeling, in her boots.

"We need someone who can talk to all the dracs," Dulit said.

"I can feel you fighting your panic, Lieutenant," Roop said, her expression shifting toward the cookie-baking grandmother part of her
~~~~~

personality. "No fear. I am the last person who wants to take you away from your ship and the dracs assigned to it. We need someone as strong as you, but we'll have to settle for someone who is not you."

"Maybe you can bring in a batch of candidates once the eggs are laid," M'kar said. "If the parents let any of them near the eggs --"

"If they let us find the eggs," Flinders added.

"If." She grinned, imagining the egg hunt. "The one the parents approve will be the best choice for working with the station's dracs, and hopefully strong enough to get some control over Granny."

~~~~~

Ashrock sent up a letter newly arrived from Desra. It was heavy with new data taken from the surbda craters. Jasper's newest innovations had enabled the sisterhood to recalibrate their sensors and work around the sensory-blanking field surrounding the craters. Over the years, they had learned through shipping damage and theft that it was easier getting instructions and schematics to the sisterhood, than smuggling the devices through the blockades and policies of Nisandros.

The new data was half a year old, but Jasper was certainly excited, muttering under his breath as he read through the files she gave him. Her father's friends in the Diplomatic Corps reported that many of the blockades were coming down. Nisandros was more open to negotiations with the Alliance.

Desra reported that B'keerimo hoped to come to the Academy to study. M'kar didn't know what to think of that bit of news. Why would her cousin's scholarly ambitions matter to Desra? In her last letter, her vow sister had sworn off B'keerimo and his lukewarm courtship. He wavered between supporting and vilifying the new generation of rebels, who wanted to depose the Upper and Lower Halls of the clan leaders. Ke'Niq led one of the louder and more troublesome factions of the rebels, and Desra believed B'keerimo supported Ke'Niq because he was her favorite cousin. If he was going to choose sides, she wanted him to have good reasons. Letting his emotions and his lust lead him didn't earn her admiration.

M'kar put aside that minor bit of news when she read what else Desra had to say. A newcomer, an off-worlder, had the attention of many clan leaders on both sides of the question of Alliance membership. He traveled under many names, to confuse enemies who might try to silence him. Desra couldn't describe him because he kept his face hidden in a dark hood and cloak. He spoke glowingly of the benefits of Alliance membership. Every time he vanished, and people were sure he had been ambushed and tossed into a surbda crater, he popped up halfway across the planet and resumed his campaign. The man was winning over some obstinate clans just by refusing to be killed.
~~~~~

Ashrock needed to hear about this, to warn his diplomat friends. Depending on which stellar government the stranger came from, his support of Alliance membership could be intended rather to jam up the gears of the slowly grinding machinery of diplomacy and prevent membership altogether.

"Not that we are entirely in favor it, are we, *mi'sho'ki*?" Ashrock said, in a live communication link with the ship a day later. "We are both better off if Nisandros retreats behind its high walls and declares war on the entire universe." He sighed, and his wide, usually cheerful face seemed to sag and get older under the multi-colored mask of his tattoos. "That would not please Enlo, however. We must prepare to defend our kin and our homeworld, however much we would be happier to never see them again."

~~~~~

M'kar's reprieve ended. The third day after Thyal came on board, a note from Nyx to her joined the daily messages and demands from Nyssa.

"If there were such a thing as handwritten communication, we'd know if he really wrote them, or his sister did," Thyal said. They had met in his classroom to confer over the day's communication and relax with seooli tea between his class sessions.

"You do realize, she sicced him on me because she thinks I'm a rival?" M'kar retorted.

"Rivals require two to compete." His eyes narrowed and he tipped his head to one side as he studied her face. Their link wasn't open, because that subliminal note in the mental atmosphere wasn't soothing her soul. Despite that, for a moment she knew what he was thinking.

Why not become officially betrothed? Just to drive Nyssa away, once and for all? Or more likely, drive her insane, so she finally got herself discharged from the Fleet.

M'kar rejected that idea immediately. Betrothals were not to be taken lightly. When she pledged herself to someone, it had to be real, fully a union of mind, heart, soul, and body. She couldn't cheat Thyal like that. He meant too much to her. She knew they would be perfectly happy together, but she doubted her ability to be a good wife. Certainly not the dignified, graceful wife he needed, to support his climb in the hierarchy of the Academy. She wanted someone to laugh and tease and traipse around the universe with, to happily bicker and be sloppy-silly in love, like her parents. She could see herself laughing and arguing with Thyal for the rest of their lives, but could he?

"Your brain is fizzing," Thyal said, that narrow-eyed look fading.

M'kar's face warmed. She hoped she hadn't said something embarrassing while her mind was racing in circles and crashing into itself.

"You know what Genys told Battleaxe, when she was looking over
~~~~~

the crew profiles?"

"What does that have to do --" Thyal sighed. "No, I don't know."

"Axe picked up her negative reaction, so she asked what was wrong, and why did those flat people make her angry."

"Flat people. Appropriate. At least now we know dracs can look at images and equate them with the real thing."

"Genys told Axe the twins were bad-selfish-toy-stealers-stinky-hearts."

That got the bubble of laughter she wanted from Thyal. "Toy stealers are the lowest of the low."

"Appropriate, you think?"

"I wonder what sort of reaction they'd get if we told them Nyssa was a mate-stealer?"

"Stealing him from someone he already belongs to?" The next moment, she wished she could take back that flippant question.

"Does it matter?" He shook his head before she could respond. "I look forward to seeing how the dracs respond when the twins come on board."

"I wish she had told Axe they were monsters, although how she could visualize Mirror Monsters … boggles the mind."

The phrase generated a few chuckles from each other over the next few days. Until time ran out.

M'kar and Thyal were both teaching. He was working with the older students preparing to enter the Academy. She was in the shuttle bay, working with the littlest children. As her own experience had proven, a child was never too young to learn and use self-defense moves. All the ship's dracs were involved, dive-bombing the children, who squealed and laughed and threw themselves to the mats and rolled out of the way. Some were natural gymnasts, leaping to their feet with incredible grace. The daring ones tried to grab hold of the ribbons the dracs clutched in their talons. Sometimes a drac showed pity on slower ones and dropped ribbons on them. The children worked themselves into sweaty, sometimes bruised exhaustion and the dracs had fun.

Until Ha'ess pulled up in the middle of a dive, let out a squawk, and popped out. A moment later, several more dracs let out screeches and spun out of the game to swirl around M'kar, hitting her with the same images.

"No, no, no," she muttered, and sent Barroo to Medical, praying it was a false alarm.

Barroo popped back just a heartbeat later, his eyes swirling red with anger. An image slammed into her mind, along with the label that wasn't so much words, but perfectly matched the name Genys had coined: bad-selfish-toy-stealers-stinky-hearts.

In the image from Barroo's mind, Nyx and Nyssa stood before Tahl's long worktable. M'kar studied their faces. They both looked older, with marks of experience, lines of seriousness. She gave herself a mental slap that she found some satisfaction in seeing Nyssa's calculated prettiness hadn't fared well. Then again, maybe she no longer spent two hours every day carefully painting her face. Maybe she had grown up enough that looking "just so" didn't matter so much.

Then a snort of laughter escaped M'kar. Barroo showed her Ha'ess, crouched on the corner of the long worktable, wings spread as if ready to leap into the air, shoulders hunched, glaring up at the twins -- who watched her with more wariness than awe. No greed, no threat that they would demand a drac of their own as a right of their royal blood. That was a refreshing change, after all the trouble the *Defender* had had lately with self-important twits.

Have you seen them? Thyal asked.

Barroo just showed me.

Infrenx reports that Ha'ess says they smell even worse than Captain Genys implied. It seems Nyssa still indulges in too much expensive perfume. Why do women always think that expensive perfumes have to smell toxic?

I don't.

You're a blessed exception.

And our mothers.

True. A trickle of laughter came from him through their link.

M'kar sighed. It was nearly time to release the children from class. *Do you want me there for the invasion?*

Please. Shall we take wagers on which one of them finds us first?

I could ask Jasper to tell the ship not to cooperate with them, when they ask for us. M'kar clapped her hands to get the attention of her students.

Hmm, that is a bad example to set for impressionable young minds. He laughed but said no more until she had dismissed the children and notified the ship's system they were released to their next class. *Too many coincidences are suspicious. We don't want to give them the impression we fear encountering them.*

Since when has making it clear we don't like them done any good?

True.

Early lunch?

Early lunch.

Chapter Eleven

Norgan was in the deserted mess hall, muttering at a dispenser wall, when M'kar walked in. Barroo swooped across the long room and hovered next to him. The lanky, graying sensor technician flinched and looked up, then gave the little brown drac a big grin and turned to nod to M'kar. The dispenser bleeped at him, several green and blue lights flashed, and the door on the opening slid up.

"Thought for a minute my run of bad luck had settled back in. On my last ship," he said, pulling a bowl of dark red stew out of the dispenser opening, "either it would be out of clean bowls, or it would dispense my lunch, then drop the bowl on top of it."

"I heard one time the nozzle got turned sideways and shot the repair technician in the face when he came to check why it stopped working."

"Yeah, well." Norgan grinned and shrugged. "The guy was some kind of cranky. I think sometimes our ships are becoming aware, and they stick up for those of us who get blamed for things." He settled down at the nearest table and scooped up a spoonful to hold out for Barroo.

M'kar chuckled. That was proof Norgan was an all-around good guy. The dracs generally refused to eat from the hands of anyone but their adopted parents. It had to be good for the awkward man's self-esteem that the dracs all loved him.

Barroo chirped his thanks and settled down on the end of the table, then waited for M'kar to give him the go-ahead before delicately lapping at the stew. He purred between licks.

"Extra-spicy?" She decided that would hit the spot. It wasn't hot enough to scorch her throat and stomach, like shriek beast stew, her father's specialty, but it suited her need for something bracing to prepare for the first day of the Mirror Monsters on board the *Defender*.

Infrenx glided through the doorway and chirped a greeting. She purred, settled down next to Barroo, and fluttered her eyelids at Norgan.

"Where did she learn to do that?" he said, laughing, and picked up the spoon to reward Infrenx.

"You're not going to have anything left for yourself." M'kar tapped in the request for a second bowl.

"She says the stinky lady did that to the techs who brought her crates up to her quarters," Thyal said, his hoverchair floating into the mess hall.

"Stinky lady?" Norgan grimaced. "Glad I'm not the only one."

"You had the pleasure of meeting the twins?" M'kar tapped the request for a bowl of nasplatta, the spicy vegetable noodles dish that was Thyal's comfort food. Then she stepped over to the next dispenser and requested a large pot of seeoli tea.

"I heard Dr. Tahl ask them to show consideration for the sensitive noses of their new crewmates. She added that Life Sciences has a large assortment of creatures who might react violently to the scents they were wearing." Norgan grinned and nodded his thanks as M'kar brought the replacement bowl and set it down next to his depleted bowl. She calculated he had only had four spoonfuls, compared to the three each Barroo and Infrenx had already wheedled out of him with beseeching looks. At least Norgan had the sense to pick up a spare spoon, so he wasn't using the same one the dracs used. Bad enough he was dipping into the same bowl for them and him.

The three of them had just gotten settled at the table, with mugs of tea poured for all of them, when Ha'ess popped in with a plas-strip clutched in one paw. She dropped it on the table in front of Thyal and popped out again.

"They're on the loose," Thyal read aloud. He grinned ruefully and slipped the strip into his pocket.

Later, they realized they should have expected the mess hall to be the first place the twins went, once they had been released from orientation with Tahl and the department heads in Medical. By this time, another dozen people had settled into the mess hall for lunch.

The first warning came when the dracs raised up, wings spreading violently enough they nearly knocked M'kar and Norgon's empty bowls off the table. Every head in the room turned toward their corner table. M'kar caught the image from Barroo, so she had a heartbeat of warning. She schooled her face to blandness as she turned to face Nyssa and Nyx, paused in the doorway, mouths dropping open and eyes even wider than their mouths.

Nyssa pressed her hand against her mouth, palm out, and started to turn her head as if she couldn't bear the sight. She pointed at the dracs. "That cannot be good for your health, darling!" Cringing, she took two steps forward.

Infrenx and Barroo leaped into the air and put themselves between their parents and the twins. They hovered at eye-level, wings beating in perfect unity, eyes sparkling with red, orange, and black defiance. Thyal ignored her. Nyssa flushed red when she had to say his name three times.

"Oh, hello, Nyssa. Nyx. I heard we had two new medics joining the crew." He made his hoverchair turn to face them. "Infrenx, that isn't polite." He beckoned. The little drac let out one last hiss-shriek, darted upward, turned a backward somersault and came in for a graceful landing on Thyal's shoulder.

"You've got dracs too?" Nyx grinned and held out a hand to Barroo. The brown drac hissed at him and did a triple somersault to land on M'kar's shoulder. "How do you get him to come to you?"

"It's more like how do you get them to go away," Norgon offered. The two dracs chirped laughter.

"I don't understand," Nyssa said. "Those ... things are supposed to be confined to Anwesta. It makes no sense. We're medics. We should have boarded this ship from Anwesta, not from the Fleet station. I just don't understand the prohibition --"

"You don't know anything about the cocoon project, do you?" M'kar said.

"-- any more than I understand why you never respond to my communications," Nyssa continued, her eyes narrowing as she flicked a glance at M'kar. "I mean, yes," she took two more steps, stopping when Infrenx hissed. "I understand you've been busy, but you attained your Master status years ago, yet you never resumed communication --"

"There was no communication to resume," Thyal broke in smoothly.

"Oh, I forgave you. I knew that was a mistake."

"The mistake was on your part," M'kar said.

Nyssa glared at her. Barroo blew raspberries. That got a single chuckle from Nyx, a longer one from Norgan, and a grin from Thyal.

"And now that -- that -- that disgusting reptile is sitting on your shoulder, inflicting all sorts of alien microbes on you. That can't be good for you on top of your tragic injury. You need me. You need our soul bond to heal you. That's the reason you haven't healed yet."

"You know," Norgan said, standing and gathering up their empty dishes. His tone of voice implied he was speaking to everyone and to no one. "Self-delusion is not good in a healer."

Nyssa let out a steam whistle shriek that broke with a crack. For once, she had been rendered speechless.

If she didn't think Norgan would collapse in shock, M'kar might have kissed him. He was her hero of the hour. Possibly he was Nyx's hero, too, because he grinned and watched Norgon walk over to the slot for returning dishes. Nyx got away with it because he stood behind his twin, where she couldn't see him.

Maybe, just maybe, the perfect harmony between the Mirror Monsters had died? Would that be a good thing for the crew of the *Defender*, or just a harbinger of more deadly things to come?

Nyssa turned her back on Norgon and stepped closer to the hoverchair. Again, Infrenx hissed and spread her wings.

Familiar territory, M'kar told Thyal, as tears filled Nyssa's eyes. *Prepare for drowning.*

He muffled a chuckle but couldn't muffle his grin fast enough. Nyssa stomped.

"You at least owe me an explanation. No one will tell me how you broke your back."

"I didn't break my back." Thyal reached up and slid Infrenx down, to cuddle her against his chest. "My paralysis is due to dymcrait venom, which takes quite a long time to wear off."

"How can you lie to me like that?" she wailed, again with the hand pressed against her forehead, palm out. "Darling, you know dymcrait aren't real. They're just stories to frighten bad little children into behaving." She looked around the mess hall, as if she expected everyone to pay attention. "If that isn't proof that your condition is affecting your mind, and you're not behaving rationally --"

"They're real," Norgon said, coming back to the table. "I've seen them and yeah, I'd reform if I needed to, after seeing those nasties."

Nyssa turned more to put Norgon behind her. He winked at M'kar, who grinned and didn't care if Nyssa saw. Norgon hadn't seen the dymcrait, only the results of their attacks.

"Dymcrait are very real," Thyal said. "If you were up-to-date on new medical data released by the Academy, you would see references to the effects of dymcrait venom on the nervous system, and the breakthroughs being made in treating cocooning victims, now that we have identified the species that causes it."

"But that's -- that's -- "

"A gift from Enlo," Nyx said.

"-- all the more reason they should have allowed us on Anwesta!" she wailed. "I have a right to be on the front lines of fighting those horrid things, if they did that to you." She gestured dramatically at Thyal.

"You have no rights in connection with me or my injury, not by any stretch of the imagination," Thyal said. "The dracs don't like you, and they are quite emotional little creatures. I would recommend that you keep as much distance between yourself and them as you can. And since Infrenx is always with me --"

"How can you do that to me?" Nyssa went pale when Infrenx and Barroo hissed, long necks outstretched, eyes swirling red and orange. "I demand you send that awful thing away."

"Infrenx is bonded to me, my comfort, my constant companion, my legs and hands, and even tattles on me to the healers, when I push myself too far. I don't know how I ever lived without her. I am eternally grateful to M'kar for risking her career to bring her to me."

"You did that to him?" Nyssa raised one hand as if she would swing at M'kar.

Barroo let out a harsh bugle that drew the gazes of everyone in the mess hall who had been trying to ignore the confrontation. He launched off M'kar's shoulder, aiming for Nyssa, who covered her head with her arms and fled. M'kar caught hold of him and had to fight not to burst out laughing. If Barroo had really wanted to hurt Nyssa, he would have teleported in and out, confusing her by being everywhere at the same time. M'kar had seen him do it. It was awe-inspiring.

"I'm sorry," Nyx said, backing up, trying to watch his twin as she vanished through the door and down the corridor. "This isn't exactly how I imagined our reunion --"

"What reunion? You *gasquac*, we were never together and never will be. Go away and stay away!" M'kar struggled to keep hold of Barroo, as his attention shifted from Nyssa to her brother.

"I'm sorry!" He turned and fled.

Several onlookers applauded. The two dracs trilled laughter and popped out.

"Why do I have the awful feeling they're meeting up with the others to tell them the fun they had, scaring the bad-selfish-toy-stealer-stinky-hearts?" Thyal muttered.

"The what?" Norgan sputtered. He laughed when they explained the drac name their captain had created for the irritating twins.

"Well, what do you know?" M'kar murmured, once Norgan excused himself to go back to his duty station. "Dymcrait and Mirror Monster repellant, all rolled into one adorable, mischief-making package."

~~~~~

Over the course of the next several days, the twins struggled to get to M'kar or Thyal and speak privately. The dracs found great amusement in popping in whenever the twins got within five meters of their targets. Nyssa was clearly frightened of the dracs. She did extensive research over those few days, when she wasn't on duty or trying to sneak up on Thyal. She clearly didn't like the answers and argued with the crew in Life Sciences, as if she could change the nature of dracs by force of will. M'kar found some amusement in Nyssa's irritation at being told constantly that M'kar was the drac expert, and she should talk to her to get definitive answers. She went into nearly a full day of depression when asked how Thyal could have a bond with a creature who clearly disliked her, if he was already bonded to her.

Nyx reluctantly accepted the fact that Barroo generally reflected M'kar's feelings. If the drac disliked him, then so did she. Despite what his sister insisted. He approached M'kar with his conclusions on the eighth morning after the twins came on board, after her hand-to-hand combat class.

"Face it, Nyx, you were only interested in me because your sister *told* you to be." M'kar almost felt sorry for him.

"You're probably right." He gave her a somewhat abashed smile that
~~~~~

made him seem much younger and less arrogant. "Tell me, if it's not just Nyssa's jealous imagination, are you two together?"

"Me and Thyal?" She nearly laughed at the lighter-than-air sensation that shot through her. "Yes." She knew she was being cruel, but she paused for a moment. "Entirely Nyssa's imagination. Thyal is my hearth-brother. We are bound together in the mind-circle of Infrenx. We faced death together. Of course there is closeness, but ... nothing like what Nyssa wants from him."

"I wish we had figured that out sooner."

"So do I. Look at all the time you two wasted, haunting us, when you should have been focusing all that energy and attention on your education. Use that energy now to make a place for yourself in the ship. Make friends."

"Is there a chance we could be friends?"

"Focus on making friends with other people. It's a big ship." M'kar left it at that. She knew better than to give him hope, but she didn't want to be cruel, either.

~~~~~

Less than a dec later, Genys received a high priority communication from Fleet Command. Coding attached to the communication prompted her to take it in her ready room instead of reading it on the bridge. Two hours later, she called M'kar to her ready room.

M'kar asked Battleaxe about Genys's mood, as she approached the door on the level below the bridge. Both dracs reported the captain was angry and tired and sad. When M'kar stepped into the ready room, Genys was in the circular seating area, instead of at her desk. She handed M'kar a tablet.

"Read first, all the way to the end. Then we'll talk. Just be aware I've been pulling all the strings and filing all the complaints I could. I burned up a lot of favors people owed me, trying to ward off the Mirror Monsters." She sighed. "I honestly have no idea what else I can do."

M'kar tapped the screen to awaken the tablet.

Fleet Command, Le'anka
Admiral Harrendon
To Captain Genys Arroyan, AFV Defender

Captain Arroyan, you will soon receive official orders to proceed to Tierfallon Station, to transport a team of diplomats for a high-priority mission.

This advance warning is a courtesy and in recognition of the invaluable service you and your crew have provided the Fleet and the Alliance.
~~~~~

Forget the fancy military protocol, Genys, this is a sincere apology. I have filed every protest I can, to shield you from risking scuttling your career.

The mission is -- brace yourself -- to Nisandros.

I am well aware of all the notations filed everywhere possible, requesting, recommending, and warning that Lt. M'kar must never be sent to Nisandros, with full details of the personal danger she faces, as well as the diplomatic repercussions if any of the competing elements on Nisandros ever get custody of her person. Starting with her ability and willingness to commit mass murder to stay free, and ending with Nisandros having a temper tantrum and declaring war against the Alliance.

However, those in higher authority, with louder voices (I must doubt their intelligence and common sense) believe the mission, to open negotiations with Nisandros to finally join the Alliance, is of high enough priority and sensitivity that sending her as a representative of the Fleet, the Alliance, and the Le'ankan Academy to her homeworld, will do far more good than harm.

I'm sorry, Genys, from the bottom of my heart. Even though you cast doubt on its existence often enough when you were my favorite student. Say a prayer for me. Now I have to notify Ashrock about this whole mess.

I'll be praying for you, and depending heavily on the bizarre, inexplicable luck of the **Defender***. If anyone can survive this mission with their sanity, skins and the Alliance intact, you can.*

Enlo's starlight guide you.

"Well ..." M'kar put the tablet down and finally dropped into the seat opposite Genys. "What's the saying about really wretched news or luck coming in threes? Wonder what's the next blow to hit." Barroo let out a piteous little trill of concern and rubbed her cheek with the side of his head. "Knew I should have saved that last box of mezipa for something really important."

"All I can think is that someone got word to your clan about you bonding with a drac, or maybe they think you can control dymcrait or something, and they're desperate to make nice," Genys offered. "To get to you, they have to make nice with the Alliance first."

"It doesn't really say who made the first overture to resume talks about membership, does it?"

Genys could only shake her head. She looked thoughtful when M'kar told her about the letter from Desra talking about the stranger advocating Alliance membership.

"When do we get the full mission briefing?" A truly horrific thought occurred to M'kar and she went cold.

"At the station, when we pick up the diplomatic team. What?" Genys blurted.

M'kar suspected her face had gone white. "Do you have a list of the diplomatic team?" She swallowed hard against an imminent whimper.

"Who are you afraid of running into?"

"Camola."

"I thought of him. Nobody has heard from him for the last eight years." Genys shook her head. "He's not part of the diplomatic party we're picking up at Tierfallen."

"And Enlo shows us great mercy once again." She tried to smile. From Genys's concerned expression, she had probably failed. "I need to send a message to my parents, see what they've heard. This would be the perfect time for the clan to try to marry me off again. This whole thing could just be a ruse to get me there for the wedding."

"Look on the bright side," Genys said with only a slight waver in her voice. "We could be bringing you home for a ritual sacrifice."

"Thanks, you're so encouraging." M'kar wanted so desperately to be able to laugh. She wondered what Genys would say if she suggested they thumb their collective noses at the Alliance, confiscate the ship, and turn pirate.

~~~~~

Genys didn't trust Nyx to have learned his lesson. She was sure Nyssa would continue to encourage her brother to pursue M'kar to eliminate her as a rival for Thyal. Genys wanted M'kar and Thyal together and sometimes considered banging their heads together to wake them up to what they had. However, now was not the time for that eye-opening confrontation. Preventing Nyx distracting M'kar as she prepared for a life-threatening mission was more important.

She had Battleaxe recruit the other young dracs to keep an eye on Nyx. When he took to haunting the corridor outside the cargo bay during M'kar's classes, Genys decided it was time to act, as captain and friend.

Besides, he was part of her crew now, and she had to stop him from endangering his life. While there would be some satisfaction in M'kar beating the snot out of Nyx and some common sense and common courtesy into him, Genys had a duty to protect all members of her crew, whether she liked them or not. She headed to Medical to catch Nyx when his duty shift ended.

"Medic, a word please?" She waited only long enough for Nyx to meet her gaze with a "Who, me?" look, nodded, and backed out into the corridor outside Medical.

"How can I help you, Captain?" Nyx fell into step with her.

"I was roommates with Lt. M'kar, back at the Academy." She waited for recognition to change his polite, inquiring expression.
~~~~~

"Oh."

"Yes, oh. I've been there from the beginning."

"I don't suppose I can ask for your help --"

"That's what I'm here for, Medic." She held up a hand to stop his relieved smile. "You have ignored some details of our mission."

"We're heading to Tierfallon Station to pick up the diplomatic party handling the negotiations to bring Nisandros into the Alliance. What have I missed?"

"Are you aware of Lt. M'kar's clan association, her background?"

"Everything I can find out about her. Yes. Nyssa says that's just more proof --"

"How about the genetic manipulation of the Nisandrian genome, attempting to create immunity to known diseases, to speed healing, to increase longevity, and especially that general immunity to alcohol? Do you know about that?"

"Umm … the basics. Is there something I missed?"

"M'kar is the first daughter born to her clan in I don't know how many generations. She's also the first half-blood. The clans have been battling to make her a political tool since before she was born. Chances are very good her family married her by proxy for political benefit. We could be walking into a marriage festival, the moment we set foot on Nisandros."

"But -- but -- it's against Nisandrian tradition to force marriages."

"Yes, well, when you have a couple hundred lunatic prophets pretending to hear the Ancestors speak, a lot of traditions and laws get tossed aside for expediency."

"But she's -- I know M'kar has been a little reluctant --"

"*You're* trying to force her into a marriage she hasn't chosen, just like half her homeworld, you narding indiferp." Genys clasped her hands behind her back, when she wanted to grab Nyx by the shoulder seams and slam him against the wall. "She doesn't even like you."

"But I love her." He barely managed not to whimper.

"You don't know her. All that research you did should have scared the unholy spit out of you. What kind of an idiot makes a nuisance of himself to a *Nisandrian*? Do you have a death wish? And by the way, keep insisting you love her, and you're going to face a couple dozen honor challenges and death threats from all the political suitors waiting to pounce, the second she steps foot on native soil. Are you ready for a Nisandrian ritual circle of challenge? To the death?"

Maybe she had gotten through to Nyx. His mouth froze into a round "O" of protest, and his eyes were wide in his ashen face.

"Just something to think about, Medic. I have a duty to protect you. But Enlo save me if I'll risk my neck and these negotiations and the safety of my ship, to protect you when you're stuck in some misguided romantic delusions that you didn't even choose for yourself. You let your sister decide you were in love. And let me tell you, according to all Neoma's teachings, that ain't love at all." She took a step back, because now her palms were itching to grab and shake him until his eyes rattled. Or maybe until he started breathing again. She seriously doubted he was breathing. Maybe he was having a seizure? "Are we clear?"

"Yes, Ma'am. Captain." He nodded and swallowed. "Thank you for the ... the warning, and the information and ..." Nyx's lips twitched an attempt at a smile.

"If you have any questions or ideas, come to me, not to M'kar. She has enough on her plate, with either forced marriage or ritual assassination waiting for her."

"Ritual ..." His mouth moved without sound, then he nodded. Somber.

Maybe she had gotten through to him after all.

"That'll be all, Medic."

"Yes, Captain. Thank you." He stayed there, his gaze dropping to the deck, as Genys turned and continued down the corridor.

That evening, after the briefing for the command crew, Decker approached Genys. Spitfire hovered over his head, visibly edgy. The little pink drac's eyes sparkled with brief flashes of orange amid the blue that signaled amusement. What worried Spitfire and yet made her want to laugh? Perhaps the better question was what made the Chief of Security worried and amused simultaneously?

Decker waited until the door of the conference room slid closed, leaving them alone for however long it would take for someone to come up with more questions. "We've got a bit of a situation,"

"As in?"

"That kid hounding M'kar." He waggled his eyebrows.

Genys told herself to be grateful Decker left it at that. He had found the situation with Nyx and Nyssa chasing M'kar and Thyal funny. Until Barroo and Spitfire had a mid-air snarling argument for maybe ten minutes. Then suddenly Spitfire flew shrieking to Decker. She circled him for a good five minutes, eyes red and yellow, spitting fury. Very rarely was Spitfire upset with her "Daddy."

Chapter Twelve

"What about him?" Genys said with a sigh.

"He's scared to death, and he doesn't know how to get himself out of trouble." Again, Decker waggled his eyebrows.

"What kind of trouble?"

"Turns out the same day we learned about our mission to Nisandros, boy genius used his diplomatic connections to send a message to M'kar's clan ..." His eyes glinted with amusement.

"No. Please tell me he didn't."

"Yep, asked for permission to marry her, and basically implied she was willing, but hesitating because of traditions and family honor and such. Gave his whole pedigree, proving he's just as royal as she is --"

"In what warped version of reality? He's so far from the throne on Qahngress, he's in another solar system. M'kar is so royal she's nearly a deity, plus being a figure out of prophecy." She groaned, leaned back against the wall, and thumped her head against it twice. That didn't help, because it proved this was real and not a bad dream.

"Yeah, well, he said you had a talk with him and showed him what a mess he had made, and now he's worried about honor challenges from M'kar's groom. He asked me what it would take to learn the Nisandrian honor battle rituals and some moves to save his neck."

"What did you tell him?"

"Well, I started to recommend he ask M'kar for help, and the guy nearly puked right on my boots." Decker snickered. Spitfire made an almost perfect echo.

Genys wondered what sort of Human habits and gestures Battleaxe was picking up from her. Just how were they changing the drac race?

"Then I told him poison was always a time-honored method of dealing with rivals." Decker's version of an innocent expression didn't fool her. He was enjoying this far too much.

"Not a good tactic on a ship charged with a diplomatic mission."

"Nope, but the guy seemed to perk up for a few seconds. Then I suggested he plead temporary insanity and withdraw his request."

"How did he take it?"

"Seemed kind of relieved, said he'd work on it, maybe he'd ask for help from the diplomats when we meet up with them at Tierfallen." Decker shrugged. "I think he's finally catching on."

"But way too late to prevent him messing up the mission. We need to spend a lot of time praying for Enlo's protection."

"Already on it."

~~~~~

Jasper sent a message to M'kar via Tress the next morning. The little girl delivered the much-folded and sweaty plastic packet after the children's exercise session. Inside were several sheets of printouts of various devices Jasper had theorized over the years, for piercing the energy fields and sensory distortion of the surbda craters, along with a map he had pieced together of fly-by scans done by the Alliance's orbital station. The map showed details of the surbda craters scattered over the planet, along with computer-generated energy lines connecting them to each other.

Scribbled on the map were the words: *Almost got it. Need time dirtside. Best kept quiet. Crazy idea: the whole planet is a Gate.*

M'kar's hands shook a few times as she looked over the schematics of the devices. Jasper was on his way to retiring very rich, with his own starship, to visit engineering mysteries and disasters. Rich, that is, if the devices he designed worked as intended.

She composed a message for Desra, proposing they set up a clandestine mission for the *Defender*'s engineers. Just how could they send an entire shuttle of equipment down to Nisandros without rousing the ire of the clans who wanted nothing to do with the Alliance? One wrong move could start another planetary war, like the one when Etrusca thumbed her metaphorical nose at the Ancestors and declared her allegiance to Enlo.

~~~~~

The gossip chain on the ship included the children. When Tress and her gang realized that the twin medics were chasing Thyal and M'kar, and wouldn't take no for an answer, they got indignant. Dafna approached M'kar and Thyal after an exercise session in the zero-g tank. She knew how to stop "those stupid, sorry, I know we're not supposed to call people stupid, but they are, they really are."

"Oh, stop them from what, exactly?" M'kar asked. Without thinking, she knew, and her gaze raised to meet Thyal's.

He grimaced and finished sliding from the hatch of the zero-g tank into his hoverchair. Infrenx chirped and flew over to settle on Dafna's shoulder and rub the girl's cheek, before returning to the arm of Thyal's chair. For a few seconds, the little girl looked starry-eyed with wonder.

"Stop who from what?" M'kar prodded her.

"Oh." Dafna blushed. "We decided how you can stop them from trying to make you marry them."

"From the mouths of babes," Thyal murmured.

"I have the awful feeling I don't want to know," M'kar said.

"You don't?" Dafna's blush faded.

"That's not ..." Thyal sighed. "That's sort of what she meant, but if you're talking about the Mirror --"

"Don't!" M'kar glared at him. Then they were both laughing. She didn't want to have to explain the label slapped on the twins when they were in Basic. Sighing, she went down on one knee to look Dafna in the eyes. "Tell me. What should we do to stop them?"

"Master Thyal is your best friend, right?" The little girl waited. M'kar fought not to look at Thyal. She nodded. "My Grammy says you shouldn't marry anybody who won't be your best friend for always."

"That's very wise," Thyal said. M'kar wanted to slap him.

I've got a horrid feeling where this is going, she thought to him.

So do I, but better to get the agony over with, so it can be dealt with.

I think I should be insulted. She was grateful that she felt like laughing. And that they had the ability to have this kind of conversation without being overheard.

"So you and Master Thyal should get married." Dafna grinned. "And then Barroo and Infrenx can mate and have babies and we can all have dracs when we're grown up."

"Oh, so that's your reasoning behind it all." Thyal chuckled. "You're just plotting how to get your own dracs."

"Well ..." Dafna giggled, blushing again.

"You're going to be late for your next class." M'kar stayed down on one knee until she was sure they really were alone. "You do realize we're going to be in even worse trouble now, if the children think we ... you and me ... "

"What do you want to wager Maenta will torment us by letting the children plan our wedding?"

"Oh, they can *plan* all they want. Doesn't mean anything will happen."

"Would it be so awful?" He tilted his head to one side and fluttered his eyelashes at her, exactly like Nyssa.

"Wedding ceremonies are exhausting. Especially Nisandrian ones. My father said sometimes he was sure the games, the feats of strength, were to kill off either the bride or the groom so someone else could take their place."

"I meant being married to me. It's not like I can enforce my husbandly rights."

"That is an old-fashioned concept that could get you killed on quite a few planets." Despite the twisting, dropping sensation in her gut, M'kar laughed. If the strangled sound that escaped her tight throat could pass for a laugh.

"As both our fathers stated long ago, our bond could be considered marriage on some worlds."

"If you're referring to Eyran, where the people are so paranoid about germs, viruses and bacteria, there is no physical contact between the genders, and children are bio-engineered and gestated in mech-wombs -- shall I go on?"

"No." His lips twitched, then flattened, pressed so hard the skin around them went white.

"Besides," she hurried on, "you're the one who would be in trouble. Stuck with me. You have no idea when my mixed-up biology might deteriorate and send me into insanity. Violent insanity. And with my Talent, I could override Infrenx's defensive reactions, so you'd never stand a chance."

"Are you --"

"Insane? Upset?" Her voice cracked. She was terrified if she went on, she would either shriek or burst out laughing so hard she would fall to her knees.

Neither of us will ever marry because of this bond between us, because nothing and no one will ever come between us. Thyal's mental voice had a quiet tone she had never heard before. It made her shiver, because she couldn't interpret it. *The only reason, at this point, to marry is for physical reasons. That is the only change marriage would make in our relationship. As I am unable to perform, indeed, as I am physically unable to feel lust --*

"You're an idiot!" M'kar's voice cracked. "Get out of my head."

"I had to prove I was telling the truth."

"Yes, and I think I would be flattered if you ever ... well, I would be relieved and overjoyed for you, when you recover to the point you can feel any kind of lust for a woman."

"But terrified if I felt it for you?" The left corner of his mouth twitched.

"Thyal, this conversation has gone on about twenty minutes longer than it should have."

"You're afraid of considering anything more between us than what we have now, aren't you?"

M'kar took a deep breath and stared into his eyes and fought for the words. She fought to understand what she was feeling. Well, turnabout was fair play, wasn't it? She spoke into his mind in return.

Right now, with a dozen different possible receptions waiting for me when we reach Nisandros ... I am feeling rather ... allergic to the whole concept of marriage in general. And yes, the physical aspects of marriage, in particular.

Any man who tried to force you deserves all the damage you do to him. And I demand to be allowed to watch.

That made her laugh, which released the pressure building up.

"Would you do something for me? As my hearth-brother?"

"Anything. You know that."

"Don't ever tell anybody about this conversation."

"Especially your father?"

"Knowing my Po'pa ..." She leaned back against the wall of the zero-g tank. "Knowing him, he would knock us both nearly unconscious and walk us through the bare minimum ceremony, and then roar at us and tease us until we give in."

Infrenx and Barroo chirped at them, sounding so much like, "Yeah," they grinned at each other, let out deep breaths, and finally moved to leave the rec deck.

~~~~~

Once they reached Tierfallon Station, M'kar spent most of her on-duty time with Ambassador Defrayn and his team, preparing them for every contingency when they arrived on Nisandros. That kept her away from the children, who had done exactly as she feared, and asked E'bett and Maenta to help them research a Nisandrian wedding ceremony. It also kept her out of reach of Nyssa, who had hysterics when she found out about her brother training with Chief Decker, to prepare to defend his life.

The journey from Tierfallon to Nisandros took two decs, and passage through four jump gates. It seemed to pass in a few breaths. Preparing for both trips down to the planet's surface, official and unofficial, threatened M'kar's patience and her control on her temper.

When the *Defender* reached Nisandros, Desra managed to send a message up to her, hidden among a packet of messages from Ba'e'do'stra Clan, and a handful of requests from enemy and ally clans, insisting M'kar confer with them before the welcoming ceremony. She guessed most of those clans wanted to talk about a marriage alliance or trick her to come close enough for them to kill her.

Desra reported that the sisterhood had pledged their lives to defend Jasper and his team as they studied the surbda craters. That was good. Several rebel factions, whom she swore were rebels just for the fun of it, had agreed to create distractions during the diplomatic mission. They would keep the attention of the entire planet firmly off the skies and the craters and any hints that off-world visitors had landed.

She included a note from Great-grandfather Aquid, who looked forward to seeing her. He wanted M'kar to stand with him when he got married, for the fifth time. She had no idea who the intended bride might be. It was entirely possible he had a sweetheart hidden away somewhere, because the aggravatingly active, spry, clever old man managed to vanish from the clan house for days at a time, and no one could ever figure out how he got out or where he went.

The next news from Desra shocked M'kar. She and B'keerimo had just gotten married. Would her vow sister help them sneak on board the *Defender* so they could claim political sanctuary and sponsor them going
~~~~~

to the Academy to study?

They needed to get off Nisandros as soon as possible, because the remainder of the letter broke orders of silence from the clan and the Upper Hall of the clan leaders. B'keerimo would be in trouble for telling Desra, and she was in danger for passing the information along to M'kar.

First, Chieftain Ba'shiq, her grandfather, had mentally and physically deteriorated to the point that the clan had forced him to step down. His successor hadn't been chosen yet, and the other clans were being kept ignorant of the in-fighting so Ba'e'do'stra could retain its position as the leader of the clans.

M'kar shuddered, imagining stepping out of the shuttle at the welcoming ceremony and finding the worst of her uncles had already pronounced a death sentence on her. A massive headache threatened, as she calculated how little time she had left to prepare Ambassador Defrayn for dealing with all the new variable in clan leadership.

Desra warned her the next news had two poisoned edges. First, she had uncovered the real name of the off-worlder who had convinced Nisandros to reopen negotiations with the Alliance. He had revealed his true name when the *Defender* sent a message to Nisandros indicating when the ship would enter orbit. Desra recognized him because M'kar had told her about him, and she apologized for not discovering the man's identity so she could kill him before his plan unfolded.

The architect of the Nisandros-Alliance negotiations was none other than Arys Camola.

That wasn't the worst part of the news.

Camola had announced that M'kar had agreed to a diplomatic marriage to seal the unity between Nisandros and the Alliance. The twelve clans that supported him followed prophets who called her the child of prophecy, to heal Nisandros.

"Of course they support him," Ambassador Defrayn said, when M'kar shared the news with him and Genys in her ready room. "They hope to control you through him, and wrest control from your clan." He bowed his head, cupping his forehead with both hands. "I cannot apologize enough for the gross arrogance my colleagues and I have allowed to guide our actions and decisions. And for ignoring the warnings from those with far more experience and yes, wisdom."

M'kar admired the ambassador for his humility and for not going overboard in apologizing. He shared some information that wasn't exactly encouraging, but did offer her some comfort. Camola hadn't been allowed to just run off and do whatever he pleased all these years. After he had scuttled his career, the Diplomatic Corps had kept an eye on him to make sure he didn't use his knowledge and training to harm the Alliance. Someone who had showed so much potential for a meteoric career needed to be watched after he destroyed that career for the sake of a grudge. He had been last seen two years ago on a colony ship that had been taken by Hivers. He was presumed to be in a cocoon somewhere. Obviously, that report was mistaken. He had eluded his watchers and had been free all this time to work his newest mischief.

"You can't just call him a filthy liar, can you?" Genys said. "Not without endangering the negotiations."

"Marriage, especially diplomatic marriages, are pretty serious business on Nisandros. If I challenge his honor, that throws the marriage question wide open." M'kar didn't care if she looked as nauseous as she felt right that moment. "Anyone who wants can enter the competition. Nisandros is big on proving honor through blood and pain. I can't refuse to go down to the planet, since they know I'm coming. Unless I get the support of whoever leads the clan now, and most of the current lunatic prophets, I'm not leaving Nisandros without getting married."

Barroo, who had been curled up with Battleaxe on the front corner of Genys's desk, crooned and leaped off to land in her lap. He crawled up the front of her jacket and curled himself around her neck, vibrating with the intensity of his croons. The image that passed from his mind to hers made her choke on a chuckle.

"What did he ask?" Genys said.

"He's reminding me about my vows." M'kar touched the corner of her eye, indicating the blue lines of her Etrusca vow. "Sorry, Troublemaker, but even my vows to Enlo and Etrusca won't protect me from this."

Barroo made a "hmph" sound, echoed by Battleaxe.

M'kar and Genys and Defrayn talked for nearly two hours, trying to come up with something that would excuse her from going down to the planet, or free her from the trap Camola had set for her. M'kar's head hurt so much at the end that she wasn't able to laugh when Genys remarked that it would serve Camola right if she did marry him. And spend the rest of his very short life showing him what a big mistake he had made.

She retreated to the observation dome to sit in the quiet and think and pray. Thyal was waiting, with the entire ship's complement of dracs, and two boxes of mezipa Ashrock had given him, to save for emergencies. M'kar shuddered, pulled between furious tears and what she feared was hysterical laughter. She wasn't sure how, but she ended up curled up against him in his hoverchair, clutching at the front of his shirt and shaking. The dracs covered them both. It was an engineering miracle the hoverchair didn't burn out its anti-gravity thrusters from the weight.

You really are an idiot, Thyal told her, when her brain and body had quieted enough she could hear him through their link.

M'kar growled and didn't even try to come up with words.

Our betrothal tattoo. You avoid the honor challenge because you have proof Camola is a liar, because you're already promised to me.

She sat up, tumbling five dracs off the hoverchair. She pressed both hands against his chest to put enough distance between them to see his face.

"That will get you killed," she rasped, her throat so tight with fury and choking fear she was amazed she could speak at all. "The moment I show them my tattoo, yes, it frees me of Camola and calls his honor into question. And endangers the whole diplomatic mission. Which I would gladly flush into the netherworlds. But you idiot – I have to identify who wears the matching tattoo."

"So?" He gave her a lopsided smile. "Ashamed to be seen in public with me?"

M'kar growled and punched his left shoulder. He didn't even flinch, which frightened her. She thought he had regained more feeling in his torso.

"You'll have to come down to the planet's surface to face all the challengers. And there will be. Dozens of them. All eager for a chance to gain power over the other clans through me. I'm not risking your life."

"Especially when I'm totally useless to defend myself?" The lack of any emotion in his face or voice chilled her.

"That's beside the point."

"Maybe." He winked when she huffed, searching for words that weren't mostly curses. That yanked the breath from her lungs. "Why exactly will there be challengers, if our betrothal tattoos protect you from Camola?"

"Because of stupid ritual and pretenses of being fair, and my honor will be called into question along with his. We're telling two conflicting stories, so both of us are judged liars until one is proven right. With blood. And preferably someone's death. And meanwhile, anyone who wants to challenge Camola's claim to being betrothed to me, and my claim to be betrothed to you, has the right. And they will do it. With the bloodiest, loudest ..." M'kar caught her breath as an idea seemed to jump up and down at the edge of her mind, demanding her attention.

"What did you just think of?"

"We need a distraction to get Jasper and his team safely down to Etrusca's Wall."

"What about the rebels?" He shook his head, frowning, clearly lost.

M'kar snorted. "You can't depend on them for anything. I always knew I'd have to come up with a contingency plan, but a bridal competition might be just the ticket."

Her legs shook slightly as she slid out of the hoverchair, dislodging most of the dracs. She hit the deck of the observation dome and nearly went to her knees before she could get her balance.

"This might work. I need to think, get all the details straight in my head, but … it might work."

"Let me help." He gestured at the boxes of mezipa sitting on the empty equipment pedestal. "I brought provisions."

~~~~~

M'kar arrived on Nisandros in full dress uniform of the Fleet, wearing the pins that marked the honors she had earned in scholarship and service. Barroo rode proudly on her shoulder, sitting up straight, head raised, one paw intertwined with the metallic cord braided into her hair.

Silence swept across the plaza as she was the last to emerge from the shadows of the shuttle and into the harsh, late afternoon sunlight. When she stepped out onto the pavement of the welcoming plaza, painted with all the clan symbols, Barroo's eyes were red and black with ferocious threat, and sparks of blue glee that only M'kar could see. He opened his mouth and bared his fangs and extended his tongue in a silent shriek of defiance.

"I told you!" a harsh, tenor voice called out, sending up shrill echoes off the stonework. "Didn't I tell you? None of you listened to me. The Ancestors mocked you every time you failed --"

A dull clang and a thud echoed across the plaza as the waiting crowd turned, trying to locate the shouter. M'kar knew that sound quite well. It was the sound of the wide, bronze blade of a booliwac, referred to as a peacekeeper, hitting a hard head. In this instance, the rock skull of one of the many filthy, raving, self-appointed prophets who outnumbered the venomous birds and ground-burrowing creatures of Nisandros. Her father often speculated that the booliwacs were designed specifically to deal with the cranky old men and silence them.

A flutter of movement caught her attention. A crumpled, thin, dark figure toppled from over the balcony of one of the towers surrounding the plaza. It was a public tower, lacking clan symbols, which anyone could enter for a good view of the ceremonies. A flash of light on the bright polished blade of the booliwac caught her eye, then the guard vanished back into the shadows. The crowd on the pavement below scattered in time to avoid cushioning the man's fall. Knowing how holiness and devotion to the Ancestors were closely tied to wretched personal hygiene, M'kar supposed the smell alone moved people aside before they realized the madman was falling down on them.

The interruption took all of ten seconds, and M'kar calculated her pause was barely long enough to be noticed. Besides, she had to give the naysayers and enemies and power players time to get a good look at her. She put her right boot on the dark green pathway painted on the pavement, to follow the ambassador and his party. Barroo chirped
~~~~~

happily and turned to look all around. Someone chuckled, someone muttered, and whispers trickled through the crowd.

Good. No one was quite sure what to make of her. They were still digesting the statement she had made by appearing in uniform, rather than wearing her clan's colors. M'kar wished there were legends of dragons on Nisandros. Emberwings, yes, with feathers that dripped with flames, and all sorts of vengeful creatures in the service of the Ancestors, but nothing that would work for her or against her, from having a miniature dragon riding on her shoulder.

A muffled pop, more felt in the back of her head than heard, warned her just as the entire ship's complement of dracs burst into view. They flew circles around her. Barroo chirped happily and leaned down to brush her cheek with his head. The images coming from him were pride and amusement and relief -- he hadn't liked keeping a secret from her. She was rather proud of him that he was able to, then worried, because essentially someone had been teaching her drac to *lie* to her.

Was this what you were whispering about with them? she asked Thyal.

Impress them with wonder, and hopefully scare some of them into at least hesitating to ambush you, he responded. *How do they look?*

Infrenx came in for a landing on her other shoulder. M'kar bit the inside of her mouth to fight down a wide grin.

Whispers and mutters spread through the crowd. She caught flashes of avarice on far too many young male faces, all of them attached to bodies in full ceremonial robes and decorative armor painted with clan colors and sigils. They were young enough to have large swaths of skin untouched by tattoos from bloody and clumsy performances in the hand-to-hand combat that passed for good clean fun among the nobles of Nisandros.

It's a wonder the noble houses didn't wipe themselves out of existence centuries ago, with all the stupid, life-endangering games they consider necessary to prove themselves and get the Ancestors' approval.

Proof that Enlo is merciful? Thyal asked.

Proof that Enlo has a totally vicious, warped sense of humor. Then she grinned, because while the welcoming ceremony was shaping up to be just as involved and tricky as she had feared, that was also a relief. Her plan with Desra depended on the greedy reaction of those staring young men, all in the right age range for courtship battles. Yes, oddly, it *was* comforting to come home and find out nothing had changed.

Chapter Thirteen

The dracs continued their aerial dance and formed a canopy over M'kar's head as she crossed the plaza to join the diplomatic team for the official welcome. Amazingly, every clan was represented. How often had that happened in the history of Nisandros?

More important, how long could these cranky, battle-hardened, scarred, teetering-on-the-edge-of-insanity-from-brain-trauma old men be gathered in one place before planet-immolating civil war broke out? According to legend, none of the clan heads had gathered in one place since the Gatekeepers vanished -- if the mysterious, nameless, all-powerful beings who slapped the ancestors for their arrogance and told them to shape up or die actually were the Gatekeepers. Many on Nisandros insisted the Gatekeepers weren't real because no Gate had ever been found.

That wasn't proof there had never been a Gate. Gates got buried by time and weather, geologic changes, and even cataclysms. Sometimes legends only mentioned the continent, or hemisphere where the Gate had stood. Sometimes the Gates were found under massive piles of rock that defied all attempts to analyze or take samples for study. Sometimes Gate technicians armed with the sensor power of a starship had to search for years before they found a Gate. Nothing had been found yet on Nisandros, but in all honesty, those with the technology to find Gates hadn't been permitted to search. That would change if Nisandros joined the Alliance.

Ambassador Defrayn stepped forward, up onto the raised platform that faced the council of clan leaders. He took up his position, parade rest, shoulders back, hands clasped behind his back, and began the long greeting in high Nisandrian that he, Treinna and M'kar had revised and rehearsed until they all had splitting headaches.

Is the nosepicker there? Thyal asked, as she showed him what she saw, and told all the dracs except Barroo and Infrenx to leave. No sense in distracting everyone so the ceremony got muddled.

Her gaze slowly slid across all the clan leaders and their heirs and heirs-of-heirs seated around them. *According to the big pretty-boy wearing his clan colors and the mark of the heir, yes.*

How pretty?

M'kar nearly laughed at the slight sharpness of his tone.

Po'pa says some clan leaders deliberately scar themselves for artistic purposes. He certainly supports the theory. M'kar kept her gaze away from

Ke'Jor. One glance had been enough. The young man standing behind the seated head of Rissor Clan had a square jaw and sharp cheekbones, too artistically scarred with four parallel, straight lines marked in a shade of green that glowed against his mahogany skin. He had a burn patch along his jawline, at just the right angle and height so it didn't interfere with the neat, sculptured line of his beard. It just wasn't fair that someone as whiny and dominating as Ke'Jor had grown up to be so wide-shouldered and elegantly tall. And yes, gorgeous. In a masculine, overly jeweled weapon sort of way.

That was it. She would think of him as a weapon that had been rendered useless for anything but ceremonial purposes because it had been unbalanced with too many jewels.

Probably unbalanced mentally. Why couldn't he have whined to the wrong person, irritated them so ... well, I can't in all good conscience have hoped for the bratty nosepicker to get himself killed, but couldn't he have done something stupid to get himself disqualified as the heir?

You're thinking very loud, lupi, Thyal said

Please, Enlo, just get me through the next four hours of ceremony. Would it be wrong of me to hope the entire ambassadorial party gets sick on the feast, so we have to retreat in shame back to the ship?

Thyal laughed, and Infrenx trilled. M'kar fought not to react when the people standing to her right, almost within arm's reach, startled at the sound. Her gaze met several of theirs. A few nodded to her, one winked, and she wondered if any of them thought she recognized them.

The ambassador finished his speech with a flourish and a low bow that threatened to topple him off the platform, nose-first. A moment of silence, then the clan heads thudded out their approval with the butt ends of the upright spears in their hands on the echo boxes placed next to their massive chairs. The booming sound made the tiles of the plaza vibrate under her feet.

From the corner of her eye, M'kar saw several drac heads peer over the edge of the pavilion on her right, watching the proceedings. She held her breath and narrowed her eyes, or she might laugh. How many dracs could cluster together in one spot, creating enough weight to tear through the cloth of the ceremonial canopy? Not a good impression to make.

She asked all the teacher dracs to go sit on balcony railings where they would have a good view. Then she directed the other five *Defender* dracs to glide under the pavilion canopy and take up positions where they would have a good view of everything that happened, to share with their parents.

M'kar focused on the scarred, tattooed, bearded, weathered faces in front of her for any hint of resentment, excitement, fear, or just old-man grumpiness. Too much beard and too many overlapping tattoos made them hard to read. When the last banging echoes faded away, the figure wearing the ceremonial robes of her clan stood up and moved forward, close enough for her to finally see his face. M'kar sent up last-minute prayers for Enlo's mercy. Who had taken over leadership of the clan? Friend or foe?

Well, who is it? Thyal asked, as the old man stepped forward. *The betting pools need to know.*

M'kar muffled a snort and had to hold her breath for several seconds. Barroo and Infrenx trilled, and the old man looked over the heads of everyone in the diplomatic party to meet her gaze. He winked and turned his head enough to show a red and gold pinwheel tattoo on his right temple. The tightness in M'kar's chest loosened a few notches.

Uncle Rokas. She crossed her eyes at the old man because her dignity wouldn't allow her to grin and laugh aloud in giddy relief.

He tipped his head back and let out a couple barks of laughter.

Which one is he? Thyal sounded slightly irritated, slightly impatient.

My father's triplet. The good one. The clan scholar. Still is, I assume. Sorry, he's talking now.

M'kar kept gazing straight ahead, at parade rest, her expression impassive, her shoulders as straight as she could keep them under the weight of two dracs. She listened as her uncle welcomed the diplomatic party. Her father had often joked that such ceremonies were as much an endurance test as a chance to show off the clan wealth and power. Ritual guided everything, including the exact positioning of the pavilions and the chairs for the clan leaders and where shadows should fall at what time in each phase of the ceremony. M'kar had drilled the diplomatic party on just how long the ceremony would last, the timing, and how crucial poise was to success. Still, she caught at least a third of them surreptitiously shifting their feet or checking the progression of the sun across the sky.

She couldn't wait to get away from all these laser-focused eyes and retreat to her parents' old quarters. Just for a few minutes, to catch her breath and report to the ship. Desra had assured her that the suite of rooms had stayed sealed since the day her family left Nisandros, and had been thoroughly cleaned and prepared for M'kar to use them while staying in the clan house. Desra and B'keerimo had promised to make sure any nasty surprises, such as boobytraps and spying devices, were found, dealt with, and removed, so she could relax.

Finally, the welcome and introductions on both sides finished. One more official waited to be introduced from the Nisandrian side. His position as last in the ceremony indicated just how important he was. Would Camola give her the necessary opening here at the welcome ceremony, or would he wait until the feast at the clan house to press his claim to the fake betrothal? Timing was everything. If she repudiated him here and announced the bridal games, chaos could result. Did she want that?

It took all her willpower and discipline not to give the slightest reaction anyone could warp to their advantage. Or give Camola any satisfaction at startling her. Let them assume she didn't recognize him. That had to be a nasty blow to his ego, at the very least.

The man in his long, plain black robes now stood high enough for his features to be visible. Those robes signaled that he had taken vows to serve the Upper and Lower Halls of the clans and made their goals and the security of their discussions his highest priority. They also meant he put Nisandros before any blood ties or honor ties. That was all very idealistic and honorable and didn't fit with the spoiled brat he had been on Le'anka. She believed Camola was a conniver who could turn around and reason his way into breaking every single vow he had ever made, so he could proclaim with offended innocence that he had done nothing wrong -- he had followed his conscience.

She wasn't going to give him the slightest opening to do that. He was going to tangle and strangle himself in his own plot, if it was the last thing she ever did.

It took all her discipline and focus to listen to Camola's words and say nothing, show no reaction. Such as shout that he was a liar, every time he paused. With great relief, she caught the gleam of the sun from the corner of her eye, at just the right angle to mark the end of the ritual.

Rokas stepped forward and slammed his staff down five times, concluding the ceremony. With no talk of betrothals or impending wedding feasts. M'kar kept her face impassive as she marched out of the plaza with the ambassadorial party, climbed into the waiting land transport, and prepared for the ride to the clan house, where they would all be housed for the duration of the negotiations.

She was directed to a private compartment in the transport with the ambassador and her uncle. M'kar thought perhaps her face had frozen into disciplined impassivity through utter weariness. She wasn't going to have to endure the stares of clan guards and her uncles and cousins on the ride, but she wouldn't be alone with the ambassador, either. She couldn't relax.

"Welcome home, Little Blade," Uncle Rokas said, when the door of the private compartment slid shut. He grinned and eyed the two dracs sitting on her shoulders. "Interesting pets, your Fleet provides for you."

Barroo blew raspberries at him.

"Barroo, be nice to family," M'kar murmured as she and the ambassador took the wide bench seat facing the one Rokas sank down into. Infrenx trilled laughter.

"Ah, and is your little friend as vicious as his namesake?" Her uncle nodded. "A warning, perhaps? That is good. We are meeting here, this way, so I can warn you."

"I already know about Camola's false claim of betrothal."

"Ah ... good." His eyes narrowed for a moment. "If you are your father's daughter, you have a plan?" He glanced at Defrayn. "Forgive me, Ambassador, but surely you know my niece's history? The complications resulting from her conception, surviving childhood, fears that she is a figure of prophecy, and her parents' flight to the Alliance?"

"Most certainly," Defrayn said. "We are aware of the implications and complications and possibilities."

"Aware does not always mean ready." Rokas sighed and rubbed his eyes with two fingers on each hand. For a few seconds, he was just an old man who preferred to be a scholar, two heads shorter than M'kar's father, pale and quiet and dangerously intense. "This business must be handled immediately, before we are overrun ... Niece, where is your suitor?"

"My suitor." M'kar tried not to clench her fists. "You're not referring to Camola, are you?" She swallowed hard. "Now that was a complication I hadn't calculated ... Nyx of Qahngress contacted you. I assume he didn't send his withdrawal letter?"

Rokas shook his head. M'kar thought she saw a glimmer of amusement in his old, dark eyes. She said a silent prayer of thanks that the ambassador was fully informed on the whole Qahngress twins problem, so she didn't have to waste time rehashing the idiotic mess.

"Why do I have the feeling you've known all along Camola was lying about marrying me?" A chuckle escaped her when her uncle's lip twitched in a momentary smile. "Let me guess. Word somehow slipped out that the betrothal is open to challenge? Other politically motivated suitors are lined up?" She took a deep breath and closed her eyes for a moment. "Thank you, Enlo, for mercies great and small."

"This is a good thing?" Defrayn said.

"The more suitors for my niece," Rokas said, "the more complicated the situation becomes ... and the easier it is to add conditions to the resulting bridal challenge without anyone noticing or protesting."

"As in?" M'kar tried not to hold her breath.

The transport's bumping and humming slowed, meaning they had entered the main courtyard of the clan house.

Rokas shrugged. "We are not setting any historic precedent here. Other brides have resented being turned into prizes. They tricked the *gasquacs* pursuing them into agreeing that if they didn't like the winners, they didn't have to take them."

"Uncle." She choked for a moment. "Thank you. I was hoping to do something like that, but I wasn't sure I could." M'kar wished she knew her uncle better, so she could hug him.

"Enlo does show great mercy. In this instance, in ensuring that the chieftain who writes up the bridal challenge contract is the clan scholar and knows how to tangle lesser minds with complicated language." He sat back and rested his hands flat on his thighs. "Besides, I do not like any of the contenders who have already put their names on the list. I don't want them to be part of our family. We have standards to uphold, after all." He smiled genially.

The ambassador laughed first. Then M'kar found enough breath to join in.

Thank you, Enlo. Thyal, have you been listening?

Oh, yes, he responded, and laughter vibrated warm through his mental voice in her head.

The transport door slid open. Rokas led the way, stepping out into the main courtyard. All the rest of the diplomatic party had disembarked and were being led into the house by the wives of her uncles and cousins.

Tell Decker if he can figure out any way to cheat, big-time cheating, start putting it together, and prepare Nyx to come down here on a moment's notice.

~~~~~

Great-grandfather Aquid hadn't changed. He sat in the dark in the front room when M'kar opened the door of her parents' suite. For the moment she was alone, with only Barroo for company. Infrenx had gone back to the ship with the other dracs. Aquid sat on a bench and leaned on his two canes carved to look like battling slitherfangs, grinning at her, blinking in the beam of light coming from the corridor. He was just as shaggy and gray and skinny as the last time she had seen him. Maybe insanity had some benefits, in terms of longevity.

"Have you had fun, *kis'ka*?" he said, after M'kar turned the lights on, studied him for two heartbeats, then stepped inside and shut the door.

"That depends. Have you decided if I'm allowed to live, or are you here to obey the Ancestors who say I'm a threat?"

"Most of the Ancestors are too busy enjoying the Afterworld to bother with us," he said, waving his hand in a dismissing and semi-obscene gesture. "The ones who do communicate are even worse raving lunatics than me, so you're better off ignoring them."

"Uh huh."

"I like your little friend." He tipped his shaggy head to one side and grinned at Barroo. "Hello, are you taking care of my cub?"

Barroo trilled and lifted off M'kar's shoulder. He flew circles over the old man's head, then abruptly dropped down and landed on his shoulder. The impact nearly knocked him backward off the bench where he had been sitting. Aquid burst out laughing as he struggled to sit upright. M'kar was surprised the laughter didn't turn into wracking coughs. The old madman was in good shape, despite his years and skinny, ragged frame.

"Have you had fun?" he asked again, when he got himself upright.
~~~~~

Barroo settled on the bench next to him. His eyes sparkled blue and green, and he seemed fascinated by the old man.

M'kar trusted Barroo's impressions of people, and she was already inclined to trust her great-grandfather. He had always been the most reliable and constant among all her relatives, when she was a child. Despite his bouts of lunacy, talking to people who weren't visible in the room. Still, that didn't mean she was willing to relax her guard and trust what anyone said. Not until the *Defender* had left Nisandros and put three jump gates between them.

"Yes, often enough," she finally said, and stepped around him in a wide arch as she came into the room. She decided to be pleased that the furnishings seemed to be unchanged since her parents had left. The cleaning looked thorough enough to let her be comfortable, and she trusted Desra to have cleared out all the spying eyes and listening bugs and the odd assassin's bomb or poison traps.

"Ready to come home and set things aright?"

"As in?"

"The boy needs your help. Not just pulling this world forward a few centuries, but cleaning out a lot of idiotic traditions." Aquid snorted. "Starting with listening to a bunch of moldy old grumpy ghosts."

"If you're in the mood for some fun, we could argue whether ghosts have any corporeal substance that would retain mold."

That got him laughing again. "The boy says you were good partners when you were children. Now you can be more."

"Which boy are you talking about?"

"Don't play games, *kis'ka*." He shook his head. "You're wise to be cautious, but there's only one boy who was worth anything. You liked him. You even considered accepting him, if his *ba'scwaka* cousin would step out of the way."

"You're in contact with … Ke'Niq?"

His grin widened, and that was all the answer she needed. Before M'kar could think of what question to ask next, there was a thump on the door behind her. She nearly called permission for whoever was out in the hall to enter, but this wasn't her cabin on the *Defender*, where the doors would open on her command. She stepped to the door and opened it.

"M'kar?" The woman who peered up at her blinked a few times, as a smile slowly spread across her face. She was petite, with gray eyes that clearly marked her as coming from the northern mountain clans, her face unmarked by scars or tattoos.

Except for two royal blue lines extending from her eyebrows, marking her as a follower of Etrusca. M'kar knew that face, she knew those eyes, and she was so glad to see them she might have hugged the woman, but that was never a wise move when it came to vow sisters.

"Desra?" she whispered.

"Is it safe to come in?"

M'kar could think of a dozen smart-alec or philosophical responses. She stepped aside and reached to close the door once Desra was inside.

"There you are, child." Aquid held out a hand, beckoning for Desra to join him on the bench. "Any new messages?"

"Not yet." The wide-eyed look Desra gave Barroo was quite satisfactory.

Barroo jumped up, popped out, then popped back in, hovering over M'kar's head. She decided to be amused and grateful for the high ceilings in all the rooms. Her drac came in for a gentle landing on her shoulder, crooning softly to her as he settled into his usual perch.

"All of them obey you?" Desra said, staring at Barroo.

"Hardly. I'm not going to waste my time explaining the whole social structure and hierarchy of dracs to you. Not here and now, anyway. Are you ... in league?" She gestured at Aquid.

"Did you know that Etrusca also allows men to vow? But their tattoo dye is made to glow in the dark and be invisible in daylight."

M'kar snorted. She believed it. Her head was too full of other considerations to make a smart retort. "What does that -- Oh. Great-grandfather, are you a vow ... brother?"

Aquid chuckled and wagged his head from side to side.

"So was Ke'Niq ... for a while," Desra added with a sigh.

"For a while? Were his men providing distraction while the sisters gathered data from the craters? Are they helping us now?"

"They say they will, but you know how men are here. They want to be in the title of the story, not in the list of weapons-bearers." She shuddered. "I'm just glad we didn't tell him why we need the distractions when your friends come down."

"More distraction when hostilities cease, so we can all enjoy the entertainment of fighting for a pretty bride," Aquid said with a chuckle.

"I can't stay long. The old aunties seem to think I need constant supervision, or someone will try to steal me from Beek." Desra wrinkled up her nose.

"Beek?" M'kar nearly choked when she realized it was a pet name for B'keerimo.

Amazing, the things people will do for love, Thyal commented.

You, hush. I don't need more distractions. She found it hard not to laugh, but Desra might be offended if she did. M'kar settled herself more comfortably and shared the rough, adaptable plan she and Jasper had made to bring him and his team down to Nisandros.

In less than half an hour, Desra hugged her, fighting down a smirk of delight and mischief, and hurried out to send messages to the sisterhood, to prepare for their part in the plan.

"Well, Great-grandfather, what do you think?" M'kar asked, in the few moments they were alone together. She was due to meet with Ambassador Defrayn and Uncle Rokas soon, and still had to wash and dress for dinner.

"I think you are indeed a figure of prophecy. I think you make your father very proud, even as you terrify most of our bloodline." Aquid chuckled. "Do be careful, cub. I want you in one piece and able to attend my wedding."

M'kar shuddered, remembering something she heard in a lecture at the Academy. History proved that prophetic figures didn't survive their pivotal moment in history. She would much rather be a footnote in multiple mission reports, maybe with a couple of reprimands on her record, than be the main figure in a story full of sacrifice and earn a noble eulogy.

~~~~~

When M'kar reported to the guest suite, Ambassador Defrayn looked like he at least had a chance to rest after the strenuous welcoming ceremony. His deputy and his secretary were both present. Everyone spoke High Le'ankan, as a security precaution. M'kar knew better than to trust the assurances of clan security that the room would be not only soundproof, but regularly swept for listening devices.

The diplomatic party needed to know what would happen next, and especially how the developments on Nisandros had dovetailed perfectly with the plan she and Thyal had cobbled together. They needed to simultaneously support the mission while defeating Camola, and let her remain free of marriage, becoming a high priestess, or being sacrificed.

The diplomats didn't need to know the part of the plan where Jasper brought a shuttle full of equipment down to Nisandros to conduct experiments that weren't exactly forbidden, but not exactly approved. The sisterhood groups across Nisandros were nominally in control of the surbda craters. They were the only ones able to go into them and come out again untouched by the warping of time or their minds. They wanted help from the Alliance in understanding what happened within the craters. That didn't mean Jasper and the members of his team wouldn't face charges of insubordination and endangering a diplomatic mission if something went wrong and they were caught, or some damage occurred to all that equipment that belonged to the Fleet.

M'kar explained the traditions surrounding the bridal competition that would be announced at the feast. Rokas had sent messages to the other clans in anticipation of M'kar's cooperation, inviting suitors to come during the feast for the ceremonial start of the bridal challenge.

"It's an ancient and time-honored tradition, especially where there is
~~~~~

only one high-ranking bride and a multitude of suitors who all feel themselves worthy."

"You're not going to actually go through with it, are you? How will you get away with that?" the deputy asked.

"Oh, we barbarians are very fond of long, wordy, convoluted legal documents when it comes to marriage alliances." M'kar grinned, finally feeling a little peace about the whole tangled situation. Enlo was indeed answering her prayers. "The terms of the competition will be so very difficult that most will forfeit. My uncle is rewording the contract to allow me the right to declare no winner at all. The contract will state it is competition to prove worthiness to be my groom, rather than allow one of them to claim me as a bride. That difference is all the grace I need."

When she met with Rokas to look over the contract and the terms of the competition, M'kar seriously considered shedding family blood, because he seemed to be having far too much fun with this. The document was far longer than she thought it needed to be. After reading the first third, she realized all the repetition was to discourage the suitors from reading all the way through, and thereby miss certain key items that would protect her.

Nowhere did the document promise a marriage ceremony. Everything focused on the hopeful suitors, the boundaries of honor, the progression of tests through the games and the penalties imposed on anyone who exceeded the acceptable levels of violence and brutality. All the promises and rules focused on the suitors, with no requirements for the bride.

Then she realized what was missing – and what had been added.

For that, Rokas was indeed her favorite uncle.

Chapter Fourteen

The suitors were forbidden to approach M'kar unless she sent for them. Even better, there was no promise she wouldn't interfere with the games, wouldn't strike out against anyone who irritated her, or that she would stay to observe all the excruciating phases of the competition. In two places, the wording could be interpreted to imply that M'kar should be busy elsewhere during the contests.

She thanked her uncle multiple times, and they laughed together as they walked down the sloping hallway to the grand feasting hall, where the guests had gathered.

On the voyage to Nisandros, she had helped the diplomats practice for the welcoming feast and the games that would follow. Every aspect, from the food to the entertainment to the contests of skill that followed, was calculated to prove the cleverness and the physical strength of the guests. It was crucial that Defrayn's team impress the Nisandrians with their capacity for eating until on the verge of passing out, while keeping themselves awake with riddles and games of skill. M'kar thought the entire team was ready, but she still prayed for Enlo's mercy and protection, and warped sense of humor. Everything seemed to be proceeding according to custom, up until the moment the platters for the welcoming bread were being removed. *Bread* being a very loose term, because it was thin and tough, wrapped around enormous hunks of falling-to-pieces-tender meat, spicy enough to draw tears of blood.

A doog horn blast rattled the ceiling beams two stories overhead. Dust and debris better left ignored rained down on the feasting tables. The wide double doors at the far end of the feasting hall rattled with three hard blows, silencing those who had ignored the shrieking bellow of the horn. Then the doors swung open.

Five men, hooded and cloaked in gray, marched through the doors together, each carrying a white banner tied to a spear. Rings of gold and precious stones bound the long banner to the spearhead as long as a man's forearm. Normally the banners would carry symbols indicating what sort of truce was being demanded. The bridal truce, when all feuds and disagreements and honor vendettas were put aside until a suitor was declared winner, didn't need symbols.

M'kar watched as understanding skittered through the room and one head after another turned toward her, at the high table with Rokas and the ambassador. When those five men were ten steps into the room, another five stepped from the shadows into the light of the feasting hall. And five more after them. And five more after them. They were relatively anonymous under their hoods and flapping cloaks, nothing to differentiate them other than their height and the width of their shoulders. Legend said the first suitor who had defied an honor vendetta to win the bride of his heart had come to her clan's hall in disguise.

Barroo chortled his delight when M'kar showed him what she wanted him to do. He flew from the perch he and Infrenx shared behind the table and glided across the open pit in the center of the room, where the rows of suitors had come to a stop. Several in the first row flinched away from him as he approached, close enough the breeze from his wings fluttered their hoods. He looked into a few faces, and M'kar watched through his eyes. She didn't recognize any of those faces. Not that she expected to, considering most of those suitors would have been children when she last saw them, if she ever met any of them. This move was to impress and intimidate, not to scout out her options.

The bench she shared with her uncle and the ambassador rocked slightly. Rokas stood and held out his hand. His assistant hurried from the far end of the table where he sat in readiness, wiping one hand on the front of his tunic. A messy tunic at the end of a feast was a compliment for the cooks. He held out a long scroll wrapped around a ceremonial baton.

What is he doing? Thyal asked.

He's going to yell at them for interrupting the feast before it got started, then welcome them and tease me a little for inspiring passion in my suitors, then he's going to read as fast as he can the terms and conditions and warnings, in the hopes that they don't hear half the things they'll agree to. Then he'll make them all come up one by one, declare their names and pedigrees, and sign with their blood, which will hold them to the agreement, on pain of being disqualified, dishonored, their clans mocked, and their more prestigious tattoos modified into something silly.

So this is why Nyx left in such a hurry. Your uncle sent an invitation for him to come down and join the fun?

I assume so. She sighed. *So the idiot didn't get some sense at the last minute and decline to participate. I can't imagine Nyssa encouraged him to come down here and risk his life.*

Actually, no, she didn't, but she didn't have much chance, either way.

What did you do? M'kar bit the inside of her mouth hard to keep from laughing aloud. The mischievous tone of his mind was infectious.

Barroo finished his perusal of the rows of suitors and soared up and over, to return to her, chirping happily. He landed on her shoulder instead of returning to the perch with Infrenx. She called the other drac over and fed them the remains of the welcoming bread. The dracs' reaction to the heavily spiced meat, shaking their heads and squeaking at the first few bites, earned some chuckles from those sitting closest to the table.

I didn't do anything, Thyal finally said. *Nyssa went into hysterics when Nyx blew up at her, putting the blame for his problem directly on her shoulders.*

Too little, too late. He should have taken control of his life years ago.

Tahl hit her with a strong tranquilizer she had been holding in reserve, just for her. You didn't hear it from me, and I didn't hear it from her -- at least, not directly -- but Tahl has a few theories of subliminal programming that she would like to test.

M'kar was saved from laughing aloud by hearing Rokas speak her name. Time for her to address her suitors and verbally agree to the contract, encouraging them to agree before they had time to think about what they had heard.

Other than making that speech, M'kar didn't have to face her suitors that evening. The welcoming feast had to continue, for the sake of the cooks if no one else. There was a great deal of pride invested in the massive amount of cooking done.

Her mother was right, M'kar realized. Nisandrians focused on the basics of enjoying their food, proving who was tougher, and getting their feelings hurt over trivial matters. They were children in far too many ways, with none of the charm and easy laughter and swift mending of feelings that children enjoyed.

She didn't have much opportunity to enjoy the feast, however. Her appetite died when she made the mistake of looking at the list of the suitors present, as well as those still to arrive. Ke'Jor and Ke'Niq of Rissor Clan were present, and Arys Camola was due to arrive in the morning. M'kar couldn't decide if this was supposed to be the prelude to a tragic comedy or a black farce.

Then Nyx arrived, halfway through the sweet course. Someone had provided him with the ritual clothes, but clearly few instructions on what to do or not do. He pushed the doors open wide enough to walk through them. They should have been barred to keep them from being opened again before the feast was over. A spreading ripple of quiet announced his presence, rather than a horn blast. He tugged back his hood, revealing his face, which none of the suitors had done yet during the entire feast. His chin went up a little higher as he wove his way between the tables to approach her. His shoulders went back a little bit with each table he passed. A few times he flinched, and M'kar speculated some of the other suitors had said things to him. They wouldn't have the sense or the courtesy to speak in Alliance Standard, and M'kar doubted Nyx had studied enough Nisandrian to understand, but the tone of voice wouldn't need any interpretation. He had to feel threatened, and she hoped the fury that marked his high cheekbones was directed toward his twin sister, at long last.

What does Decker think his chances are? she asked Thyal, as Nyx crossed the cleared area of the floor to stand before her table.

His endurance and lung power and agility are his best weapons. If he can make his opponents chase him until they pass out, stay out of their reach, and evade anything they throw at him, he might stand a chance.

~~~~~

M'kar knew better than to trust her uncle to entirely follow through on the plan to frustrate her suitors while ensuring the negotiations between the Alliance and Nisandros succeeded. That meant she had to get Jasper and his team down to Etrusca's Wall, leave them with a guard from the sisterhood, and come back to the clan house to support the mission. She spent half her restless night regularly waking to beg Enlo for guidance and grace -- or a natural cataclysm that would throw half the planet into chaos and cancel everything.

She took advantage of her right to design the contests for her suitors. The next morning, she gave them their first challenge: help the members of the diplomatic team learn about Nisandros up close and personal. M'kar divided up the diplomats and assigned them to her suitors in pairs, two diplomats and two suitors in each team. Their assignment was simply to spend the day together and learn about each other. Then on the second, third and fourth days, they would go out together across Nisandros, to the suitors' clan territories, to explore, and to meet the people. Besides supporting the diplomatic mission, the plan had the added advantage of keeping the suitors separated. If they weren't together in one group, they couldn't expect her to be with them. She could do whatever she wanted, go wherever she wanted. In theory.

Rokas called the plan clever, and thanked her for sparing the clan the expense and trouble of feeding suitors, cleaning up after them, setting up the arena for the contests of skill and strength, and tending their expected injuries.

M'kar retreated to the upper chambers of the clan house where her grandfather and great-grandfather spent their days, sitting in the sunshine and living in the past. She hoped to run into Desra to check on the progress of their plan without being overheard, but her vow sister was nowhere to be found. M'kar visited with Ba'shiq and Aquid for a short time. Seeing how much more her grandfather had deteriorated, mentally and physically, than her great-grandfather chilled her. Something strange was going on here, and instinct said she needed to find out why, and how.

"I hear Etrusca calling to me sometimes, when the moons are all full and hanging low over the crater," Aquid confided to her, when she commented on how little he had changed. "She sends me strength and youth from that place where time stands still."

"We could use an Etrusca around about now, to beat some common sense into the clan leaders," she said, intending the comment for humor.
~~~~~

Somehow it didn't sound very funny once it left her lips.

"We need an Etrusca to cut out their lying tongues and beat the scheming and lies out of their heads." He broke down snickering like a nasty little boy holding a box of venom-squirmers, ready to drop them from a third-floor balcony into the center of a feasting hall.

M'kar shuddered but managed to smile back at him. She wondered, not for the first time, if the Nisandrian genetically engineered resistance to alcohol was the source of their insanity. Maybe the attempt to trigger psionic gifts in the royal bloodlines had created a warped kind of group or hive mind. Maybe the madmen and prophets heard whispers from all the minds on the planet, rather than the Ancestors. After all, as her father had pointed out, the souls who had passed on to Eternity had far too many things to occupy their minds and their time, to spare any attention for the limited, time-bound fools still trapped within their flesh and their senses.

That conversation got her thinking, and she was a little startled to find herself going to the clan archives next, in search of all the information she could find on Etrusca. B'keerimo wasn't present, and she didn't ask for him, but his assistant fell over his own feet several times in his eagerness to give M'kar anything she wanted. Most of the volumes were full of tales of people who had stumbled into surbda craters, and claimed they saw or heard Etrusca. M'kar searched all the legends of Etrusca escaping her pursuers by fleeing into the craters. They became forbidden ground because everyone who entered them emerged insane. Or never emerged at all.

When she shared her research with Thyal, he told her that Jasper and Taggert had been muttering and snickering over the data they had gleaned by scanning the surbda craters from orbit. They had been holed up in Taggert's workroom long enough to make Treinna concerned.

I think that's my cue, she responded. *Please, Enlo, let this be good news.* She said goodbye to him, left their link, and headed up to her parents' suite to unpack and activate the communication pack Jasper had created just for this private mission. For two heartbeats, she considered scuttling the whole secret mission right there.

One slip or something going terribly wrong at the worst possible time could scuttle not just this diplomatic mission, but her career, and the careers of Jasper, Taggert, and the handful of engineers and Gate team members who had volunteered for the project. They had to do it this way to protect Genys, if that something did go wrong. The *Defender* was there solely to serve the ambassador and his team. Until requested to do so by the clans, no scientific studies could be conducted on Nisandros. That especially meant studying the energy emissions that swirled and surged and died away to nothing in the craters. M'kar hoped, but tried not to hope too hard, that her rank and unusual position in the clan would provide some wiggle room and a large portion of grace.

"We're going to need a lot more time than what we've budgeted into the plan," Jasper stated, as soon as the communication link opened between them.

"Why?" M'kar winced, knowing that was the wrong question to ask. Especially if his head was full of all sorts of figures and formulas and theories. When he was excited about a new idea or radical new data, Jasper tended to speak in a language only engineers could understand, and he got irritated when he had to stop and translate.

"A lot of what we've harvested bears some twisted resemblance to burping Chutes and that freaky anomaly growing near Draxonis." The hissing of the warped energy generated by the surbda craters filled the silence between them for a few seconds.

"So ..." She waited a few moments longer, silently begging him to resume talking so she wouldn't sound as lost as she felt. "What does that mean? We have a Chute trying to ... no."

Jasper made a raspy sound that might be his version of an evil chuckle. "Bigger. Quantum dimensions bigger. What I'm theorizing compares to Chutes the way Chutes compare to jump gates. All those stories about people who went into those craters, and the time warping you experienced, mixed with this new data, gives me some fun ideas. And theories that could blow Chute science totally out of normal time-space." He exhaled loudly. "I'm going to need years to study that thing, but you know I won't be able to. Just like that anomaly by Draxonis, somebody else has all the fun."

"Jasper!" She fought the need to reach through the link and throttle him. "Bottom line. What do you think we have here? No matter how crazy it is, tell me."

"We might have found Nisandros's Gate," Taggert broke in. "Some way, I have no idea how, but it's the only explanation even if it isn't really logical -- some way, it exists in all the craters at the same time. Maybe the time warping is an effort of the Gatekeepers to keep the Gate open. Maybe that's where the Gatekeepers went when they left the Human races on all the worlds. Either into the future or the past."

"Time only travels one direction," M'kar retorted, echoing one of the tenets resulting from many late night, fun, slightly crazy discussions of time-space theory and the truly warped science that came from popular fiction. "Forward."

"That we know of." Jasper gave that pseudo-evil chuckle again. "Can you speed up the schedule, get us down there a day early, let us stay a day longer?"

M'kar wanted to shriek at them, but she swallowed the sound and turned it into a sigh.

"I'll do my best."

She was relieved to end the communication.

I think I'm sorry I introduced you to Jasper, Thyal said, startling her. She had been too wrapped up in the engineer talk to sense he had opened their link. *Although I must admit, the mystery has been entertaining all these years.*

This is all going to blow up and blow us into another dimension of reality, I just know it, she said, and was relieved she didn't have to give him the gist of the conversation. *Presenting Nisandros with the missing Gate will throw the whole planet into a few decades of war, between those saying, "Told you so" and those saying it's a fake and they're cheating. I should just resign my commission right now. Steal one of those merchant ships docked at the orbital station and start running.*

Don't frighten me like that, he retorted. *You wouldn't leave me alone on this ship with all those children who will blame me if their favorite teacher and playmate vanishes. Would you?*

Hah! Is that genuine terror I hear? I thought you liked all the ship's children. Well, most of them, anyway. There are a few rotters who are pretty good indicators of what kind of trouble we can expect at the worst possible time from their parents, but ... M'kar sighed and collapsed back across the couch in the front room of the suite.

I love quite a few of them already. What frightens me is you trashing your career so casually.

Not casually. In utter terror. Maybe Great-grandfather's insanity is heredity and I'm crumbling already.

You are not. Come up here so I can slap some sense back into you.

She muffled a chuckle. *What if ... that crazy old man isn't crazy? What if the visions are true? What if the craters are an anchor point of some crazy power fluctuation that warps time and space? Anyone who goes in is changed physically, so they can't handle reality anymore? What if what they see isn't hallucinations, but reality in another dimension?*

That is quite a theory. And unfortunately, I agree with Jasper and Taggert. They are going to need even more time than you schemed for. If my mother were here --

She would team up with Tahl to tranquilize all of us and throw us into hibernation until the diplomatic mission ended.

True. Thyal's chuckle came through their link like a warm embrace. *However, I believe she would counsel us to take this one step, and one day at a time. Bring Jasper and his people down as planned, and then if they need more time, perhaps what they discover in the one day you give them will be enough foundation to reveal the truth without plunging us into interstellar war.*

Pray for me?

I always do.

~~~~~

Common sense said to keep an eye on the suitors, but M'kar couldn't
~~~~~

be everywhere at once, especially once they headed out of the clan house to show Nisandros to the visitors. Fortunately, she had reliable spies on call, who she could communicate with and never fear someone could overhear or steal the information they gave her.

The ship's dracs came when she called them, and they seemed eager enough to spy and explore. They spread out through the sprawling clan house, peering into every room, flying through every window left open, settling down to get into staring contests with servants and family members, but only occasionally allowing themselves to be scratched or stroked. They never took food from anyone, which was a relief. M'kar didn't know what she would do if someone decided to be nasty and poison a drac, or try to drug them to make them prisoners. There were plenty of people just as foolish as the Maniterri who tried to capture dracs with nets or boxes or sacks and tie them up, completely ignoring the demonstrated ability to teleport into and out of anywhere.

M'kar assigned a drac to each team of diplomats and suitors when they left the clan house, with strict orders to keep out of sight whenever possible. When the teams returned to the clan house for dinner, the dracs reported to her one at a time, to share their memories and show her what the teams had done, where they had gone, and how well they had gotten along. Then she gave the dracs permission to explore anywhere they wanted, as long as a drac was watching Camola.

She had them change off at short intervals and wasn't surprised that with so many dracs flying around, never stopping anywhere for more than a few minutes at a time, the residents of the clan house grew used to them, and then ignored them. That was what she wanted, to have her spies always present, but essentially invisible.

Camola couldn't be trusted. He was following the rules too well, so he had to be up to something. She wasn't surprised when he stepped away from the small hall where the suitors ate together. She wasn't surprised when he went down the hallway of the wing that housed the guests before anyone was expected to retire that evening. She wasn't surprised when he knocked on a door once and then opened it and stepped inside, without waiting for an answer. She contacted Thyal, showed him what she had seen, and sent Barroo into the room to spy. She could always see and hear through Barroo, even if keeping up that link gave her a bit of a headache.

The little brown drac popped into the guest room and settled down in the vent hole of the privy box. M'kar was glad she couldn't smell through her drac. The opening was at the perfect angle to give her a good view of Camola settling down in one of the two chairs at the small table in the guest room. The other chair held Ke'Niq. M'kar was disappointed, but not really surprised. Ke'Jor was among the suitors, so Ke'Niq would join the list, just to frustrate his cousin. Desra had told her Ke'Niq had been pushing the boundaries, focusing on his own profit rather than the rebels' agenda for years now. Such an attitude and history made him the perfect co-conspirator, or at least tool, for a schemer like Camola.

Interesting, Thyal said, after Barroo showed her that Infrenx had joined him in the small opening. *But not entirely surprising.*

No, I suppose it makes sense.

I wonder which cousin wants to win you, and which one wants to prevent Nisandros joining the Alliance or share the glory of making it happen.

Camola is here for his own profit. Hurting me is just a bonus. It's only a coincidence if he helps Ke'Niq.

The two conspirators spoke about their competitors. Camola shared news he had received from the Alliance and information on Draxonis and the dracs and cocoons. He mentioned the names of two members of Defrayn's team, but what he said didn't reveal if those men were Camola's contacts, leaking information, or just targets he hoped to influence and use. M'kar and Thyal only needed a few seconds to agree to warn the ambassador and let him deal with the problem.

After half an hour of listening, they didn't gain much more information. Most of the discussion was what Ke'Niq's rebels should find out or do next to influence the leadership of Nisandros and take over the government entirely.

That meant they wouldn't be helping with the distraction the sisterhood needed to help bring Jasper and Taggert and their team down to the planet undetected. Another non-surprise for M'kar.

One drac could spy on the meeting with no trouble. M'kar took Barroo with her when she went to see her uncle. She needed to get permission from Rokas and arrange for supplies to go out into the Barrens tomorrow. She needed to head out early in the morning to go Etrusca's Wall. Tomorrow was her true reason for coming to Nisandros, and she didn't want anything to go wrong.

Rokas didn't quite understand her interest in the crater when she told him partial truth: she wanted to follow up on her experience there when she was a child, for scientific purposes. He accused her of using the field trip as an excuse to get away from her suitors. M'kar laughed and agreed. Yes, she needed to get out of the house. Rokas laughed when she related how MedTech Brea called it a mental health retreat. He wrote out orders to have a gyphel saddled and provided with food and water, and temporary shelter, if a sand-devil appeared, and called a servant to take care of the preparations. Then he kept M'kar another half hour in his office, asking questions about Le'anka and her parents, and reminiscing a little about when he and Ashrock and Be'dosho had tried to convince everyone they were identical triplets.

"It was easier when we were younger, before your father had his growth spurt and started growing a beard at ten years of age." Rokas chuckled and slumped a little in his chair. "We were idiots. We didn't realize until years later how dangerous it was to be identical. The Ancients believed at least one child born identical was a malevolent spirit, sent to wreak havoc. The only way to be sure the threat was eliminated was to kill all the children, not waste time testing them to determine which wasn't Human."

His expression grew pensive, and M'kar decided that would be a wise time to leave. She wished him a good night and left.

To avoid more people trying to get her into a private conversation, and perhaps a compromising situation, M'kar cut through the garden courtyard outside her uncle's office, taking the long way back to her parents' suite in the opposite wing of the house. She had barely reached the halfway point when Frostfire, one of the teacher dracs, popped in so close she nearly ran into him. The drac projected images into her mind with such force, it gave M'kar a headache. Frostfire was the oldest of the teacher dracs on the *Defender*, so named because his dark orange and deep red mottled hide was streaked with white and silver. He held back his panic enough to give her a clear image: Ke'Jor attacked Camola in another courtyard with a k'ta paddle. K'ta was a game played by hitting bags of multiple layers of hide, sewn around a core of dried mud and excrement. The object of the game was to hit the bags hard enough to break the ball, so opposing players were doused with a shower of foul-smelling dirt. The paddles were as tall as a man and as thick as the smallest finger.

In the images pounding from Frostfire's mind into hers, Ke'Jor battered Camola's head and gut using a k'ta paddle with the markings of a minor clan. M'kar had no idea what political upheavals would come from framing that particular clan's suitor. She didn't care. Ke'Jor had violated several laws of hospitality, along with the bridal challenge truce.

On her call, five dracs joined Frostfire and teleported to drive Ke'Jor away from Camola. Running down the halls to the lower-level courtyard where the attack had occurred, M'kar realized what else Frostfire had showed her. He had scratched Ke'Jor across the side of his face, up into his scalp. How was he going to lie and explain away that injury?

Chapter Fifteen

The dracs were silent when M'kar reached the courtyard. The moons were nearly at zenith. She sent Barroo for lights, Raspberry to Ambassador Defrayn's quarters for a memo pad and stylus, and Boomer to Brea, for a medical kit. She had barely begun to examine Camola, checking for his pulse and breathing, before both dracs returned. She set up the lights, pausing to wipe Camola's blood on the legs of her pants, then wrote a note on the memo pad and tore a sheet off. She sent Raspberry and Frostfire to Nyx, with careful instructions to bring him back with them. Then she got to work examining Camola. It amazed her how much medical knowledge she had picked up from Tahl and Brea, just watching them work.

Once Nyx came and started working on Camola, M'kar sent for Rokas and the ambassador. This was a matter that bled into several areas. A guest in their clan house had been assaulted. A suitor under the truce flag had been injured by another outside of the games. And a citizen of the Alliance involved in a diplomatic mission had been attacked by a native.

She couldn't tell Genys or anyone on the *Defender*, other than Thyal, because they were required to stay back and wait, until the ambassador summoned them or requested help. Genys could only send people down without the ambassador's approval if he didn't check in with her at set intervals.

M'kar needed to talk to someone, get some feedback, maybe even a really bad joke. She wanted to be able to tease Genys about the silence order being necessary to keep her from becoming another Captain Shryne, intervening when she thought it best, even against orders.

I am writing all this down for you, Thyal said, *so you don't have to go over it again when you finally do make your report.*

Thanks. She sat back, watching Nyx working on Camola, and felt like she could finally catch her breath

Then Rokas appeared. She was still telling him what the dracs had seen and done when the ambassador and several of his aides came, following the map M'kar had sketched on the notepad for him. After that, everything sped up.

Household security entered Ke'Jor's room while he was still trying to glue together the long scratch Frostfire gave him. He didn't have the k'ta. A servant found it early the next morning, broken in half on the edge of the refuse burning pit. Most likely to destroy genetic evidence such as skin cells, that would prove him guilty.

~~~~~

Even if she had scheduled the meeting at Etrusca's Wall for a different day, M'kar still would have headed out the next morning. She needed to get away from the clan house, from the prying eyes and the whispers and the aunts and the servant girls asking who she favored now, was she glad Camola was injured, was she sad, was she angry with Ke'Jor, did she believe his insistence that Ke'Niq had attacked Camola and put the blame on him? On and on.

Desra and B'keerimo were gone, overseeing the distractions being carried out by sisterhood teams and two reliable rebel teams in the territories of clans surrounding Ba'e'do'stra. The only person she could grumble to about the idiocy of the entire situation was Thyal. They talked on her way to the stables long before sunrise, to claim the waiting, saddled gyphel. She had borrowed the tough outdoor clothes of a patrol rider, so no one would be curious if they saw her. Just another patrol.

Maybe you should give the impression that you went into the crater and didn't come out, he said after several moments of quiet.

The gyphel was as close as Nisandros could get to a horse. The long-legged, scaled quadruped had a long nose horn, huge, taloned feet instead of hooves, and a serpentine tail with a stinger. Gyphel were once used as battle mounts. They could lope over sandy wastes with as much ease as they climbed steep rock faces.

What if I do -- go in and can't get out?

I was thinking more of you getting in the shuttle and having Tahl put you into hibernation so the mind-hunters can't catch you. If no one sees the shuttle with their own eyes, if Jasper's sensor-baffle works like he thinks it will, the planet's sensors won't register it coming and going. Decker says he has enough dirt on the commander of the orbital platform, he'll have the man hide the record of the shuttle coming and going, and no one will know what happened to you until the negotiations are over.

That sounds lovely, just sleep away my troubles. She sighed and thanked the waiting servant with a nod. She waited until the girl had gone back into the house, then led the gyphel out the stable doors, under the dark sky with a thin gray line of dawnlight far to her right.

But?

But with my luck, someone will distract Uncle Rokas while someone else revises the rules of the contest, and I'll be married by proxy before anyone can call a halt to the entire ugly mess.

And then you'll wish you had gone into the crater and not come out.

You'd come after me, wouldn't you? She swung up into the saddle and clamped her mind firmly down on the gyphel's instinctive need to arch and spin sideways, to attempt to throw her off in those first few seconds.

Always.
~~~~~

~~~~~

What do you think we'll find out there? M'kar asked, after an hour of blissfully silent, solitary riding. She had passed the four arches marking Ba'e'do'stra Clan territory, and the terrain had changed from rocky, coated with a tough, mossy growth, to the shattered slate and sand of the Barrens as they gave way to the Ring Mountains.

Insanity? There has to be a reason why all those holy men and self-proclaimed prophets went mad. Besides being Nisandrian.

You are so encouraging. She managed to laugh.

She wished for Barro and Infrenx, but she had sent them both to the ship and had given all the other dracs orders to repeat their performance of the day before. Hopefully, no one would realize she was gone because the dracs were distracting them. While she would have enjoyed their company, having them fly alongside her as she crossed the Barrens would give away her identity. She had borrowed these clothes to be as anonymous as possible.

M'kar was out in the open, racing across the Barrens, in full view as the sun rose. The moment the bottom edge of the sun cleared the ragged horizon, the distinctive grumble of an overland skimmer roared into life somewhere far behind her. The acoustics in the Barrens were notorious for confusing riders. She knew better than to look around and try to locate the direction and the route of the aircraft. The timing wasn't right for a patrol flight, so common sense said she was the hunted. Pausing to look would only slow her. Speed was vital, and Etrusca's Wall was still a kilometer in front of her, just over that first sharp rise and drop in the landscape.

The distant rumbling could be only a few hundred meters away, or four kilometers away, or even so distant she wouldn't see the skimmer for another half hour. Through the rumbling, she heard voices.

Men, calling her name. Men cursing. Men arguing. And through that, the thudding of gyphel feet when they crossed that patch of drum sand she had swerved around maybe thirty-five, forty minutes ago.

M'kar looked back and saw six riders, racing across the sand and patches of wind-swept stone, in a straight line between her and the clan house. Clan flags dragged out behind them in the wind of their passage. Did those indiferps think this unannounced race across the Barrens was part of the competition? Right this moment, they should be having breakfast with their Alliance teammates.

Whoever piloted that skimmer that hadn't become visible yet was probably a suitor too. Several suitors. Cheaters, with the help of someone in the house. Who was chasing her? High-born idiots who were raised to believe the rules applied to everyone else? Or someone who knew they would be disqualified for making contact with her, but came anyway, because they never wanted to win a bride in the first place?
~~~~~

Her pursuers had just shot her scheduled meeting with Jasper and Taggert to the netherhells. On the bright side, if she didn't have to fight for her life soon, she could legally disqualify all the suitors chasing her. At least she had something to look forward to at the end of what was shaping up to be a major disaster.

Knew there was a reason I chose not to tell Genys what I was planning. Let's hope we all have a good laugh when the dust settles, she remarked to Thyal, when she wasn't even sure he was listening.

She used her Talent to urge the gyphel to run faster than it ever had in its life and cursed her pursuers in every language she knew. M'kar barely exhausted a third of the vocabulary Treinna had taught her before she crossed the last stretch of flat Barrens and reached the upward slope of Etrusca's Wall and the iffy sanctuary of the surbda crater. The rattling scrape and thunder of the gyphel's feet on stone and sand grew louder, and she called for Barroo and all the dracs of the *Defender*. There was no use trying to be discrete now, and she could certainly use their offended feelings and utter loyalty to keep those interfering idiots away from her.

If all else failed, she would have the dracs shriek that dymcrait-repelling, peel-your-skin-off-with-your-own-fingernails note, if anyone tried to recite love poetry in her hearing.

Just steps away from the top of the slope, the gyphel reared up and nearly flipped over backward, shuddering in physical pain and terror that M'kar felt, through her loose touch on its mind. She tightened her physical and mental grip and borrowed the gyphel's senses. A note similar to the dracs' shrieks clawed at her mind. The sense of having sand injected under her skin overwhelmed her for a few heartbeats. Shuddering, fighting not to heave her scanty breakfast, M'kar pulled out of the gyphel's mind, soothing its terror and physical pain as she retreated. She wasn't going to get it to go down into the crater.

Hastily, she yanked the saddle-mounted knife free as she dismounted, and slashed at the saddle straps, rather than take the time to fight with the gyphel and remove her gear. The thin pad and three straps twisted and tumbled free as the beast leaped up and stumbled down the slope. M'kar knelt and yanked her gear free of the saddle, and looked back.

There it was now, just breaking the horizon: the black, ominous, squat shape of the skimmer. It clearly came from Rissor land, not from her clan. That was interesting. What did it tell her about who had betrayed her plans? She flinched when a happy trilling broke through the slowing rasp of her breath.

The dracs circled over her head, flying blithely out over the crater and back toward her. Not a flinch in their wing strokes, not a sound of protest. Didn't they hear what the gyphel heard? Or were they immune because they could create that note on an audible level? Scrubbing at her arms, which still felt like there was sand under her skin, she took a few deep breaths, focused, then asked Barroo and Infrenx if she could borrow their senses. Both dracs dropped out of the circling formation to land on her shoulders.

Are you getting anything from Infrenx? she asked Thyal, before sliding into the dracs' minds.

She's more focused on those riders catching up with you, he responded after a few moments.

M'kar groaned and turned to look. How had she forgotten about those idiots? She estimated they were maybe five minutes away from the base of the crater wall.

Nothing about the crater? No energy or sonic fields or something telling her to stay away?

Something, he said after a pause. *It's odd. Not strong enough to get her attention. I can't quite describe it.*

M'kar thanked both dracs and linked their minds to hers, like using two sensors pointed at slightly different angles, to get a better picture of the area being scanned. She had to fight the moment of disorientation that came from adjusting from her height to the height of the dracs, and multiplied images. Spreading her feet for more steady footing, she turned to look down into the crater. The dracs saw in infra-red, while picking up sonic readings. She flinched at the tickling sensation that spurted over her skin, as the sonic "peeps" the dracs emitted every few seconds bounced back at her, giving the density and location of rocks and sand within the barren landscape spread out before her. It looked like nothing more than a crater impact site. The infra-red vision showed her where the rising sun slowly crept across the sand and shards and pillars and piles of rubble, and the minerals absorbed and radiated heat in different ratios.

The other dracs slowed their circling while rising higher in the sky. A few gave the equivalent of knocking politely, trying to get her attention. When she widened her focus and let them join the link, they called her attention to the approaching riders. A few were curious why she was standing there, looking down into the empty landscape. Hadn't she wanted to get away from those men? Why wasn't she moving? M'kar snorted, nearly yanked out of the scanning link, when she got the distinct impression from several dracs that they wanted to dive bomb the riders and scare their gyphels and steal their decorations, like the dracs on Anwesta Station had attacked and stolen from the Maniterri invaders.

Obviously, while they don't have a racial memory, dracs do share memories they consider important, Thyal observed, when she shared that with him.

Or amusing.

True. I think I hear something. Maybe my link with Infrenx is stronger, despite the distance. If you pull out and just hear through Barroo, maybe that will make the sensation clearer.

You're right, M'kar said, after narrowing her focus to just her drac's senses. *It reminds me ... it reminds me of the hibernation mode of a teaching monitor. The old style that blanked the screen if you didn't do anything, didn't move on to the next lesson. That hum just on the edge of hearing, more felt in the hairs on your arm than heard.*

Or an old-style communication pickup.

A passive sensor array? M'kar suggested after a moment, trying to simply relax and let the impressions come to her. She had run into enough situations where trying to sharpen her focus and locate the source of the muted signal or sound or smell had served to push it away, or silence it.

Something is waiting in the crater?

That kind of makes sense ... but what? Or who? Her thoughts switched back to the old woman who had only ever been referred to as "our reclusive friend," by the elders of the sisterhood. Could she be there, hidden from sight? Could she have stepped sideways into another dimension, if Jasper's theories about the crater and the lost Nisandrian Gate were even partially valid? Was there warping of time, so the woman only experienced days when the world outside the crater experienced luns and years?

A queasy sensation tugged at the base of her throat when an idea she had no time or energy to consider right now tapped on her metaphorical shoulder and cleared its throat, asking for her attention.

We'll have to wait to answer that question later. If you don't flee now, Thyal said, *you'll never get away from your sweethearts.*

Very funny. M'kar checked her chrono on her tool wristband, hoping Jasper and Taggert hadn't launched the shuttle yet.

She needed to get rid of her pursuers before the shuttle arrived, or everything would be an even bigger mess than it was already. She wouldn't put it past some of her more muscle-brained suitors to attack the shuttle and crew, and claim they were defending her as well as Nisandros. The ones pursuing her for purely political reasons would probably attempt to blackmail her into choosing one of them, in payment for their silence. Then there was the threat of that approaching skimmer, probably loaded for war. She wouldn't put it past some of her suitors to be in the pay of the really nasty old prophets who had been shouting for her death since before her birth.

"I wanted some time by myself," she called down to the first riders dismounting at the base of the sloping outer wall.

Their gyphels refused to climb. Most of the riders struggled to control their mounts when the beasts clearly wanted to flee. Two looked up. Both were faces she did not want to see, today or any other day.

"It isn't safe," Ke'Niq called. "You have enemies."

"Your cousin is locked up safe and sound, to await judgment from the council."

"He has supporters, and there are all those old lunatics who want you dead." He took a few steps up the slope and paused to look back as other riders lost control of their gyphels, which shrieked and bucked and broke free in unison.

Nyx stepped up next to Ke'Niq and they shared a look that made M'kar cringe. They weren't working together now, were they?

"Ke'Jor has -- or had, now -- several of your servants in his pay, and they overheard you talking with your uncle about this morning, and have been spying on Desra and B'keerimo." Ke'Niq shrugged. "Fortunately, many servants like Desra better than most of your aunts or their sons, and they've been keeping watch, so we know who is spying. It's been kind of fun, actually, planting all sorts of false information, to trip --"

"Could you get on with it?" She tried not to watch the approaching skimmer, getting bigger and louder. "I kind of have a few deadlines. If you all start walking now, you should get back to the clan house before the really scorching part of the day hits."

"I overheard them telling Ke'Jor what they found out, and the messages he gave them, to pass on to his people." Nyx slipped and fell behind Ke'Niq a few steps as they continued climbing the slope to the top of the crater. "I still had my translator on, so I got it all recorded." He grinned like he had just won a Brain Blast tournament.

M'kar seriously contemplated, just for a moment, launching herself at the two of them, hitting each in the center of their breastbones with a foot, and sending them sliding back down the slope. What part of "go away" didn't they understand?

"Don't quote me that idiotic rule about healers being sworn to keep secret anything they overhear in the sick room," he continued, looking very proud of himself. "I was going to tell your uncle, but I ran into Ke'Niq and figured he had a right to know, and we decided to come out and help you." He hooked his thumb over his shoulder at the approaching skimmer. That gesture threw him off balance and he slid downward nearly a meter.

"This one was too loud." Ke'Niq shook his head, giving Nyx a look that would have had a seasoned warrior hunching his shoulders in embarrassment. "The others overheard, and they came after us." He gestured down the slope at the other riders who were arguing with each other and gesturing at the fleeing gyphels.

"It really isn't safe out here," Nyx said. "Why did you take the chance to come out all alone?"

"First of all, I'm not alone." She muffled a snort of laughter when Barroo chirped his "so there" response. Then she pointed upward at the other dracs, circling overhead, diving down and rising up again, and still not sensing whatever frightened the gyphels. "And second, I want to be alone because all of you are driving me to the point of violence."

That got a grin from Ke'Niq. For just a moment or two, he was the boy she had liked so much more than any of her cousins or uncles.

Nyx blanched, which showed he was finally getting some common sense. Too late.

Half the dracs dropped down to circle around her, coming close enough to whack Ke'Niq and Nyx's heads with their wings. Barroo sat up and hissed, and M'kar latched onto his senses.

"We're out of time."

The rumble-roar of the skimmer shot up in volume and the sandy rock under her feet vibrated.

"The safest place right now is in there." She hooked her thumb over her shoulder, into the crater. Both men opened their mouths, visibly ready to protest, then the skimmer shrieked as it arched upward, clearing the last ridge in the landscape, maybe two hundred meters away. M'kar sensed the cushion of air pressure pushed ahead of the oncoming craft.

She snatched up her packs and turned to race to the top of the crater and take that plunge down at a dead run. Instinct had her snarling silently, scolding herself for wasting all this time. If she had ignored her pursuers, she could have been deep into the crater by now, with no company but her dracs, and hidden by whatever warping of senses turned this place into the doorway into madness.

And she wouldn't have felt a bit of guilt leaving her unwanted suitors to face that skimmer.

The dracs trilled and spiraled down in clusters. A touch on their minds showed her something radiating from the oncoming skimmer, sonic waves that felt like ash being ground into their skin. So, whoever was in the skimmer knew enough about dracs to employ a weapon against them. That was fighting dirty.

Everybody back to the ship, she ordered, and pushed with her mind as hard as she could.

All the dracs vanished, except Barroo. He hunkered down on her shoulder and gave her a look that clearly said he wasn't happy, but he wasn't leaving her. She was grateful. Shielding him from the worst of that sonic field wouldn't use up that much energy or take much concentration, once she got started. Shielding nearly two dozen dracs who weren't bonded to her, however, would take too much out of her.

Do you want me -- Thyal began, just as Barroo chirped and rubbed her cheek with his head, clearly feeling relief.

Whatever you do, don't tell Genys. She started down the slope. *Just keep this quiet, between us, for now. Did Jasper --*

The skimmer roared into view, arching up, guided by the angle of the outer slope of the crater.

The roar scaled back to a purr. M'kar turned and slowed and stared.

The transport hung there, as if pinned to the sky,

"What's going on?" Nyx blurted, as he and Ke'Niq and the other four men stumbled down the slope and caught up with her.

M'kar mentally slapped herself for standing still. That was stupid. Especially with the skimmer hanging there in the air, directly overhead. Putting them in the perfect position to be squashed if it suddenly fell on them. She shook her head and backed away, keeping her gaze fixed on the craft.

"Why is the sky green?" She could almost laugh, but her head felt strange, and she had the awful feeling her brain was as frozen as that skimmer.

"Surbda crater," Ke'Niq said.

"Right." Then she realized Thyal had gone silent.

Thyal?

Nothing.

Oh, great …

Now there were two things that could interfere with their inexplicable mental bond. And maybe this just verified Jasper's theory about the craters being connected to Chutes, or maybe linked to that dratted missing Nisandrian Gate.

"What does that mean?" Nyx demanded.

"You explain." M'kar took one last look at the skimmer and turned around. She dug in her equipment pack and pulled out a handful of the small, specialized sensors Taggert and Jasper had created for today's expedition. The plan was for her to scatter the sensors around the crater, to gather up data that would then feed into the larger, hard-to-hide equipment they were bringing down in the shuttle.

At the edge of her perceptions, she heard Ke'Niq talking, and Nyx interrupting. She ignored them as she aimed for the first big upthrust pillar of rocks, intending to put a sensor on top, then go to the next cluster of pillars and do the same. The sooner the sensors were placed and activated, the more data Jasper and Taggert could play with.

Barroo crooned, sounding curious but not at all worried. M'kar reached up her free hand to rub his chest. What would she do without her little brown baby? He was an entirely trustworthy measuring rod for situations and conditions and the temperaments of people. If he wasn't worried, if he didn't sense anything dangerous, then the energy normally used for watching her back could be used on exploration.

"Huh." M'kar stopped and pulled out a recorder wand to get an image of the pillars in front of her. Were those the same ones she had seen when Ke'Jor crashed them here all those years ago?

"Those don't look right," Nyx said, coming to a stop next to her.

He was right, but she wasn't yet in a generous enough mood to agree with him. For one thing, "pillar" implied a solid piece of stone, or at least something symmetrical and balanced. These pillars were stacks of rocks that somehow stayed together, despite the visible unevenness. Some rocks looked way too thin to be holding up the huge, lumpy chunks resting on them. This could be the place where she had stepped into another dimension, if some of Jasper's theories were correct.

Barroo squealed and a whiplash of pain crackled from his mind to hers, a stabbing sensation through her head, in one ear and out the other. M'kar ducked and dropped the wand and reached up to touch her ear, fully expecting to have blood on her fingertips. Barroo hunkered down on her shoulder, urging her to run.

So she ran, and obeyed the aching need to look over her shoulder.

Behind them the purr of the paralyzed skimmer returned to a roar. The impression of it being pinned to the sky shattered. The sky cracked and crazed like pottery. The skimmer broke free and it shrieked higher a good hundred meters, as it finished its upward arc.

Then the roar died, the engines suddenly dead. The men behind her shrieked and cursed and bellowed and fled as the skimmer did a belly-whopper downward. M'kar ran and didn't waste her breath urging the others to run. If they couldn't figure it out, she was all for letting catastrophes weed out the idiots who hadn't learned to think for themselves. Maybe that ran against the principles of Enlo and how her parents raised her, but right now she didn't much care.

The impact of skimmer hitting sand lifted her off her feet. M'kar's feet kept moving with air underneath them. Any other time, she might have laughed, but in those few seconds there was no air whatsoever. A massive hand seemed to slap gently at her, sending her flying forward. Bodies flew past her, moving at two and three times her speed. She floated, bobbing slightly. She watched the men tumble forward, arms and legs pinwheeling.

Chapter Sixteen

The wand she had dropped went tumbling past her. M'kar reached for it, even though it was out of arm's reach. Against the law of physics, her momentum changed and she caught it between two fingers. The action of pressing it against her chest changed her direction. She turned on her side. Barroo leaped off her shoulder. His launch pushed her in another direction.

She slammed into the sand and bounced and rolled and kicked up clouds of sand and debris. She clutched her packs tight until the ride finally stopped and let go of her.

When she opened her eyes, clouds of dust and debris slowly settled as if the air was thicker than water. The pillars of rock were right in front of her, just a few meters away. She had to roll onto her back to look up at them. They wobbled and the individual pieces rocked in different directions and at different speeds, and some even spun around ... but the pillars didn't come apart. M'kar sat up and gingerly felt herself for damage, all the while watching those rocking, gyrating, should-have-disintegrated-but-didn't pillars. It was like they were somehow attached to each other, with invisible hinges or maybe elastic loops that kept them from pulling so far apart that they fell.

The delayed crash of the skimmer hit her in a wave of sound, metal crumpling and ceramic shattering as broken parts jammed up and disintegrated with clatters. M'kar sat still, only her hands moving as she scrambled to get hold of her sensor wand and turn it on the pillars.

Please, please, please, Enlo, let Jasper have found the right frequency to let the sensors work here, when nothing ever --

The sensor wand lit up, scrolling data across its small screen so rapidly she couldn't read most of it.

A strong magnetic field wrapped around the pillars. Several fields, according to the different colors on the screen, indicating intensity and polarity. They were like thick bands, wrapped tight around the pillar, one band going upward, and the other band, peeking out between the gaps of the first, spiraling down. They stretched, the colors shifting in intensity, as the pillars moved.

So who had bound the pillars together, and for what purpose?

Thyal, are you there yet?

Nothing.

Barroo settled down on her lap and tipped his head to one side, looking up at her, then turning to study the pillars, then up to her again.

"What do you see, what do you sense, Troublemaker?"

He chirped, and his eyes sparkled blue and green with excitement.

M'kar's head hurt a little when she reached with her mind to hitch a ride through Barroo's senses. She had a sensation of pressure, like when she dove too deep underwater, all the kilos of water weight trying to compress her.

Then she forgot all that. Swirls of colors filled her eyes, hung like a gossamer sheet blowing in a gentle breeze between the two pillars. The colors spun outward from the sheet, visibly evaporating in the air. Sometimes they stayed together in long streamers and twirled and knotted and wrapped around chunks of rock littering a rough sort of pathway up to the pillars.

"What does it do?" she murmured. "What else do you see that I'm not picking up yet?"

Barroo chirped and lifted off from her lap. He arched upward and turned a backward somersault, lightly slapping the top of her head with his tail before darting away. Straight at the pillars.

He flew between the pillars.

And vanished.

"Barroo!"

She tore herself free of the slow, sucking, languid sensation by the force of her shout. M'kar snatched up her sensor wand and ran, digging up clods of sand and clay-sticky soil underneath, toward the pillars.

Barroo reappeared. Chortling, he dug his talons into her shoulder and wrapped his tail around her neck and pulled her forward, between the pillars.

M'kar fell, hitting the ground on her knees and sliding, down a short slope lined with juicy leaves. The crushed green perfume enveloped her senses and washed away the dryness of the sand that had filled her mouth and eyes and coated her skin. At the bottom of the short slope, maybe four meters, she slid to a stop and let herself fall onto her side as she looked back the way she had come.

"No, no, no, no ..."

Trembling, she could only stare.

It was simply blackness, shimmering with every color for just a moment, then seeming to fade away so all the thick, humid jungle surrounding it was visible, then darkening again. It was tall, stretching up to the sky, and then pulsing down so it was barely higher than her head, then massive again. It was a crackling yet soft sheet of light, giving an impression of more density than a dozen black holes slapped together. It hummed, tickling along her nerves, yet deafened her a moment later with silence that spoke of killing cold combined with the scorching of a star.

It was a Gate, as artists and visionaries had imagined the dark, dead, dull, impenetrable things should be when they were alive and awake and functioning.

Alive and awake and ...

M'kar swallowed hard, terrified by the thousands of theories she had heard, the arguments and philosophical ramblings and petty disagreements and even malice that the most radical Gate scientists flung at each other in the name of the pursuit of the truth. There was no way to prove their theories true or false, because the Gates were so utterly quiet, they were considered asleep.

This Gate was awake.

More important, it was *aware*. The same instinct and sense of "This is the way it is, don't fight it," that had settled in her when her psionic Talent woke up, told her so. M'kar knew better than to doubt that instinct.

This Gate was alive, just as some of the deepest thinkers had postulated. It was a living being, aware because of the immense power invested in creating it. She felt as puny and worthless as she would have felt standing -- not standing, but falling, trembling -- in the presence of one of Enlo's bright spirits.

Perhaps Gates were bright spirits?

But how could Gates be bright spirits, if there were sleeping, quiet, waiting Gates scattered through the known universe, on every Human planet? Bright spirits were just that: spirits. Awareness mixed with energy. Not flesh or any other material being. Bright spirits didn't need to be corporeal to serve Enlo. So how could a Gate be a bright spirit?

Barroo chortled and settled down on her shoulder. He trilled and bobbed his head and looked all around. He wanted to go exploring, and he was very proud of himself.

A shudder took her. She hunched her shoulders and wrapped her arms around herself and didn't care if she looked like an idiot. There were no people to see her, so what did it matter?

She had gone through a Gate.

Without a ship. Without being guided or protected by a Gatekeeper.

Maybe ... this was the world the Gatekeepers had vanished to, when they finished rescuing all the Human races and tribes and genotypes from the cataclysm that threatened Core?

"Barroo, can you sense any other minds around here? Any people?" M'kar laughed at herself for that. What rule was there that the Gatekeepers had to be *people*, as she knew people?

Her brown drac chirped at her and looked around. No response to her question, not even that confused, thinking look when he tipped his head back and forth and blinked as he tried to understand what she had said or imaged to him. Maybe the lack of response meant there were no people? No other minds?

Maybe no other living things, besides plants? While there was a sense of a breeze fluttering leaves far overhead, there was no sense of animals or even insects. Just the plants. The light was green because so much lush plant life stood between her and the sky.

"Enlo ... help?"

She struggled to her feet. Simply standing made her inner ear turn cartwheels, so she felt like she might fall off the edge of the planet if she wasn't careful. M'kar spread her legs for secure footing and stood as still as she could, taking deep breaths and fighting for a sense of balance.

"Get hold of yourself. You are a lieutenant in the Fleet. So what if you're not a Gate technician or astrocartographer or whatever would be able to handle a meeting with the Gatekeepers?" M'kar took another deep breath, and this time she thought she smelled sweet, fresh water. Her heart finally slowed down to a normal pace, so it wasn't rattling in her ears. Maybe she could hear the trickle of water? A drink would help settle her. "This is the chance of a lifetime, and you are going to do your duty as an officer of the best E&D vessel in the Fleet." A snort escaped her. "Let's see Captain Shryne and her crew top this one."

Taking small steps, arms spread to help her keep her balance, she followed the sound of water. In moments, the thick walls of leaves bigger than her head parted, and she saw the stream. She followed it with her eyes, and discovered a stairstep series of pools, spilling downward for several meters.

"Is it safe?" she asked Barroo.

He blinked and looked at her. Looked at the water. Then he hopped off her shoulder and fluttered down to the pool just above where she stood. He chortled and bent his head and drank. Then another chortle and dove in, splashing.

"Oh, thank you very much. Just mess up the water that I'm going to drink." It didn't matter. She got on her knees and bent down and scooped up water from a pool that trickled into Barroo's pool. The water was cool and tasted green and silver. M'kar didn't wonder until later, when she shared her memories and impressions with Thyal, why her senses crossed over. Colors had tastes. It reminded her of going through Chutes, where the physical senses were turned inside out.

"*Das'qua*," she muttered, as the enormity of what had happened hit her again, so she almost toppled forward into the pool. "I went through a Gate. Chutes are related to Gates. At least, this might be proof, but ... Stupid, stupid, stupid." She struggled to her feet and hurried back the way she had come, swaying and slipping and sliding sideways into trees because her inner ear kept sloshing and telling her she wasn't standing upright. She kept trying to correct and compensate when she didn't need to. She wiped the sweet water off her face, and nearly ran into a tree, distracted for a few steps by the discovery that the water tingled.

"Thank you, Enlo," she whispered, as she burst into the clearing and nearly tripped over the sensors and the two packs she had dropped when she slid to a stop. Tears touched her eyes as she tipped her head back and looked up at the Gate.

It looked semi-transparent and seemed to have solidified a little bit. At least it no longer softly throbbed and changed density and size and colors. It didn't vanish entirely and make her think she had hallucinated.

Of course, she had landed in a surbda crater, where hallucinations were standard practice. For all she knew, she was kneeling where she had fallen in the sand, suffering a hallucination so strong she thought she had moved and drank sweet water and was right this moment staring at an active, live, aware, awake Gate. The dream of every Gate technician and starship captain in the Fleet, and the goal of the council that had formed the Alliance.

"Enlo … please don't let me be going insane." M'kar went to her knees and opened her bag of provisions. She had packed enough food for a day of exploring and wandering. Enough food to share with the dracs when she felt safe enough to call them down to help her explore. More important, she had a medical kit, and a good, field-level medical scanner. Maybe she didn't understand all the readings the equipment would give her, but she could at least check herself to make sure she hadn't suffered some injury, attacked by some energy wave that fried her brains.

If she wasn't hallucinating the equipment working …

"Probably all those prophets and visionaries went insane just doubting themselves." She gripped the medical scanner a moment, silently prayed for protection, and turned it on.

The physical stresses and strains it detected in her body made perfect sense. Surely if this was a hallucination, she would imagine herself in perfectly normal shape? She opened a packet of dried meat, and ended up having to open three, because Barroo wanted his share. M'kar choked on the first mouthful, because even though she expected the strong, hot Nisandrian spices, she hadn't really been ready for them. She made a mental note to bring a whole crate of Nisandrian spices up to the ship, because obviously the spices her parents paid exorbitant prices for were either diluted or had faded from age by the time they reached the family kitchen on Le'anka.

She had brought two waterskins, but that water tasted flat, with a bitter aftertaste. Had that happened through Gate travel, something essential leached from the water, or was it truly that bad, compared to the freshness and sweetness of this world? M'kar spent a good twenty minutes using the different sensors on the water in her waterskins and comparing it with the water from the cascading pools.

"Maybe this is what Neoma meant when she talked about living water coming from Enlo's Rest?" she asked Barroo, after filling her waterskins with the Gate world's water, and then drinking until her stomach almost sloshed from fullness.

Then like a blow between the eyes, she realized she had been wasting time.

Maybe time was strange here, elongated, and no time at all had passed on Nisandros?

"No, with my luck ... think, you idiot. Think! How many days passed when you thought you had only been there a few hours, when that idiot crashed the aircar?" M'kar got to her feet and hurried back to the clearing where she had first landed. Another check -- the Gate was unchanged since the last time she had seen it.

Like it was waiting for her to do something?

"No, no, no, no, please don't be asleep now," she muttered, and dug the sensors out of the pack again. What was wrong with her that she couldn't seem to keep her duty clear in her head for more than a few minutes at a time? "Okay, Gate, let's see what we can learn about you before we ..." She swallowed hard, fighting down the first real, solid sense of panic that had washed over her since arriving here. Wherever *here* was. *We can go home. Barroo went through and came back, and he brought me through, so he can bring me back. Right?* She looked up, relieved to find Barroo hovering over her head, his eyes that reassuring swirl of happy blues. "Can you take us home -- well, not home, but back to the crater?"

Barroo chirped and dove down for a landing on her shoulder. He bobbed his head several times and nuzzled her cheek.

"I trust you. Let's get some scientific work done and earn my pay for the next couple luns and then ... I guess we need to go back." M'kar had no idea of how much time had passed here, much less back on Nisandros.

The Gate, she discovered quickly, was unwilling to give up any of its secrets. Just like decades of studying the sleeping Gates on every planet in the Alliance had yielded no useable scientific data, this one also seemed impervious to sensors. The sensors admitted there was a solid object, but the measurements of size varied by a good forty percent in both directions, never stabilizing no matter how long she held them against the sometimes black, sometimes starry, sometimes gossamer surface. Most of the time, M'kar almost couldn't feel it, though there was definitely a stopping point when she couldn't move the sensors any farther forward. She couldn't get any more energy readings than a vague measurement of low-level radiation, in the range a Human body would generate. No mineral or metallic readings. No temperature readings. She knew it was useless to try to cut or chip or even burn off samples to study. Not that she had anything stronger than the knives she had brought with her. New technology had been developed in the fruitless effort to pierce the surface of Gates, to take samples for analysis.

Essentially, M'kar had managed to do little more than prove this was indeed a Gate like all the other Gates found in the Alliance. Except in one important detail: this Gate was functioning.

At least, it had been functioning when she came through.

The light hadn't changed in all the time she had been here. For all she knew, no time had passed. Did that mean there would be no night? Even if night did fall, she wasn't sure how she would be able to see the stars through all this heavy foliage. Recording the night sky to study the stars later and try to locate this planet was impossible. It would have been fun to see the ship's astrocartographers drive themselves frantic, trying to locate this planet by the view of the stars from dirtside. Maybe on her next visit, if she could come back, she would stay long enough to get those images.

She needed to go back to Nisandros before she could plan her next visit.

"All right, Troublemaker," she whispered, when there was nothing left to do but find something to ease the low-grade ache throbbing at the back of her neck. "I think it's time to go home." She flinched. Nisandros wasn't home. The *Defender* was. "Can you take us back where we started?"

Barroo tipped his head from side to side, studying her face, unblinking, for what felt too long a time. Had she confused him? Was this place affecting him? Then the little brown drac chirped and nuzzled her cheek before leaping off her shoulder and heading for the Gate. She ran after him, remembering how he had grabbed hold of her just before she touched that shimmering gossamer wall of rainbows. There were no rainbows or shimmers here, however. Just that black wall that seemed suddenly too solid. M'kar closed her eyes and braced to hit it hard enough to break something. Barroo trilled and slammed into her shoulder and dug his talons in.

Heat and blowing sand and the shouts of men and the screams of tortured machinery wrapped around her, muffled somehow. M'kar opened her eyes as she stumbled a few steps through a shadowy haze. Sparks stung her bare skin and burned her eyes, so she gasped and flung up her hands to defend herself.

All the ship's dracs swirled around her, caroling excitement and questions and then concern for her. She went to her knees as the dracs surrounded her, some hitting the sand and pebbly ground around her, others landing to catch hold of her jacket and pants. Infrenx landed on her other shoulder and proceeded to scold Barroo at a high pitch that made M'kar fear her ears would start bleeding in another moment.

"Stop that! Right now!" She pressed her hands over her ears, nearly knocking both dracs off her shoulders.

The drac cries faded into a few chirps and trills, and then silence.

The men around her had fallen silent also. The only sounds were the moans of the wind wrapping around the pillars, and the crackles and groans and clatters as the skimmer continued dying. Everyone was watching her, weren't they? And there she sat, huddled on the ground with her hands pressed over her ears like a child.

Now would be a really good time for all of you to learn to work together and teleport people and get me out of here.

No response from the dracs.

She opened one eye. Her head was bowed enough all she saw were a few sets of feet. By the angle, yes, their owners faced her. M'kar muffled a sigh and opened the other eye and sat up straight. At least, as straight as she could. She ached all over and her head throbbed twice as much.

"Are you all right?" Nyx pushed his way through the other men and dug through his medical pack, to pull out a scanner wand.

"Why?"

"You're glowing like you were bathed in ..." He shrugged. "Something phosphorescent. Or you ate something bio-luminescent?"

M'kar held out her hands. She pulled up her sleeves. She saw no glow coming from her skin. Either she would have to take his word for it, or he was hallucinating. Which made sense, since they were in a surbda crater.

"What do the rest of you see?"

"You're glowing," Ke'Niq said.

"Well ... maybe that's what happens when you go through a Gate." She focused on the other dracs, asking what they saw. The older dracs gave her tiny glimpses through their eyes. A soft, rainbow shimmer moved over her bare skin, and wove streaks through her hair. The younger dracs didn't see anything. That was something to put aside and investigate later.

"A Gate?" He snorted. "We don't have a Gate on Nisandros."

"Have you studied Gates?"

"No." His face twisted for a moment, so he looked too much like Ke'Jor. "Unlike you, the rest of us haven't been able to leave the planet and travel the universe."

"Well, I have. Studied Gates." She levered herself to her feet. "Theory, anyway. Maybe Chutes are Gates without any controls rigged to them."

"What does that have to do with us?" a man asked from the back of the group gathering around them. From the darkening bruises on his face, a torn shirt, and bloodstains on his clothes, he had been chasing them in the skimmer. Which meant he was most likely an enemy.

"Nisandros messed up big-time." She gestured at the pillars behind her. "That is probably what's left of Nisandros's Gate. Probably all the surbda craters, surrounded by rings of rubble, are what we got when someone managed to shatter our Gate. Only Nisandrians are stupid enough to destroy a Gate."

A few of the men facing her grinned and nodded or made sounds like they were proud of that distinction. M'kar marked them as either mentally damaged from the crash, the effects of the crater hit them especially hard, or they were just mentally deficient to start with.

"Maybe someone wanted to stop the Gatekeepers from coming back through to check on them and slap them around for breaking the rules. Doesn't matter," she hurried on, when several opened their mouths, most likely to argue with her. "You can't destroy a Gate, just change its shape. Those pillars still work as a Gate."

"You're crazy." Ke'Niq's face twisted in a sneer, and now he even sounded like Ke'Jor. "Your mixed blood or just living away from Nisandros or --"

M'kar leaped and grabbed him by the throat and pushed hard enough to make him stumble backward. He was taller than her, and a good twenty kilos heavier, but with her fury, maybe aided by whatever made her glow, she kept going. Barroo and five other dracs grabbed hold of her and Ke'Niq as they hurtled through the darkening rainbow gossamer wall.

"Gate," M'kar spat as they stepped through a star-shot, stinging haze.

This world was predominantly blue and green, and stars filled the dome of the sky, multiple colors, some of them close enough to see rings around them in dark glowing purple and red. The air was thick in her mouth. A sensation like bubbles zinged from her lungs through her blood. The zinging traveled to her heart, and raced with razor-sharp cold pulses to her extremities.

A vast plain spread out around them in all directions. Ke'Niq gasped and dropped to his knees, struggling to breathe. Maybe he didn't like the air? She liked it just fine. All her bruises from that fall in the sand vanished, scrubbed out of her flesh with another inhalation of that zinging, thick air.

"What do you the rest of you think?"

The dracs answered her in a trilling chorus of notes and chords she had never heard them make before. They glowed in all their colors and spiraled upward, as if they could reach for the stars and touch them. Barroo chortled and flew in circles over her head, upside down.

"What is this place?" Ke'Niq wheezed.

"Obviously some place where the Gatekeepers didn't want to drop Humans."

"With good reason," a woman said. "You'd better take him back before he suffocates. Males don't last very long here." She faded out of the darkness, a soft, rainbow-tinted glow emanating from her. It grew stronger with every heartbeat, like turning up a lamp.

She spoke High Nisandrian. The language of the oldest records. M'kar shuddered, seeing the scars around the woman's eyes and mouth, highlighted with multiple small, thin lines of blue.

The woman from her crash-landing visit when she was eight years old. The reclusive friend of the sisterhood.

Could she be ...?

"Go," she said, as M'kar struggled to put words to the thoughts that didn't want to penetrate the zinging in her blood. "I'll be right behind you."

M'kar called to the dracs, who had flown far enough away they were just tiny glowing dots of color, weaving intricate patterns in the sky. All but for Barroo, who crooned and dropped down to hover in front of the woman and give her one of his endearing doggy smiles.

Ke'Niq yowled when the woman caught hold of his upper arm and yanked him to his feet with the ease of picking up dirty clothes from the floor. The glow grew stronger where her fingers touched his flesh. The dracs popped back in and surrounded them. M'kar took one last breath of the zinging air and leaped into the Gate's surface.

This time it did feel like she slammed into a solid wall. Before she could wince or cry out in pain, they stumbled back to the sandy floor of the crater and out from between the pillars.

Several men bellowed in outright fear and ran as far as their battered, bloody condition would allow. Others hurried forward, wide-eyed, shaking a little, to jerk Ke'Niq out of M'kar's and the woman's grip.

"Etrusca?" M'kar blurted, her brain finally breaking through the barrier.

Chapter Seventeen

"Well, a child who knows her history." Etrusca smiled, which did odd things to the scars and tattoos around her mouth and eyes.

"I took your vows and your marks." M'kar touched the lines at her eyes, then laughed and gestured at the men huddled on the ground or standing, stupefied, staring in wonder or on the verge of terror. Nyx just looked confused. "Suitors. They ignored the warning from my marks."

"Fools." Etrusca laughed, her head tilted back, and took deep breaths of the dry, warm air. "Enlo shows me you are already bound to another in all the ways that matter."

"Excuse me, ma'am?" Nyx stepped forward. "Where did you come from? M'kar and Ke'Niq were just gone for maybe twenty, thirty seconds. Where did they go, and where did they find you, and why are you glowing like that?"

"Like this?" Etrusca held up her hands. Power swirled around her fingers, rainbow streaks with star-shot blackness around their edges. "Dwell long enough in the vastness between the worlds, listening to the echoes of Enlo's voice as he commands all creation into being ... you will soak up a little of that power, even undeserving."

"Through there?" another man said, gesturing at the pillars.

"How come it was different, the second time I went through?" M'kar moved over to block the doorway, even knowing she couldn't stop more than one or two men from going between the pillars. Something in their eyes, the sudden intensity radiating from them, chilled her.

"When the vortex was broken centuries ago, the focus was shattered." Etrusca stepped forward, addressing the watchful men. "There is no anchor place, and the power of the vortex reaches out constantly, trying to lock onto the vortices on other worlds, one after another. Again and again, constantly seeking and never finding wholeness."

"How many worlds are there?" Ke'Niq sounded like he had swallowed sand. He stayed seated, but his color looked better.

M'kar didn't like the way he looked at the doorway. As if it could hold all the most important answers in life.

Thyal, can you hear me? She had to at least keep trying to reach him through their link.

Silence.

Etrusca studied Ke'Niq's face for a long, silent moment. "I have not counted in many years."

"Empty worlds, like the one where you were trapped?"

"Child, I was not trapped." She smiled, and M'kar made note of those who shivered and those who looked offended or angry, and the few who smiled, either in idiocy or wonder.

"We call the vortices Gates," M'kar offered. "All that we've ever found have been asleep, or maybe even dead. We all have legends of how we were brought to our different worlds by the Gatekeepers. No one can agree on the reasons, if it was to save the Human race or scatter it to punish it. Do you know? Have you met the Gatekeepers, and have they told you?"

"Other than the fools who try to follow me inside, or the unlucky who have not yet learned to listen to Enlo's voice, who stumble through the portals on this world ..." Etrusca shrugged and spread her arms, as if to encompass the entire planet. "I have been alone. Finally able to hear Enlo's voice and learn and be healed. My life's duty has been to share wisdom, and seek eyes that clearly see, ears that clearly hear, and hearts born to obey."

"My great-grandfather said he has met you many times."

"Ah, and who is he?"

"Aquid of Ba'e'do'stra."

"Yes, of course, I thought I caught the scent of his spirit, clinging to you." She laughed, and it was a warm, welcoming sound. Not touched with the scorn that she gave the men gathered around them. "There is another scent in your spirit ..." She stepped over and clasped M'kar's shoulders and looked deep into her eyes. "A scent of other worlds, of many friends and growing wisdom, and gifts. These little ones are fond of you, but this one." Her eyes crinkled with amusement as she gestured at Barroo, who leaped up from the place on the sand where he had settled, with the other dracs. "This one loves you with the complete adoration and trust we owe Enlo."

"What about the Ancestors?" The man who asked was from the skimmer. "What do they say? Shouldn't we obey them?"

"The Ancestors?" Etrusca's lip curled up in scorn. "I am an Ancestor. Are any of you bowing down in worship of me? No, children, the Ancestors are not to be listened to, and not to be obeyed. Not if they tell you to ignore Enlo's words. The Ancestors broke the anchor point and scattered its pieces all over the planet, for the sake of control, of power, to tell everyone else what to do and what to think. They cut themselves off from the other worlds, and from the ones who brought us here and reminded us of Enlo's teachings before they moved onward and outward."

"The other surbda craters are portals too?" M'kar shuddered as some theories snapped into place in her mind. Where was Taggert when he needed to be here to hear all this? "There are stories of you appearing in the other craters. You can go to all those other places, because the pieces of the broken Gate -- the broken vortex -- they link all together?"

"Indeed, and that violation of Enlo's gift brought madness. They thought to hear each other, watch each other, control each other, but only earned madness. Those fools decided they heard voices from beyond the grave. They only heard the senseless babble of many voices, speaking all at once, each trying to drown out the other." She tipped her head back and gestured at the pillars. "This is all that is left, with enough energy to reach to other worlds, but there is no control, no consistency or anchor. "

"So we can go to hundreds of worlds, but we won't know where we're going until we get there? And no one can follow us?" Ke'Niq asked. "How long after someone steps through does a door close?"

"There is no way of knowing. Those who thought to chase me became lost through their own foolish choices. Do not follow that dream I see in your eyes, child. It is a fool's selfish arrogance."

Ke'Niq sneered, but he said nothing. He didn't need to.

"Come." Etrusca beckoned to M'kar. The dracs leaped up instantly and swarmed around them.

Ke'Niq and several others shouted and scrambled to follow, as the two stepped through the gossamer wall between the pillars. They stepped out almost immediately into what looked like the same place. But there were no men, no crashed skimmer.

"We're still on Nisandros?" M'kar guessed. "Another crater?"

"Clever child." Etrusca patted her hand, then turned, nearly tugging M'kar off her feet. "Ask your friends how many follow us. They can see and hear into the vortex."

"How do you know that?"

"Learning to hear and see Enlo everywhere grants much knowledge, and over time, wisdom as well."

M'kar asked the dracs. Her head ached a little from the effort. All the benefits of breathing that zinging air had faded. For a moment, she thought about asking Etrusca if they could go back to that world and recharge. "All but four are following us. Nyx and the worst injured stayed behind."

"Good. We shall lead those selfish children on a merry chase, and then ..."

"What?" M'kar clutched at Etrusca's arm as they stood and faced the pillars of pieces that rippled with gossamer light. Waiting for what? For their pursuers to come out? Or something else? Such sadness wrinkled the woman's face for a moment, it made her ache deep inside.

"Taking apart the frame of the doorway will not be so hard, but keeping it apart, keeping it from regaining its shape ..." Etrusca shook her head. "It must be denied them."

"How many pieces of the pillars do we need to get away, and keep away, and how far away?"

Etrusca had no time to answer. The men stumbled and staggered and leaped out of the shimmer of light between the two pillars, one after another. In those few seconds while they fought to regain their balance or their breath, or struggled with heaves, the two women tightened their grip on each other's arms. M'kar called the dracs to her as they plowed through the men and back through the energy, to another portal in another surbda crater.

They repeated the process, until she got too dizzy to count, too breathless, and her head pounded with an odd combination of exhaustion and buzzing, zinging energy. Each time, it took longer for their pursuers to follow them. And then, every three or four passes between the pillars, one less man staggered out of the wall of light.

"We're losing them," M'kar said, as they clung to each other and fought for balance and air. "Is that what we wanted to do?"

"I had hoped ... with the strain of so many going through, again and again, perhaps we would drain enough energy we could knock the frame over. Maybe pull the pieces far enough apart they do not rejoin. We cannot allow those greedy children a chance to go to other worlds and pillage them."

"Maybe we should take the pieces to other worlds," M'kar said.

Then she got an idea.

The next time they came out of the light, she tugged her arm free of Etrusca and stumbled up the slope of the crater, to the top. It was only half the height of Etrusca's Wall.

Thyal, can you hear me?

No response.

She took ten steps down the outside slope.

Thyal?

Still silence.

Ten more steps, until she was nearly off the slope. Now she had a better idea of what energies generated the interference with equipment. Breathing was easier, as if the energy that swirled among all the broken pieces of the Gate had been pulled from her own flesh.

Thyal?

What's wrong? His voice clattered inside her head for a moment. *I'm getting all sorts of chaotic impressions from you. Where have you been for the last ten hours? They're worried enough they called up to Genys.*

I'll explain later. Where are Jasper and Taggert? Did they launch? How soon until they can meet me at the crater? Do they have the ability to set up isolation fields around big chunks of stone? Whatever it takes to cut off energy and communication and ... I don't know. We just need to keep something from regaining cohesion. And keep it silent. I don't care how many regulations you have to break, don't let anyone know what we're doing. Please, Thyal, you have to trust me on this.

Silence.

Her head throbbed hard enough she pressed her fists against her temples to fight the pressure, the sense her skull would split open.

Always, Thyal said, and a warm surge of concern pulsed through their link, soothing the exhausted ache from her chest, outward. *The shuttle has been hovering, waiting for your call. Jasper said he can be there in less than half an hour.*

M'kar returned to Etrusca before the last handful of their most determined pursuers came out of the wall of light.

"Can we go back to our starting point? Do you have that kind of control?"

"Yes." Etrusca's eyes narrowed for a moment, then her tense, weary expression relaxed and she patted M'kar's arm. "Enlo bless you, child. I think your plan will work. And the wonder is that all the portals are joined. They are all mirrors of the first. Remove one, and all are removed." They took a deep breath, and as Ke'Niq and the last four pursuers came through the light, they pushed past them and went back in.

"How do you know what my plan is?" M'kar asked, as they came out.

The dracs trilled weary relief and settled down on the trampled sand around them.

"Are you all right?" Nyx hurried away from the side of a prone man.

"How long have we been gone?" She nearly laughed when he gave her a confused look. Yes, it probably was a ridiculous question.

"Maybe ten, fifteen minutes. I'm not sure."

"How long do you think it's been since the skimmer crashed?"

He turned his wrist to check his chrono, frowned, and tapped it. "I'm not sure. This hasn't ticked over a single second since we got here. It feels like maybe two hours at the most."

"Thyal says we've been missing ten hours. So if we're lucky ..." M'kar's knees buckled at the mere thought of climbing that ridge again, to get out of the interference field of the broken Gate pieces.

Fortunately, she could send the ship's dracs to look, with instructions to come back to her when the shuttle appeared. Even with her suspicions about the passage of time outside the crater, she flinched when the dracs flew back to her and reported that the shuttle had arrived. She noted that while they could teleport inside the crater, they couldn't teleport into the crater or out of it.

"Are you ... is it safe for you to step out of the crater, out of the energy field of the Gate?" she asked Etrusca, as the two of them, with Nyx following, started the climb up the slope of the crater wall.

"Do you mean, will I be hurt by dismantling the frame?" Etrusca shook her head. "I know not. But do not worry for me, child. I have lived long enough ... death does not frighten me. I know where my soul belongs, and who holds it safely for eternity."

The sight of the shuttle waiting at the foot of the crater wall was the most beautiful thing she had seen since stumbling through to the first Gate world. Jasper and Taggert ran to meet her while their team kept working, hauling equipment out of the shuttle. M'kar eyed the shuttle, hoping she was right and they had brought the biggest one, with enough cargo space to fit all the pieces of the Gate inside, and room to spare. What had Jasper been planning to do? Take samples, huge samples, back up to the ship? From every surbda crater?

She thanked Enlo that Jasper was a practical man who planned for big successes.

M'kar didn't have time to explain, only outline the plan. Her urgency was clear enough that the two men just gave each other a look, then got to work, calling for their team. Jasper and Taggert ignored everything and everyone else, once they got inside the crater and readings spilled through their equipment. They were nearly incoherent with fascination over all the data caught by their custom-made, one-of-a-kind sensors, outside the crater and then inside. M'kar gave them ten minutes to gabble incoherent engineer's talk at each other, then she pointed at the pillars, and the dracs screamed for attention.

Most of the blocks had to be pulled apart, wrapped in energy dampening fields or isolation fields or whatever they could come up with, and hauled away from the base blocks before the pillars reassembled themselves. No one questioned when she and Etrusca said the pillars could indeed reassemble themselves.

More important, they came up with simple solutions that worked.

They got the pillars knocked apart before the last exhausted stragglers could come back through. M'kar had a few queasy moments, when she wondered about all the men who had pursued them from one crater to another, the numbers slowly depleting. Had they become lost forever in the energy between worlds? Or had they simply become too tired to keep going, and had fallen one or two at a time, in the craters? Would removing enough of the parts of the pillars negate or disperse the energy that warped time and perception?

"Okay," Jasper said, when they had hauled the pieces out of the crater and loaded them into the shuttle. "What sort of trouble are we in?"

"And which of our theories did we prove or shatter?" Taggert asked, staggering up to join them, grinning like a madman, and sweating like a waterfall.

"It all rests on me. Let me handle my clan." M'kar gladly sat down on the rocky ground outside the crater. All she wanted to do was curl up in her own bed in her own cabin and sleep for a dec. After gorging on an entire roasted wacuzu, and sweet-spice bread and enough mezipa to explode. Maybe that was one of the biggest problems with time travel, so no one was able to attempt it? The energy drain?

"Don't worry, those chunks of rock are locked away good and tight, so none of that weird energy leaks out and messes with the shuttle and the ship. I hope." Jasper rolled his eyes. "The chrono in the shuttle says we landed four hours ago, but the personal chronos each of us are wearing are all messed up, the more time we spent in that crater. We're going to have half the Academy and all the Gate technicians and theorists going nuts, once we turn over whatever we learn on the voyage back to Le'anka. What did we just mess with? I know you told us about the sensory warping and time differentials, but ..." He grinned and whistled long and low. "Was all this here when your ancestors arrived, or did they make it?"

"Oh, they made it." M'kar wished she was more awake, so she could enjoy this moment. She wished she had something to record his reaction, because she knew it would be priceless. "Those chunks of rock are pieces of a Gate that my ancestors broke."

He just looked at her. Blinked a few times. Pursed his lips in thought for a moment or two. Then he took a deep breath and looked to Taggert, whose grin was slowly fading under a mixture of wonder and terror and disbelief.

"Say that again?"

So M'kar did.

"So, Jasper ... is it safe, with all the isolation fields and blocking tech we have in place?" Taggert asked, after a dozen rabbity twitches of his nose. "I mean, safe to take up to the ship? And travel with it?"

"As safe as I can make it. Considering we don't have the equipment to read even a tenth of the energies that thing is giving off, and the evidence we've already had about how it messes with time, or at least the awareness of time and ..." Jasper sighed. "Trust me, if I had any doubt, I would not take that thing up to the ship and have it within ten light years of my wife and daughter."

"Good enough for me," he said after a few more seconds of thought. "But M'kar has to tell the captain what we've got here."

"I will. Just not now. I need to clean things up down here before I go up to the ship." M'kar wished with every fragment of her aching, exhausted body and soul that she could ride up to the ship with them, even if she had to sit on top of that questionable cargo.

"So ..." He smirked a little. "Any closer to deciding who the lucky man is?"

M'kar had no idea what expression she wore, but Taggert went ashen, so it must have been fierce.

"Have no fear," Etrusca said. "I will speak with your elders, and I will call on the sisterhood to support you. Your way will be smoothed to allow you to return to your ship and your family." She patted M'kar's shoulder and turned to go back up the slope of the barrier wall of the crater.

"You mind telling us who that is?" Jasper said.

Etrusca had spoken in High Nisandrian, so they hadn't understood her. M'kar wondered for the first time how her suitors, and especially Nyx, had understood Etrusca. She doubted any of those men had ever spent the time to study the ancient language. Maybe that was part of the warping inside the craters, merging their minds to understand each other? Would the effect continue, now that the link between the surbda craters had been broken by the removal of the pieces of the pillars?

That was something for the sisterhood to study and decide. She was too tired, with too many other problems that would be demanding her attention far too soon.

"One of the few noble bloods who isn't a possible ancestor," M'kar said, after discarding a handful of other responses.

"Meaning?"

"She's been traveling in and out of the doorways in time created by that broken Gate and creating a lot of legends over the last few centuries."

"Uh huh …" Jasper frowned in concentration, watching Etrusca climb to the top of the wall. "That's probably something you need to put in your report to hand over to whoever gets to work on this new puzzle."

Her head hurt, but in a muffled, empty kind of way, when M'kar called the scattered gyphel to come back. Something had changed. They weren't terrified now. Either something in the crashed skimmer had scattered the gyphel, or the energy and resonances coming from inside the crater had changed. Maybe they were gone, rather than toned down? Did she really care? All that mattered was that they wouldn't have to walk back to the clan house, as exhausted or injured as they all were. It would take far too long in the growing chill of night.

They didn't talk much on the ride, which was necessarily slow because none of them had the energy to guide the gyphel. The creatures had a tendency to go crooked when they went faster than a leisurely trot. Despite that, they had a plan and an explanation when they reached the gates of the clan house. Most important was that Nyx had been sworn to silence, with implied threats. Etrusca would meet with Desra, who would send for the elders of the sisterhood, and all the mad men and women she had talked with and taught over the years. They would decide how to explain to the clan heads the danger that had been sleeping on their doorsteps for centuries. Etrusca's journeys through the pillars had been necessary to use up energy to prevent it building to the point of making the planet implode. More of the pieces needed to be removed from

Nisandros, but Jasper and Taggert had neutralized enough now that no one could travel through the pillars. That was the important part. Or so Etrusca said.

Most of the inhabitants of the clan house were waiting when they reached the gates. M'kar welcomed the brief surge of energy that came with the flare of resentment. She didn't want to slide off her gyphel and melt into a puddle on the pavement in front of witnesses. Her irritation enabled her to stand up reasonably straight and salute Rokas and the ambassador properly. That was as far as she needed to go. Aquid shoved his way through the crowd. Etrusca let out a warrior's delighted howl and leaped at him. M'kar forgot to breathe when her great-grandfather swept Etrusca up in his arms and she planted a long, passionate kiss right on his lips.

Despite the lateness of the hour, the clan house vibrated with excitement over the announcement of the imminent marriage of Aquid and Etrusca. M'kar took the opportunity to meet with Rokas, in private. After a long, hot herbal soak that wasn't long enough by at least two hours. He turned on the white noise generators and locked several doors. He never said a word until M'kar finished her story. He flinched a little when she stated that the rocks at the core of all the hallucinations and strange warping of time in the surbda craters were actually broken pieces of a Gate -- the Gate that Nisandrians had always denied existed. He finally smiled and started to breathe again when M'kar stated that according to the conditions listed in the bridal challenge document, the cheating of most of her suitors and the very clear attempts to capture and coerce her, permitted her to disqualify them. She believed she was in her right to cancel the contest altogether. There would be no winner.

He laughed when she asked him to contact the other clan houses, to send searchers to the other craters to retrieve the scattered, exhausted and most likely seriously confused suitors. Many of them probably still hadn't sensed any passage of time, no matter how long ago in the chase they had dropped out. Jasper and Taggert both agreed it would take several luns until the time and sense-warping energies that had soaked into the ground and air would dissipate.

"With your permission, Uncle, I will separate myself from the diplomatic mission and return to my ship. All that has happened necessitates a long period of isolation, and a chance to rest and recuperate and ... contemplate the implications of everything that happened, and everything that we have learned." M'kar stood. She was going to leave whether her uncle gave her permission or not, but she owed him the chance to be a good host and dismiss her politely.

"Of course. You have earned your rest." He nodded and sank back in his chair, as if the telling had exhausted him more than her. "Nisandros and the Upper and Lower Halls owe you a great honor debt. We need to move forward and adapt to work with other worlds. You have revealed the rot in the hearts of the young men we considered entrusting with making those changes. I think perhaps Enlo has given us the answer we needed, for handling this change. I do not doubt that Grandfather's bride is Etrusca herself. She is such a powerful figure of legend, after all the abuse she endured -- for teaching the very things we need to learn now, to join the rest of the universe. She is the perfect one to lead us now. Who would dare gainsay her? Lessons coming from a figure of legend -- and some proper terror -- will go down easier than lessons from young men who have revealed greed and foolishness under their masks of civilization."

M'kar would have given anything to go straight to the shuttle and up to the *Defender*, but she needed to report to the ambassador first, and formally request removal from the diplomatic team. He accepted her simple explanation: she had made a discovery of scientific importance to both Nisandros and the Alliance, she had sent it up to the ship for further study and to be transported to more suitable experts, and she had found a way to extricate herself from the cultural "problem" that had required her presence on the planet. Defrayn agreed with her request to be separated from the diplomatic team and accepted her promise that she would explain everything later. After she had rested and recuperated.

She was almost in tears from exhaustion when she climbed into the shuttle. Barroo crooned to her, clutching the front of her jacket. She was nearly asleep before the shuttle broke the atmosphere. He continued crooning to her, all the way up to the ship, so she never quite fell asleep. With his help she managed to get up and leave the shuttle and make her way through the ship to her cabin with one eye open, only partially awake.

M'kar slept for nearly a full ship's day. Got up, took a shower, ate enough breakfast for three, then curled up in the small front room of her cabin to snack and outline the report she owed Genys. Thyal had sent her a transcript of everything she had told him, everything he had seen through her eyes, and that saved her several hours of work.

Then she went back to sleep for another day.

Chapter Eighteen

M'kar ran out of food but didn't want to leave her cabin. Thyal brought her provisions from the ship's stores to restock her kitchen. He refused to leave until she told him everything that he had missed while she was inside the crater, full sharing of impressions and memories through their bond. He helped her laugh, and recognize the stupidity and ridiculousness, as well as the wonder and the terror of what she had gone through.

She fell asleep leaning against him, both of them curled up on her small couch. She slept better than she had in the previous two days. When Thyal insisted that she needed to have Tahl check her, she agreed.

They were holding hands when they went into Medical. Nyssa was on duty. She saw them holding hands and went white for two seconds, then two bright red spots lit her cheeks. Fury brought her near shooting lightning from her eyes.

Thyal tugged on M'kar's hand and brought it to his lips, to brush a kiss across her knuckles. She nearly pulled her hand free, but his iron grip was painful.

You're so nasty, she scolded him.

She deserves it. How many times does a man have to say he's not interested, he will never be interested, and she can never force her way through my mental shields to make even a fake bond with me?

Nyssa threw down the tablet she was using and stomped out of Medical. Rumors later circulated through the ship that she had had a screaming battle with her twin brother, and the two refused to talk to each other. Later rumors claimed they had deliberately shattered their twin bond, and neither wanted to repair it. Tahl assigned them to different duty shifts.

The amusement soon died for M'kar, because Tahl found all her physical stats were down, depleted, with hints of an unfamiliar energy lingering in her tissues. On the bright side, M'kar didn't glow. Tahl prescribed plenty of quiet and rest and relaxation, and thorough exams every other day, to track the progress of her recovery and ensure that strange energy was fading. Or at the very least not doing any damage.

~~~~~

Thyal and M'kar retreated to the observation dome for a private, celebratory dinner, the day the *Defender* was released from its assignment to the diplomatic party. They pulled back the shields to see Nisandros
~~~~~

receding to a dark dot behind them. Another ship had arrived to relieve the *Defender*, with additional diplomatic personnel and the first shipment of supplies and equipment to expand the orbital station the Alliance had installed at Nisandros decades ago.

"I have some good news," Thyal said,

"What could be better than going home?"

Barroo and Infrenx chirped, echoing her tone.

"The Mirror Monsters have formally applied for transfer --"

"Enlo is merciful!"

"Veylen just happened to leave his tablet open to their documents and lying where I could see it." Thyal smirked as he slid out of his hoverchair to sit on the cushions M'kar had spread on the deck. "For some odd reason, they're contemplating resigning from the Fleet. They feel they've learned so much Alliance medicine that should be applied to Qahngress's medical practices, and they have an obligation inherent in their royal blood to look after the welfare of their homeworld, first."

"Broken hearts are so altruistic," M'kar muttered.

Thyal sighed, but he didn't scold her for being nasty, which he probably should have.

"There is a slight problem, though," he added, as he leaned back against the equipment pedestal.

"Fleet won't let them go?"

"They pulled so many strings and irritated enough people in high places to get onto the *Defender*, they don't have any strings to pull to get them off quickly enough to suit them."

"Why do I feel like they're being taught a lesson, several overdue lessons, but we're the ones getting the punishment?" M'kar was just too tired to laugh right now. Maybe later. She opened up the last box of mezipa, which she would only share with Thyal.

"I have a few strings to pull," he admitted. "People who owe me favors."

"That's not fair, using up favors to benefit someone else."

"That's not how I see it. Anything is worth not seeing Nyssa giving me these martyred looks every time I turn around. Or even worse, telling me she forgives me every time she catches me alone."

"That's what you get for being totally adorable." She fluttered her eyelashes at him.

"You are utterly wretched, and I pity the man you finally track down and throw on the altar of matrimony."

The dracs joined in, their squawks and trills sounding like a mixture of teasing and scolding. Thyal waved his finger close enough to her face, M'kar had to try to bite it. He let out a yelp.

"I never got my teeth into you!" She laughed, but the sound caught in her throat as Thyal pointed his trembling finger down at his feet.

Infrenx was perched on his foot, her claws digging into his bare ankle, where the sock had slid down, exposing the flesh.

His trembling foot.

"You felt that?" She whispered, because the alternative was to shriek.

Thyal nodded. He seemed to have trouble breathing for a few moments.

"You're going to be all right. I know you've been healing all along, but now it feels real. You're going to be all right." Then she wrapped her arms tight around him and he clung to her. M'kar let herself cry because the tears would soak into his shirt, and he would never see them in her eyes.

Captain's Log
Personal

Six days out from Nisandros.
M'kar thinks she found pieces of a broken Gate!
She brought pieces of a broken Gate onto my ship!
I'm going to kill her. Somehow. When she least expects it. I am going to ambush her and pound her to within a grain of death.

I understand the stress she was under, and there was some massive time and space dilation when she and all those narding indiferps trying to trick her into matrimony were chasing her and fell through that malfunctioning Gate -- malfunctioning with not a single blip showing up on any ship's sensors, which doesn't do much for my nerves, because what's the use of all those sensors taking up half the ship's systems, focused on finding Gates, when we can't even detect a malfunctioning one sitting right underneath us?

I'm so proud of her, and so grateful she got back alive, I just want to throttle her.

Maybe I'll do worse. I'll point out the feelings between her and Thyal that neither of them seem aware of, and let her just melt down from embarrassment. That'll fix her.

THE END

About the Author

On the road to publication, Michelle fell into fandom in college and has 40+ stories in various SF and fantasy universes. She has a bunch of useless degrees in theater, English, film/communication, and writing. Even worse, she has over 100 books and novellas with multiple small presses, in science fiction and fantasy, YA, suspense, women's fiction, and sub-genres of romance.

Her official launch into publishing came with winning first place in the Writers of the Future contest in 1990. She was a finalist in the EPIC Awards competition multiple times, winning with *Lorien* in 2006 and *The Meruk Episodes, I-V*, in 2010, and was a finalist in the Realm Awards competition, in conjunction with the Realm Makers convention.

Her training includes the Institute for Children's Literature; proofreading at an advertising agency; and working at a community newspaper. She is a tea snob and freelance edits for a living (MichelleLevigne@gmail.com for info/rates), but only enough to give her time to write. Her newest crime against the literary world is to be co-managing editor at Mt. Zion Ridge Press and launching the publishing co-op, Ye Olde Dragon Books. Be afraid … be very afraid.

www.Mlevigne.com
www.MichelleLevigne.blogspot.com
www.YeOldeDragonBooks.com
www.MtZionRidgePress.com
@MichelleLevigne

Look for Michelle's Goodreads groups:
Guardians of Neighborlee
Voyages of the AFV Defender

NEWSLETTER:
Want to learn about upcoming books, book launch parties, inside information, and cover reveals?
Go to Michelle's website or blog to sign up.

Thanks for reading!
If you enjoyed this book, would you help Michelle by posting a review on Goodreads?

As a way of saying thanks, Michelle invites you to the Goodies page on her website. It will change regularly, offering you a free short story, a sample audiobook chapter, sneak peeks at new cover art, inside information on discounts and new release dates, etc.

Please go to: Mlevigne.com/good-stuff.html

Also by Michelle L. Levigne

Guardians of the Time Stream: 4-book Steampunk series
The Match Girls: Humorous inspirational romance series starting with **A Match (Not) Made in Heaven**
Sarai's Journey: A 2-book biblical fiction series
Tabor Heights: 20-book inspirational small town romance series.
Quarry Hall: 11-book women's fiction/suspense series
For Sale: Wedding Dress. Never Used: inspirational romance
Crooked Creek: Fun Fables About Critters and Kids: Children's short stories.
Do Yourself a Favor: Tips and Quips on the Writing Life. A book of writing advice.
To Eternity (and beyond): *Writing Spec Fic Good for Your Soul.* A book defending speculative fiction.
Killing His Alter-Ego: contemporary romance/suspense, taking place in fandom.

The Commonwealth Universe: SF series, 25 books and growing
The Hunt: 5-book YA fantasy series
Faxinor: Fantasy series, 4 books and growing
Wildvine: Fantasy series, 14 books when all released
Neighborlee: Humorous fantasy series
Zygradon: 5-book Arthurian fantasy series
AFV Defender: SF adventure series
Young Defenders: Middle Grade SF series, spin-off of *AFV Defender*
Magic to Spare: Fantasy series
Book & Mug Mysteries: cozy mystery series
Quest for the Crescent Moon: fantasy series